Murder at St Anne's

ALSO BY J. R. ELLIS

Murder at St Anne's

A YORKSHIRE MURDER MYSTERY

J.R. ELLIS

THOMAS & MERCER

Text copyright © 2021 by J. R. Ellis
All rights reserved.

Published by Thomas & Mercer, Seattle

www.apub.com

Amazon, the Amazon logo, and Thomas & Mercer are trademarks of Amazon.com, Inc., or its affiliates.

ISBN-13: 9781542030175
ISBN-10: 154203017X

Cover design by @blacksheep-uk.com

Printed in the United States of America

Murder at St Anne's

Prologue

M. R. James (1862–1936) was a master of the traditional English ghost story. In his subtle, odd and disturbing narratives, horror envelops clerics, antiquarians, fortune hunters, and all who disturb things that are best left alone. His stories take place in libraries, colleges and comfortable residences; in churches, cathedral closes and graveyards.

The Reverend Clare Wilcox sat in her study in the large vicarage adjacent to the parish church of St Anne's in Knaresborough, Yorkshire. From the window she could see to her right the west tower of the medieval church, and ahead a beautiful view down into the dramatic Nidd Gorge. It was a Wednesday afternoon in mid-January and the black scribbles of the leafless tree branches stood out stark against the sky. It had been a bright, cold day, but now, as the sun went down, dark clouds were looming in the north.

Clare shivered and pulled a cardigan around her. She rubbed her hands together. The vicarage had been built in the nineteenth century and had large rooms with high ceilings; it was far too big and very difficult to keep warm. The antiquated heating system generated huge bills which they could ill afford to pay, so Clare and her husband, Jeremy, tried to keep the thermostat turned down as far as possible. It was a little easier now that their two daughters were away at university, which meant that the radiators could be turned off in two bedrooms.

She looked at her screen and tried to concentrate on what she was reading, which was a very dull report on the problems of recruiting and training readers in the Church of England. Clare was in her late forties. She had had a career as an academic theologian before entering the priesthood ten years earlier. Since then, she had proved that she was also an excellent administrator and motivator. This had led to her being fast-tracked to the position of rector of St Anne's.

Clare raised her face, with its strong features and blue eyes. Her short blonde hair was beginning to turn a little grey. With a sigh she closed the file, massaged her forehead and sat quietly for a moment reflecting. Running a church like this was quite an onerous task. It was a big and important church in the diocese of Ripon, with a large congregation. There were also rifts between groups and delicate matters to sort out. She was feeling the burden of it on this winter afternoon. Maybe it was tiredness and the anti-climax of January after the hectic Christmas season. Also, a change was coming soon and she would be faced with a new challenge and significant responsibilities. At this moment it seemed very daunting and she was not looking forward to it. She sat back in her chair with her eyes closed and had an idea: call the woman who had been her mentor for many years. It would be nice to have a chat. She picked up her phone.

～

Alison Oldroyd, vicar of Kirkby Underside, a village between Harrogate and Leeds, was also in her study in a similarly oversized vicarage next to her rather smaller church when she received Clare's call.

'Clare!' she answered enthusiastically. 'How lovely to hear from you! How's it going?'

'Alison, I'm glad you're in. To tell you the truth, I'm going through a bit of a bad patch.'

'It's normal at this time of year.'

'That's what I thought. Maybe I'm a bit apprehensive about what I'm going to face soon.'

'Well you'd hardly be human if you weren't, especially as a woman, with a challenge like the one you're facing.'

'Sometimes I wonder whether someone like you with greater experience would be better in the job.'

'No, I'm too old and much too controversial a figure.' Alison laughed. 'You'll be fine and we're all behind you. You've got massive support.'

'I suppose that's part of the problem. I'm afraid of letting everybody down.'

'Nonsense! Anyway, what's going on in the parish?'

'Oh, you know, the usual stuff: warring cliques, financial difficulties, people obsessed with detail.'

'I know it well.'

'I honestly won't be sad in some ways, not to have to deal with this kind of stuff at parish level for much longer. It sounds awful; I can only say that to you.'

'Don't worry. The truth is you're wasted in that position even if it is a large church. You're bored because you're not being stretched. Remember, it's not for long now.'

Clare laughed. 'Well, it's kind of you to say that. There are some more serious issues that I'll have to tackle before I go which I can't really talk about, but I'll manage. I'll miss a lot of the church members here, but I have to say there are some batty ones. Do you know a number of them really believe in this legend about the ghost of the heretic who's supposed to haunt the church?'

'Really?'

'Yes, they won't go into the church at night unless there's a service going on. I sometimes wonder whether some people have moved on from the superstitions of the Middle Ages. I must say I've never experienced anything frightening in there.' She laughed again. 'So, how are you?'

'Oh, fine, don't worry about me. I've got this parish well under control. I think most of them are frightened of me, certainly of my radical ideas. I'm going to retire in a few years and do something different. I'm not sure what yet.'

'I'll find a job for you. It would be great to work with you again. Anyway, I'd better go. I've got a meeting with someone soon. I won't bore you with the details, but thanks, I feel better now.'

'Good. You and Jeremy should come round one evening before the big day and you move further away.'

'That would be really nice. I'll look at my diary and text you some dates when we're free.'

'Great. Bye for now then.'

'Bye.' The call ended. Clare felt alone again in the cold and increasingly dark study. She switched on a lamp. As usual, Alison had helped her to get things in perspective. She could deal with all the issues facing her, starting with the meeting which was to take place shortly. There was just time for a cup of tea first.

～

As Clare left the vicarage and walked along the path to the church, flakes of snow were beginning to fall. It was very cold. She pulled up the hood on her coat. She wondered why it was necessary to meet this person in the church at this time on a winter's afternoon. Why couldn't they come to the vicarage? They'd said they had something important to show her. What on earth could it be?

She shook her head in exasperation; probably some trivial matter, and another waste of her time.

The area around the church was deserted and there did not appear to be any lights on in the building. The door was unlocked, as the church remained open until half past five. She entered the dark silence, sensing the height of the medieval ceiling above her. The nave was on her right, and to the left was the font and the west tower going up into the gloom. She saw that, in fact, there was a light on in a small room at the north end of the base of the west tower. This was entered through an open archway. Presumably the person she was to meet was in there. She walked over carefully to avoid tripping on something in the darkness.

'Hello?' she called tentatively. There was no reply. She walked under the tower and, when she reached the archway, she heard a kind of creaking noise and had the sense of something slicing through the air above her. She stopped and glanced up. She was about to scream, but before she was able to produce a sound she was hit by a tremendous blow and fell to the ground.

Shortly afterwards a figure appeared. It was dressed in a monk's cowl with a rope around the waist. The hood was up, and no face was visible. It stared at Clare Wilcox's body and then walked soundlessly out of the church, flitting away into the dark. As it went through the churchyard, a head appeared above a gravestone and watched it disappear.

One

'Well, Jim, I'd like to say she was hit by our old friend the blunt instrument, which might make your job easier, but I'm afraid that wouldn't suffice for these injuries.'

Tim Groves, the forensic pathologist, was on his knees by the body of Clare Wilcox. It lay at the base of the tower, next to an archway. Her head was resting in a pool of blood and her coat was covered in blood spatters. DCI Jim Oldroyd of the West Riding Police, who had worked with Groves for many years, was also looking down at the body.

'What do you think happened, then?' he said. Wilcox's body had been found by a churchwarden who had come to lock the church for the night and had gone to turn off the light in the side room. The building was now animated. The murder scene was illuminated by extra lighting as SOCOs took photographs, and full of the noise of police radios and people coming and going.

'She was hit with terrific force by something large and heavy. Her left shoulder is nearly ripped out, the left side of her head is badly smashed and her neck is broken. I can't think it was anything that a person could have lifted, let alone wielded. These types of severe injuries are what you'd normally see in a bad car accident, or when someone is hit by a train or has a fall from a great height on to rocks.' He spread his arms in a gesture of puzzlement. 'I'm baffled.'

'And time of death?' asked Oldroyd, glancing upwards with his shrewd grey eyes. There was no view up to the top of the tower; a wooden ceiling had been put in about twenty feet up.

'She's not been dead long, just a few hours.'

Oldroyd went through the archway into the adjoining room. Piles of chairs stood in one corner and there was a piano covered with a sheet. It seemed to be a storage area. There was nothing in the room that could have inflicted the horrific injuries.

'Hmm.' Oldroyd frowned as he returned. 'It's a strange one, then.'

'Definitely, but don't you specialise in them?' Groves liked to tease his friend and colleague.

'A lot of strange cases seem to come my way, Tim, but I like a challenge. Routine cases are boring. Could she have been killed elsewhere and brought in here?'

'I would say not. The amount of blood is consistent with her being struck here and falling to the floor. There's also no sign of blood anywhere else in the church, including the entrance. Presumably she would have to have been carried or dragged to this point and that would have left a trail of blood. Also, you'd have to wonder, why would the killer bother to move her? But that's your area.'

'Yes, but I agree.'

Groves was packing up his things and a team was getting ready to stretcher the body away. 'I wish you the best of luck with this one. I'll send you the full report and give you a call if I find anything new that's really important.'

'Thanks.'

Just as Groves was leaving, Andy Carter joined Oldroyd. Andy was a detective sergeant, in his early thirties, and a key member of Oldroyd's team. He'd joined the West Riding Police from the London Met a few years before. The other DS who regularly worked with Oldroyd, Stephanie Johnson, was also Andy's romantic partner. Andy had been the first detective on the scene after the police were called, and when he'd seen that it was a serious case, he'd contacted his boss.

'I've talked to the bloke who found the body, sir.' Andy looked at his notes. 'Donald Avison, churchwarden. Shaken up, of course; he's sitting in the police car to keep warm. Said he came to lock up and saw there was a light in this room; came over to see if there was anybody in and found the body. It must have been very unpleasant.'

'Did he see anyone in here, or lurking around in the vicinity of the church?'

'No, but he did say something about people believing in a ghost.'

'A ghost? If it was a ghost it's out of our jurisdiction; we can't arrest phantoms.'

Andy smiled. 'No, sir.'

Oldroyd looked at the body. 'Tell me again who she is?'

Andy looked at his notes. 'Clare Wilcox, rector here at St Anne's. Avison identified her. According to him she's been here five years.'

'Hmm.' Oldroyd frowned. 'I know that name from somewhere. So in all likelihood she walked over from the rectory.'

'Yes, sir, it's just across from here, the other side of that grassy area. We've been over there, by the way. The husband, Jeremy

Wilcox, is a doctor; he was informed of what's happened by Avison before we got here. He claims he'd not been home long and was just beginning to worry about where his wife was. He's in a bit of a state, naturally. I've left DC Robinson with him.'

'Good, I'll come over now. I think he's the first person I need to talk to.'

~

Jeremy Wilcox was a tall middle-aged man with handsome features, but when Oldroyd encountered him he was sitting with his head bowed over in an armchair in the large sitting room of the rectory, diminished by shock and grief.

DC Robinson left the room as Oldroyd and Andy sat down quietly and Oldroyd introduced himself.

'I'm very sorry about what has happened,' he began. 'We want to find who did this as soon as we can, and I'm sure you understand that we need to ask you some questions if you feel up to it. If not, we can come back tomorrow.'

Wilcox made a gesture with his hand. 'Please, go ahead,' he replied in a faint voice. His head was now lolling back against the armchair, as if he didn't have the strength to raise it.

'When did you last see your wife?'

'This morning. I left for the surgery at about eight thirty; I'm a GP in Harrogate.'

'Was she OK when you left? She didn't seem worried about anything?'

'No, she was fine.'

'Did your wife have any enemies? Anyone who would have wished her harm?'

Wilcox laughed sardonically. 'Obviously she must have had, Chief Inspector, unless there's a random killer on the loose, but I know what you mean. I don't know of anyone. It was difficult to dislike Clare, she was so warm and good-hearted, but she was a campaigner on many issues and you come across institutions who oppose you.'

'What kind of campaigns?'

'CND, Greenpeace, gay rights, Christian Aid and world poverty. That's just for starters. She acted out her faith and wasn't afraid to be political. She received some nasty messages on social media.'

'Any death threats?'

'Not that I'm aware of, but she didn't tell me everything. We're not the kind of couple who do everything together . . . *Were* not.' He paused. Oldroyd had seen it many times: the shock of realising that the relationship you had was now in the past, brought to a sudden and violent end. 'I supported her of course, but I tend to lead a quieter life. I always did a lot with the girls when Clare was busy organising a march or something.'

'Was she popular here, do you think?'

'Up to a point. Clare never disguised her left-wing politics and her progressive causes. Churchgoers tend to be a conservative bunch, large and small "c", and I don't think some of it went down well. But as a person and on the pastoral side I'm sure they liked her.' He paused, shook his head and seemed to be near to tears. 'Anyway, it wasn't going to be for much longer. In a few months' time we were going to be leaving here.'

'Oh?'

'Yes, Clare's been appointed Bishop of Kendal in the Carlisle diocese. She was excited about it.' He grimaced in pain. 'That's not going to happen now.'

'I'm sorry,' said Oldroyd.

'I've already signed up to move to a practice in the town, but I tend to do my own thing. I don't get involved much in church matters. I don't play the vicar's husband, running groups and being on committees. Other people will know more about Clare's life here at St Anne's than I do. It was the same at St Bartholomew's when she was a curate.'

Oldroyd looked up. 'Was that St Bartholomew's in Kirkby Underside?'

'Yes. Do you know it?'

'Yes. My sister is the vicar there. I thought I'd heard your wife's name somewhere before. Alison will have mentioned her.'

'Oh, Alison! She's fantastic. She's helped Clare so much over the years.' He sighed. 'She'll be devastated, too.'

'I'm sure she will.' Oldroyd smiled sympathetically at the poor man. 'Look, I think that will do for now. You need to try to rest. I'll be sending someone round to collect Clare's computer and phone. We need to investigate those messages. There's just one awkward thing that I have to ask you, which is where were you this afternoon between about three thirty and five?'

'At the surgery, Spencer Road in Harrogate. I'll give you the address. My staff will confirm that I was there all day.'

'Fine. Are you here by yourself now?'

'Yes, but I'll be fine.' Wilcox got up to see them out, but at the door he remembered something which finally brought him to tears. He leaned against the door frame. 'Chief Inspector,' he said, struggling to speak, 'how am I going to tell our girls?'

❧

Oldroyd and Andy went back over to the church. Blue and white tape surrounded the entrance, where a PC was on guard. Inside, Oldroyd took out his phone.

'I'm going to have to call my sister,' he said to Andy. 'I want her to learn about this from me, not from the media.'

'OK, sir.' Andy went off to see how the work of the SOCOs was progressing.

Oldroyd's heart was thumping as he waited for Alison to answer. This was going to be an awful shock for her.

'Jim! Nice of you to call, but it's a bit late. I—'

Oldroyd cut in. 'Alison, I'm so sorry but I have some very bad news for you. It's Clare Wilcox, your friend at St Anne's in Knaresborough.'

'Yes, Jim, what about her?'

'I'm afraid she's dead. She was murdered.' He waited with gritted teeth for the impact of this bombshell.

'What? Oh, Jim! I . . .'

'I'm sorry, I know you and her were close.' He heard some faint sobs over the phone.

'What happened? I was talking to her on the phone this afternoon.' Her voice was faint.

'Were you?' That could mean that his sister was the last person, except the killer, to have had contact with Clare Wilcox before she died.

'Yes, she called me at about half past three and we talked about things. She was feeling a bit down, and . . . I . . .' She faltered. 'Jim, this is terrible; who would do such a thing?'

'I have no idea, do you?'

'No. Clare was such a wonderful person. Just the kind of woman we need in the Church to bring in the changes if we're going to survive. She would have been excellent as a bishop. She was going to be Bishop of Kendal. It's . . . Where did they find her?'

'In the church, she was struck down violently. Killed instantly – I don't think she would have felt much.'

'Oh no, how awful! And in the church, too?'

'Too cruel anywhere' were the words from *Macbeth* that came into Oldroyd's mind, but he didn't voice them.

'Does Jeremy know?'

'Yes.'

'Oh, the poor man!'

'I know. Look, Alison, I have to go now, but I'll come round to see you first thing tomorrow morning if you're OK tonight. If not, you're welcome to come over and stay with me and Deborah.'

'That's kind, but I'll stay here. I need to tell some of the parishioners. They'll be devastated; they have such fond memories of Clare and her time here. She was such a good priest. Oh, Jim!'

Oldroyd heard her weeping into the phone. 'Are you sure you're OK to be by yourself?' he said.

'Yes, yes, don't worry. I'll be going round to see people. It will be nice to see you tomorrow, though.'

'I'll be there, don't worry.'

'Thanks.'

He rang off. He hadn't experienced his sister being so upset since her husband David had died several years before. He found it quite disturbing; she was older than him and had always been a strong character to whom he'd looked up. He sat down in one of the church pews and stayed there, quiet, still and reflective, until Andy returned.

'How is she, sir?'

'Very upset. I can see that a lot of people are going to be affected by this murder, not just her close friends and family. It seems she was a very popular and able woman. She was about to be consecrated as a bishop near the lakes, in Kendal.'

'Wow. That's high up in the Church isn't it?'

'Yes, and there aren't many women at that level yet, so it takes a strong character to take on the role. Especially given the continuing hostility to women priests and bishops from some groups in the Church.'

Andy looked around at the interior of St Anne's: the pillars, the narrow arched windows, the pews, altar and organ. 'I've always found churches a bit spooky, sir, to be honest. If there's anywhere I can imagine there being a ghost, it's in an old building like this one.'

'Well, there might be a haunting after this terrible event. Who knows? You never went to church much as a boy then?'

'No, but I went to a Church of England primary school. This old vicar used to come into assembly sometimes. He sprayed spit around when he spoke and it went all over the heads of the kids sitting at the front. We used to call him Old Spitbag.'

'So I take it religion largely passed you over?' asked Oldroyd.

'Yeah, I could never make any sense of it. All those miracles; it just sounded like a fairy story to me. There were some good gory battles in the Old Testament, though. We used to enjoy those and David killing Goliath with his sling, you know, stuff like that. How about you, sir?'

Oldroyd frowned. His relationship with religion was a long and mostly unsatisfactory one. He struggled with the big existential issues in life and envied his sister's faith. Religious belief just didn't work for him. 'We used to go to church as a family when I was little, but when I was older, my dad and I used to go walking instead. My sister's different of course. She rebelled against it as a teenager but then she changed and studied theology. You'd like her, she's very inspiring, not a Bible-basher. I've tried to be like her but I'm just not.'

'It must be a good thing to be honest and not pretend, sir,' said Andy, who beneath his exterior as the cheeky chappie cockney was quite a thoughtful and sensitive person. 'When you think about what's happened here: this woman priest who people liked, she gets clobbered to death in her own church. It doesn't seem like there's a nice God in charge of everything, does it?'

'No, quite the opposite, some people would say. Anyway' – Oldroyd got up – 'we can't sit here talking about the meaning of life all evening. Where are we up to? There's probably not much more we can do tonight.'

'You're right, sir. The SOCOs have finished, so we can lock the church up when we're ready.'

'Good.' Oldroyd looked at his watch. It was nearly ten o'clock. 'Well, let's get back to Harrogate as soon as we can.'

As they left the church, Oldroyd looked back at the building. There was sufficient light from inside to partially illuminate the grotesque, grinning gargoyles peering down from the top of the walls and the dark silhouettes of gravestones in the churchyard. He agreed with Andy; despite all the efforts of people down the centuries to make old churches places of goodness, light and spirituality, they could be very spooky places, maybe because a lot of them were ancient and many things had happened within their walls. It made him think about his favourite writer of ghost stories: M. R. James. A number of his stories took place in churches like St Anne's or cathedrals, and he used the setting to create a sinister and threatening atmosphere. With all this talk of hauntings and such a mysterious death, Oldroyd had the uneasy feeling that he was living out a story by the master.

～

The short drive back to Harrogate was difficult on the cold winter night. The snow had stopped, the sky had cleared, and the tell-tale twinkle of ice crystals on the road reflected in the headlights. The night frost was taking hold and cars were driving slowly. At one point, Oldroyd had to queue to overtake a large yellow gritting vehicle, its orange warning lights flashing in the dark. Grit rattled on the side of his car like a sudden hailstorm as he passed by.

He was relieved when he arrived back at his flat overlooking Harrogate's famous green space known as the Stray. It was past ten o'clock. His partner, Deborah, was waiting for him, comfortably ensconced in an armchair reading a book. He'd texted her to say it was a serious case in Knaresborough and he would be late back. She got up to greet him.

'Jim, you look tired. How did it go?'

Oldroyd took off his coat and gave her a kiss. 'It's a nasty one. And Alison's involved.'

'Alison? Not your sister Alison?'

'Yes. She knew the victim: Clare Wilcox, rector of St Anne's. She used to be a curate at St Bartholomew's, and I think Alison's known her a long time. They're both involved in the promotion of women in the Church. Clare was apparently about to become a bishop over in Cumbria.'

'That's terrible. Clare Wilcox? I'm sure I've met her but I can't remember where. I did hear that she was well liked at St Anne's.' Until she'd recently moved in with Oldroyd, Deborah had lived in Knaresborough, and she still maintained her flat there.

'That's the impression I get, although we've only spoken to the husband, who's devastated of course – and so is the churchwarden who found the body.'

'Murdered in the church! I'm not religious, but that still seems sacrilegious somehow. A church should be a place of peace.'

'Savagely murdered in the church.' He described the state in which the body was found. 'The injuries were so severe that Tim Groves has no idea what could have caused them. It looks as if I've got another mystery on my hands.'

'Well, you're used to those. But how's Alison? She must be very upset.'

'She is. I had to break the news to her on the phone. I'm going round to her first thing in the morning. She said she would be OK until then. I told her she could come here if she wanted.'

'Oh, Jim! That must have been awful; a member of your family in something like this again.'

'I know.' Oldroyd shook his head at Deborah's reference to his daughter Louise's traumatic involvement in a murder case in Whitby. 'I'd get out while you can. I'm bad news. It could be you next,' he added sardonically.

'Never mind, I'll take the risk. Anyway, you must be starving. I've made a vegetable casserole with herb dumplings. It's in the oven; it'll warm you through.'

'Lovely, thanks.' Oldroyd went through to the kitchen, reflecting that he would have preferred one with meat. He was quite happy to fall in with Deborah's vegetarianism; he felt it was healthier and better for the planet. But on a cold winter's night like this he would have loved a thick beef stew. He brought his plateful of food back into the living room and balanced it on his knee.

'Why on earth would someone kill a woman like that?'

'That's exactly what Alison asked me. Motives in cases like this aren't always immediately obvious, but they'll appear as we delve into things.' He spooned another mouthful of the casserole into his mouth. 'This is really good by the way.' He paused. 'Unless she was killed by a ghost.' He told Deborah what Andy had reported to him.

'A spectre in a haunted church! This is beginning to sound like an old-fashioned ghost story!'

'I know – by someone like M. R. James. I'll have to find out more about that legend at St Anne's. I love a good ghost story.'

'Do you believe that ghosts actually exist?' asked Deborah.

Oldroyd thought a moment. 'Not really, but I think I take the same view as James himself. He said something on the lines of being open-minded and prepared to consider evidence. There's no doubt, though, that strange things do happen. Lots of people claim to have seen or heard things like spirits and poltergeists.'

'There's never any definitive proof of anything, is there? Which leads me to think that a lot of it is psychological; maybe hallucinations or suggestibility.'

'You're probably right, but there's always that little doubt, isn't there?'

'Yes,' said Deborah, and then she remembered something. 'Oh, by the way, you'll have to take care tomorrow. I've been watching the weather forecast and it's going to be cold and maybe snowy for the next few days. There could be some serious downfalls tomorrow.'

'Well, dark and wintry weather; it all adds to the spooky atmosphere, doesn't it?'

'I suppose so, but I'm more concerned about you running off the road than into a ghost.'

Oldroyd laughed as he drank a late-night cup of decaf coffee. Nevertheless, 'spooky' seemed to be the word that kept coming back to him. There were already a number of aspects of this case that he found strange and unsettling.

~

When Andy arrived back at the flat he shared with Steph in the centre of Leeds, the city was still buzzing despite the weather. There seemed to be no post-Christmas lull. Bright lights illuminated the packed pubs and restaurants, and street-food sellers were braving the cold and doing good business.

Steph was on her laptop as he entered the flat, and was dressed in grey lounge pants with her blonde hair tied back. 'Hi,' she called out.

Andy took off his shoes and coat and rubbed his hands as he came into the living room. 'It's bloody freezing out there. I swear it never gets as cold as this in London.'

'You'll get used to it when you've been "oop north" a bit longer. Anyway, how was it?'

'Pretty nasty. This lady vicar got smashed really badly over the head; inside the church too.'

'God that's awful,' said Steph, and then she frowned at him. '"Lady vicar"? What kind of language is that? It sounds like "lady doctor", as if she's something odd or inferior to the real thing.'

'Yeah, sorry; it's just that I suppose it's still a bit unusual for vicars to be women.'

'Not really. It must be nearly thirty years since the first woman was ordained. It just shows how long it takes for things to change with people's perceptions of women and what they can do.'

'I don't remember any female vicars coming into school.'

'Well, just because they can be ordained doesn't mean they will be in the same numbers as men. There are still parishes where they won't have a woman as a minister, and it's even worse with women bishops.'

'Apparently this woman was about to become a bishop in the north-west somewhere.'

'Really?'

'Yeah. Anyway, how do you know all this about the Church? You've never been a churchgoer, have you?' Andy was curious.

'No, but we had a "lady vicar", as you put it, to talk to our gender-equality group at work. She made it sound far harder for women in the Church than for us in the police, and we struggle enough.'

'It's getting better all the time though, isn't it? I mean, we're slowly getting rid of all the Derek Fentons.' This was a reference to a nasty detective inspector who had been dismissed for sexual harassment of women officers, as well as other offences, largely due to the efforts of Steph and a group of her female colleagues.

'Yes, but we've some way to go yet and there's no room for complacency. Even well-meaning men can be a bit blind to the concerns of women. They don't really get it until it's pointed out to them. Anyway' – she turned back to her laptop – 'I've been searching for holiday destinations. It's time we booked something. Last year we left it too late and that hotel we fancied in Majorca was full.'

Andy had collapsed on to the sofa. 'Yeah, you're right, but can I have something to eat first?'

'There're some meatballs and spaghetti, but bring it in here so we can start looking. I've bookmarked a few places. We're not going to keep putting it off.'

Andy got up. 'Fine. Actually, I'm not too bothered where we go. You have a good search and narrow it down to a few places, and then I'll have a look and see what I think.' He disappeared into the kitchen. Steph shook her head and sighed; very nice of him to be so flexible, but why did tasks like this always seem to end up with her doing most of the work? Ironically, it was an example of what they'd just been talking about.

~

Jeremy Wilcox poured himself a stiff drink and downed it before he could face the horrendous prospect of calling his daughters. He'd done virtually nothing since the detectives left, except sit thinking about how to do what seemed impossible. He had thought of asking someone, maybe the police, to contact them for him and give them the terrible news, but he knew it was something he had to do himself. He didn't want it to come from anyone else, certainly not from any of the busybodies at the church. Jenny, the eldest, was in her last year at Durham; Fiona was in her first year at Liverpool. They had only just returned to university after the Christmas holidays.

At last, he summoned up the courage to pick up the phone. With both of them, he had the awful experience of hearing their cheerfulness turn to devastation. He offered to come and pick them up, but they both insisted on returning by themselves on the train to Leeds and then on to Knaresborough.

He put down the phone, relieved that the conversations were over, and poured himself another drink. It had been an utterly draining experience. The conversations had gone as well as could be expected, but there was another problem. There was something else which the girls were probably going to find out about sooner or later, and again he wanted them to hear it from him.

Maybe now was not the time, but he would have to face it before long.

~

Snow fell again during the night, but luckily not enough to render the main roads impassable. It was a different matter on the steep and winding road up from the A61 to the village of Kirkby Underside. There had been no gritting or snow plough at work here, and Oldroyd had to drive very slowly and carefully. Even then he couldn't avoid the occasional skid and he was glad when he turned into the drive up to what he always called the 'Jane Austen vicarage' of St Bartholomew's.

His sister was three years older than him, and he'd always looked up to her. She'd always been a feisty character and had caused their parents many problems. She refused to accept traditional female roles and had initially rejected Christianity because she said the Bible was all about men. Taking inspiration from people like Father

Trevor Huddleston, she was later inspired by the crusading tradition of the Church on social issues and was one of the first women to be ordained. She remained a prominent figure in the feminist movement in the Church. Oldroyd admired her toughness, but he knew that the death of Clare Wilcox in these circumstances was a severe blow.

As soon as he got out of the car, he felt the intense cold again and looked up. The sky was fairly bright but not clear, and there were thicker, leaden-looking clouds in the distance. Deborah was right: there would be more snow before long.

Alison, a warm-hearted person who loved a hug, was usually ready to greet him enthusiastically at the door of her Regency-style house. Today, however, he rang the doorbell twice before she appeared, her usual smile replaced by a grim and tired expression.

'Come in, Jim, it's good to see you but I'm totally exhausted. Didn't sleep a wink last night thinking about that poor woman and her family.' She gave Oldroyd a quick embrace, which for her was rather cursory, and then he followed her as she shuffled down the parquet-floored hall and called back to him, 'Do you want some coffee? I've just made some.'

'That would be great, thanks. I'll go into the sitting room, shall I?'

'There's no heating on in there; it'll be better in the study.' Like Clare Wilcox, Alison was forced to make economies when heating her oversized vicarage. No wonder so many dioceses had sold off the grand old buildings and bundled their clergy into semi-detached houses instead, thought Oldroyd. He sat in an armchair in the warm and cosy study. The walls were covered from floor to ceiling with packed bookshelves. A solid wooden desk stood under the window, which gave a view over the garden. On the desk stood a Celtic cross that Alison had brought back from the Iona Community in Scotland.

Alison came in with two mugs of coffee, sat down in the armchair opposite Oldroyd and placed the mugs on a round table between the two chairs. There was silence for a moment or two as they sipped their coffee. Alison looked very upset. He'd rarely seen her so deflated.

'I suppose the first thing you want to ask me is what did I talk to Clare about yesterday?'

'Yes. I think you were the last person to speak to her, unless she had a conversation with her killer.'

Alison shook her head. 'She was feeling a bit low. Things in the parish were getting to her and she confided in me that she was feeling rather apprehensive about taking on the role of bishop. That's not surprising.'

'No. What things were bothering her in the parish?'

'The usual stuff. Groups of people falling out, problems with rotas and so on. These things happen in all churches . . . and other groups, for that matter. But she did also mention some more serious issues that she had to deal with before she left the parish.'

'Such as?'

'She wouldn't go into detail because they were confidential. She didn't even tell me the nature of the problems. It was only a brief chat. We expected to see each other before too long.' She sighed and her eyes filled with tears. 'Oh, Jim, it's just awful!'

'Take it easy, sis; I know it's hard.' He passed her a tissue from a box on the desk and waited until she was composed again. 'There might be some important clues there. Someone may have had a motive for removing her from the scene. What do you think those problems were about?'

'Well, I don't know how serious she meant. It could be lots of things. Did she suspect that someone had stolen some money? Had there been a formal complaint about someone? Had someone in an important role threatened to resign? Was there a child-protection issue? Those are the things which spring to mind, but to murder your vicar? I know church congregations get a bad press for being middle-class and small-minded, but there aren't usually any vicious killers amongst them.'

'No, but we don't know what's really going on in people's minds, do we? And as you've told me before, we're all capable of violence in certain circumstances. Someone may have panicked if they felt some misdemeanour was going to be revealed. Maybe they couldn't bear the shame.'

Alison seemed to have forgotten about her coffee, which was going cold on the coffee table. Oldroyd reminded her, and she took a drink before replying. 'Yes, I know,' she said. 'It's possible. Was there anything stolen?'

'Not as far as we know.'

'And it would be far-fetched to think there is some mad killer rampaging in Knaresborough.'

'Well, yes, but we can't rule it out completely at this early stage.'

Alison sighed. 'So, ruling out theft and random murderers, it looks as if you may be right. It must be someone who had a motive for getting rid of her.'

'It's the most likely explanation, however unpalatable. You weren't aware that she had any enemies?'

She shook her head. 'No, Clare was such a lovely person. She's happily married to Jeremy and they have two nice girls. But . . .' She paused and looked at Oldroyd. 'You're going to think this is ridiculous, Jim, but I have another idea.'

'Go on.'

'There's still a lot of hostility to women being ordained, and even more to them being consecrated bishops; some of it is surprisingly nasty and misogynistic. Clare was a very prominent woman in the Church and about to become even more so when she was made Bishop of Kendal. She'd even been tipped as a possible first female Archbishop of York.'

Oldroyd widened his eyes in surprise. 'You think someone killed her because they're opposed to women being priests and bishops?'

Alison took a deep breath. 'I know it sounds far-fetched, but if there was anyone around who was deranged enough to do that, then Clare would have been the ideal target. I have this awful feeling that there's something weird going on.'

'Did she receive any hate mail or messages on social media?'

'Not that I know of, but that doesn't mean anything. Some of these people are far too cunning to expose themselves like that.'

Oldroyd considered this before replying. The shock of someone much admired and loved like Clare being murdered often led to family and friends looking for outlandish answers to the crime. Unfortunately, the answer usually lay much closer to home. People and their circumstances were not always what they seemed to be. 'OK,' he said. 'I understand why you might think that and it's definitely a possibility, but we have to start with the more likely explanations. Most people are killed by someone known to them, and as far as Clare is concerned, we don't really know what was going on in her life, do we? This is what we need to investigate. You don't know that she was telling you everything, however close you were to her.'

'That's true.'

'I have to warn you that it's possible that something will come up. Sometimes the shock of finding out things about the murdered person is almost as shocking to family and friends as the killing itself: the secret lover, the blackmailing, the siphoning off of funds and so on. It can be very unpleasant.'

Alison took a deep breath. 'Yes, I understand. But I would be astonished if anything of that nature was discovered about Clare.'

Oldroyd glanced out of the window. Snow was falling again. 'OK, sis. Thanks for telling me what you know. I must get going or I'll get trapped here.'

Alison looked round. 'Good heavens, it's coming down again. Take care driving back, won't you?'

'I will, don't worry.'

She accompanied Oldroyd back to the front door and opened it for him as he pulled on his coat and gloves.

'Oh!' said Alison. 'There was one thing Clare said, which I'd forgotten to mention. Apparently, some of the congregation at St Anne's believe a ghost haunts the place. I can't remember the details.'

'Yes, I've heard about that. I was joking with my detective sergeant about it. Do you think it's relevant?'

'I don't suppose so, but it might give you an insight into the mindset of some of the people there. They may have resented Clare if she scoffed at the idea of a ghost. I can't imagine her having any time for such superstitions.'

Oldroyd laughed. 'Well, I'll bear it in mind but, as I said to Andy Carter, we don't deal with the supernatural. How would you get the handcuffs on a ghost?'

Alison laughed for the very first time that morning as she shut the door.

Oldroyd was thinking about ghosts again as he drove carefully along the snowy lanes. The supernatural had fascinated him since he was a boy. But haunting as an explanation for murder? He wasn't going down that road, however much some people at the church might believe it. Murders were primarily solved by the determined application of human reason to the facts, although he also believed in the importance of instinct, which seemed to operate on the sub-conscious level. Many times, the obvious solution to a crime had somehow not satisfied him, and his feelings had prompted him to look again and again at the evidence until something else appeared to put another slant on the case which led to a different conclusion. But ghosts?

Nevertheless, as he'd said to Deborah, the unsettling doubt remained. Driving down the deserted lane was a strange experience. Although it was mid-morning, it was quite dark due to the heavy cloud and swirling snow, which was very disorienting. The familiar features of the landscape were obliterated. He rounded a corner and a tall figure in a long coat loomed up in front of him. He swerved to avoid it and then increased his speed without looking back. He wondered if he should have stopped and offered help or a lift, but he hadn't wanted to. He was glad when he reached the main road and he knew where he was. There were other cars and the snow was slushy on the road surface. He could see the lights of Harrogate.

～

By the time Oldroyd arrived in Knaresborough, the snow had stopped and the sun had appeared. The little town had a picture-postcard winter beauty about it. After he'd parked in the church car park, he went over to have a look into the gorge. The fields opposite were covered in snow and the River Nidd was blue with the reflected sky. The yellow stone of the nearby ruined castle stood out against the white of the snow, and the famous Victorian railway viaduct had piles of snow on its parapets. As he watched, a train eased itself over and into the station.

He turned back to the church. Now it was daylight, he saw what a lovely building it was. Like many large English churches and cathedrals, it was a composite of styles from different periods. The tower at the west end was wide but low, while the thinner but taller tower at the east end was a later addition with a clock and presumably bells. He was just admiring the ancient stonework when the blue and white incident tape brought him back to reality. He went inside where it was much warmer. Someone must have turned the heating on.

The ever-reliable Andy was waiting for him. 'Morning, sir. I've set up an incident room here in the church. It's quite a nice space.' Andy took him down the nave and into one of the vestries. There were some clerical vestments hooked on the wall. A space had been cleared and there were some chairs. There was a large, old-fashioned safe in one corner.

'That churchwarden said we can use this room. It's where the clergy put their robes on and get ready.'

'Yes, good. Is that the same bloke who found the body?'

'Yes.' Andy looked at his notes. 'Donald Avison. In his sixties, I think. He was here early offering to help and he's gone off to get us a table and some tea, coffee and milk and stuff.'

'Not suffering from shock then? It can't have been pleasant finding the body in that state.'

'He seemed OK. We've also done a complete search of the church, but we didn't find anything significant. Down that end' – he pointed to the east – 'there's a door and a staircase down to a boiler room. It's filthy down there. There's another door which must lead out of the church, but it's locked and boarded up and doesn't look as if it's been used for years. Then there's a staircase up that other tower, which has the clock outside, to a platform where they stand to ring the bells. There's no way out of the building from there. I've checked everything with Avison.'

'OK, I think—' There was a knock on the vestry door.

'That's probably Avison now, sir.'

A stocky man in his sixties with greying hair and a neat moustache came in, carrying a tray with a carton of milk, a jar of instant coffee, teabags, some mugs and an electric kettle. There was also a packet of biscuits. He put the tray on the floor and then went out again, returning with a fold-up table which he set up in the vestry.

Oldroyd greeted him. 'Thank you and good morning. It's Mr Avison, isn't it? I'm DCI Oldroyd, in charge of the case.'

'Oh, yes. I've met your sergeant here.' He lifted the tray on to the table.

'Have a seat,' continued Oldroyd. 'I'd like to ask you a few questions.' Avison and Andy sat down, Andy lounging a little while Avison was bolt upright in the chair. 'Now, I know you've already given an account of finding the body, but I'd just like you to go through it again for my benefit. I know it's unpleasant.' Avison remained composed.

'Yes, it is, Chief Inspector, but I was in the army, you see. I was in the Falkland Islands in 1982. We were bombed on the shore at Bluff Cove and it was very nasty. So I've seen much worse things than the body of poor Rev Wilcox. It sort of hardens you. I suppose it's how we deal with it.'

'I see.' Oldroyd looked at Avison's face, which conveyed no emotion. It was the face of a tough character whom Oldroyd could imagine in the army. 'So you're the churchwarden, and you came to lock up the church yesterday?'

'Correct. There are two of us, Mrs Baxter and myself. My wife and I live quite near to the church, so I've taken on the role of locking up in the early evening. We like to leave the church open during the day for visitors and people to come and pray, but we lock up at half past five. There are too many vandals about these days. I often have to chase people out of the grounds.'

'Quite. So, what happened?'

'It was very dark in the churchyard. I saw there was a light inside, but that's not unusual in mid-winter. If anyone goes inside in the late afternoon, the lights are on a sensor and are timed to come on after four o'clock.'

'Did you see anyone in the churchyard?'

'No. When I got in, I could see that the light was on in that room built on at the base of the west tower. There's no door, you just go through an archway. I normally put all the lights on and check everything and make sure that there's no one inside before I lock up. But yesterday I could see someone lying on the floor just by the archway. We've had a few homeless people trying to sleep inside overnight and I thought it was one of them. I went straight over and found her there. I knew she was dead, and I wondered if the killer was still in the building. I picked up a metal processional cross with which I could defend myself and searched all over the church, but there was no one. So, then I locked the door, rushed home and called the police. Then I went back to the church and waited until you arrived.' Avison nodded at Andy.

'That's correct, sir,' said Andy. 'He met us here and took us in.'

'After that,' continued Avison, 'I noticed there was a light on in the vicarage and that Mr Wilcox's car was in the drive, so I went over to inform him. It wasn't an easy thing to do, but I felt it was my duty under the circumstances.'

'Yes,' said Oldroyd, thinking that this was a man who would never fail in his duty. 'When you left the church to raise the alarm, did you see any sign of anyone around then?'

'No, the churchyard was deserted, and the snow was starting to cover it over. If it had snowed earlier there might have been some footprints coming out of the church when I arrived, but the only ones I saw were the ones I was making as I walked out.'

'OK. Thank you for that clear account.' Oldroyd paused before changing tack. 'Do you know of anyone who would want to kill Rev Wilcox?'

Avison's inscrutable expression remained the same. 'No. She was a very conscientious and hard-working rector. She was the kind of person who got on with everyone. I can't see anyone wanting to harm her, but I said to you before that we've had some of these vagrants hanging around the church and sometimes going inside. They're often drunk or on drugs. I wonder if it could have been one of those. Maybe she found one inside and there was an argument. There's one chap who's around quite a lot; long hair and beard, usually smells of drink. He can get a bit aggressive if you tell him to move on; you get some vile language.'

'Has he ever threatened violence?'

'Not that I know of.'

'Do you know his name?'

'No. There's a homeless-person shelter on Niddgate. That's the other side of the Market Place. He might go there.'

'Right. We'll follow that up. Now, last thing. I'm sure you noticed that Rev Wilcox's injuries were very severe. Do you have any ideas about that? Is there anything unusual in the church that someone could have used?'

Avison shook his head. 'They were shocking injuries, Chief Inspector, and I've no idea how they could have been caused. I know what some people round here will be saying though; they'll be going on about all that claptrap about the ghost.'

Oldroyd glanced at Andy. 'You've mentioned that before, haven't you?'

'Yes,' said Avison. 'It's plain superstition in my view, and against the Bible. People don't come back as ghosts, and they don't smash rectors over the head with I don't know what.'

'I agree, but do you know what the story is?'

'Oh, it's something about a monk who was put to death here and apparently now haunts the place; I don't know the details. There are lots of people who will tell you about it: silly, credulous people in my view, who need to pull themselves together, stick to their faith and serve the church.'

He's a practical chap, won't stand any nonsense, thought Oldroyd and smiled, but then Avison went on. 'The problem is the society we live in today. Moral standards are deteriorating all the time: marriage, bringing up children to behave properly, fear of God, it's all going to the dogs.'

'Quite,' replied Oldroyd again, but thinking it was time to bring this particular interview to an end. He had no time to listen to moralising rants.

~

'What do you think of him then, sir?' asked Andy after Avison had left and Oldroyd had brewed some tea. 'He seemed a bit weird to me. His expression never changed and then he was going on about how everything's rubbish today. How do they expect any younger people to come to church if they think the way we live is so crap?'

Oldroyd laughed. 'Yes, he's the stickler-for-order-and-standards type.' He saluted. 'It's his military background.'

'He could be the killer, you know,' continued Andy. 'There's no one to corroborate his story of finding the victim dead. He could have done her in and then pretended to have found her.'

'Yes. In fact, at the moment, he must be the chief suspect. We'll have to check with his wife that he left home when he did and not any earlier. The problem is that of the three indicators, two are missing: we don't know the means by which the crime was committed, and we don't have a motive for Avison to have done it. At least, not yet. It's early days, Andy.'

'Maybe he had access to some kind of small bomb. You know, as an ex-military bloke. That might explain the injuries.'

'Well done for thinking outside the box, but you know from your training that any kind of explosive device inflicts blast injuries, and there were none on her body.'

'No,' replied Andy, still thinking about ways Avison could have committed the crime. He'd taken a serious dislike to the man.

Oldroyd finished his tea and looked around. 'Is there a sink in here? Yes, there is – look, in the corner.' There was a small sink partially hidden by the clerical garments hanging from hooks. 'Well, we've got all the mod cons, haven't we? I think you're right, this will do us fine. Pass your mug.' He rinsed the mugs out as he continued. 'So, we need to follow up this homeless character. I wonder if anyone else has seen him? You can go round to that hostel later. Now I think we should go over to the rectory and see how the husband is getting on.'

They walked out of the church and looked over to the rectory.

'It looks like someone's beaten us to it,' said Oldroyd. 'There's another car in the drive.'

~

Andy and Oldroyd walked across from the church and up a stone garden path to the rectory. The herbaceous borders were dormant and the cut-down stumps of plants were covered in snow.

The door was answered by a very tired-looking Jeremy Wilcox. 'Good morning, Chief Inspector, Sergeant; come in. I have two visitors who you may want to speak to.'

He showed them into the living room and two men rose to greet them.

'This is Michael Palmer, Bishop of Ripon, and Patrick Owen, Archdeacon of Harrogate.' The bishop was a portly, balding man with a ruddy face. The archdeacon was tall and thin with a shock of black hair and a hawkish expression behind rimless glasses. The detectives shook hands with both, and everyone sat down.

'Absolutely shocking business,' said the bishop in a voice that contained pronounced traces of a northern accent. 'Patrick and I are here to support Jeremy and the church here at St Anne's.' He shook his head. 'It's beyond words, Chief Inspector. A fine woman, wonderful servant of the Church, and getting ready to take on greater responsibilities. I'll be honest, it's a test of faith and no mistake.'

That's a very honest response, thought Oldroyd, and smiled. He recognised a straight-speaking northerner like himself.

'I know it's very early in your investigation,' the archdeacon said, speaking very precisely, in a refined RP accent, 'but do you have any idea at all about who on earth could have done this terrible thing? Clare was rural dean of this deanery within my archdeaconry. We worked together extremely well and I can only reiterate Michael's comments about her.' He fixed Oldroyd with an icy stare while Andy furrowed his brow, baffled by the arcane Anglican terminology.

Oldroyd, however, was not intimidated. 'I was going to ask you both the same thing,' he said. 'Were you aware that she had any enemies?'

The bishop and the archdeacon glanced at each other. 'I think I can speak for both of us when I say no,' replied the archdeacon. 'Rarely have I known a rector so popular with her parishioners.'

'Absolutely,' added the bishop.

'Were you aware that there were some serious issues that Rev Wilcox was facing at St Anne's?'

'Really, Chief Inspector?' said Wilcox, who had remained silent and rather distracted until now. 'She never told me about anything. How do you know about this?'

Oldroyd turned to the two clerics. 'I was explaining yesterday to Mr Wilcox that my sister Alison Oldroyd is vicar of Kirkby Underside, where I understand Rev Wilcox did her curacy.' Both men reacted to the mention of Alison's name; clearly his sister had made an impact on them.

The bishop nodded. 'Ah yes, Rev Oldroyd. A very – what shall I say? – forceful character,' he said with a warm smile, and Oldroyd returned it. He was beginning to like the bishop.

'I broke the news to her last night,' continued Oldroyd, 'and went to see her this morning. It turns out that she was probably the last person to speak to Rev Wilcox, who had rung my sister in the afternoon shortly before she met her death. They were close friends and she confided in Alison that there were some issues at the church that she wanted to sort out before she left. She wouldn't go into details because the matters were confidential.' He turned to Wilcox. 'That's probably why she didn't tell you about them.'

Wilcox nodded. 'Yes, you're right. Clare was very scrupulous where confidentiality was concerned. She never spoke about things like that to me – in fact, not much about her work at all. We tried to have a private life in which the church or my medical practice didn't intrude all the time. We all need a break from work, don't we?'

Oldroyd addressed the two clerics again. 'So, do either of you have any information about these matters? Did Rev Wilcox confide in either of you?'

The bishop and the archdeacon exchanged glances again, both shaking their heads.

'No she didn't, Chief Inspector,' said the bishop. 'I suppose she felt confident enough to deal with whatever these problems were. It would have to be something serious for her to involve either of us—'

'We're here to offer support to Jeremy and also to take on the task of helping to organise the church in this terrible time.' The archdeacon had broken in abruptly, seemingly eager to change the subject. 'Would it be possible to get on with that now, Chief Inspector? The congregation desperately needs news about what is going to happen without Clare.'

'I understand your sense of urgency,' replied Oldroyd, noting that the archdeacon seemed very uneasy. 'But I have to tell you that there cannot be any services or meetings in the church until we are happy that we have explored everything very thoroughly. It is a crime scene and must remain sealed off. We don't know how Rev Wilcox was killed, but the clues are very likely to be in that building.'

'How long will that be?' began the archdeacon. 'I mean is it—'

At this point, the doorbell rang. Wilcox looked out of the window. He had a view of the front door from where he was standing. 'Ah, that's Robin. I've been expecting him.' He turned to the detectives. 'Robin Eastby, he's the curate; young chap, he's going to be devastated. I know he looked up to Clare a great deal.'

He went to open the door and the conversation paused. They could hear muffled words and then Wilcox returned with a man in his early thirties with a pale, freckled face and reddish hair. Wilcox introduced him to the detectives. He looked rather intimidated by the presence of the police and his superiors in the Church.

'I was away yesterday and . . . just got back this morning,' he said rather haltingly. 'Olive rang to tell me the—'

'I was going to ring you, but I knew you were away last night. I'm afraid it slipped my mind this morning. I'm sorry,' said Wilcox.

'Oh, don't be. It's . . . How you must feel, I can't imagine.' He looked nervously around the room.

'Take a seat, Robin,' said the bishop. 'When these gentlemen have finished with us, we need to discuss our plans for the immediate future of the church. We will need your help; it's going to be tricky.'

'Of course,' replied the curate, and perched himself uncomfortably on the edge of a chair.

'And after that,' said Oldroyd, 'we will need to have a word with you over in the church. We've created a little office for ourselves in the vestry. It would be good if you could provide us with a list of regular attenders and office-holders at St Anne's.'

'Yes,' said Eastby with a wan smile.

'So,' continued Oldroyd, turning to Wilcox, 'I'm going to send an officer over to take Rev Wilcox's computer away for investigation.'

'Oh? Why is that?'

'We need to see if there are any threatening messages on there, any clues about who might have attacked her. The same goes for her phone. I assume that's here? We didn't find it on her body.'

'Yes, yes, of course. I've got it.' Wilcox flinched at the reminder of his wife's murder. 'Clare never mentioned any emails or messages like that.'

'She may not have wanted you to worry, or she may not have regarded them as serious. Anyway' – Oldroyd nodded to the assembled clerics – 'we'll be on our way, and we'll leave you to it.'

∾

'What was all that about then, sir? Deaneries and archdeaconries? I was completely lost,' asked a baffled Andy on the way back to their office in the church.

'So is most of the population.' Oldroyd laughed. 'The Anglican Church is very hierarchical. Each diocese has a bishop and at least one suffragan bishop, which I suppose is like an assistant bishop. Palmer will be Suffragan Bishop of Ripon under the diocesan Bishop of Leeds. In each diocese, a number of parishes form a deanery, and a number of deaneries form an archdeaconry supervised by an archdeacon like Owen. Three or four archdeaconries form a diocese, and then each diocese is part of a province – in this case York with the Archbishop of York in charge, but he's second to Canterbury who also presides over the whole of the Anglican

Church in this country and beyond. After that, the Great Chain of Being goes into the heavenly realm with hierarchies of angels, archangels, etc., until we get up to the Almighty Himself and the buck stops there.'

'Bloody hell, sir, it makes the structure of the police force sound simple.'

'Yes, and we only have to be concerned about this life, too.'

As they got to the doors of the church, they were immediately confronted by a small round woman with straggly hair, glasses and a slight squint, who'd been waiting by the door. She was wearing a house coat and rubber gloves. She pointed at Oldroyd.

'You're that chief inspector; I've seen your picture in the paper.'

'Yes. And who are you?' asked Oldroyd.

'Violet Saunders. I clean the church, but they say I can't go in; it's an incident scene or something. That's all very well, but if I don't clean up, it's going to be filthy when people come back to worship.'

'We should be done with the forensics in a couple of days. You'll be able to get in then and there won't be any services before we've finished, so don't worry.'

She stared at Oldroyd. 'I don't think forensics will tell you very much.'

'Why is that?'

'Ghosts leave no trace, do they?'

Oldroyd smiled. 'I've heard about this ghost. Tell me what you know about it.'

The woman's eyes lit up. Clearly this was something she enjoyed talking about.

'I don't know all the history, Chief Inspector, you'll have to ask someone like Austin Eliot about that. It was a monk who was put to death, I think. But I've seen it.' Her eyes took on a faraway look. 'I came into the church one afternoon when the light was failing, and there, under the tower, was a figure in a monk's cowl. There was a rope around its waist. The hood covered the face, thank goodness. It was very dim but, as I watched, it seemed to disappear. And it never came back, Chief Inspector.' She nodded her head knowingly. 'Walls can't keep in a spirit. I've also heard strange noises, groanings and wailings coming from the church at night. There's a very disturbed spirit here. I can feel such things, believe me.' She closed her eyes for a moment and took a deep breath.

Oldroyd wondered if she was about to start communing with the dead, so he posed a quick question to keep her in the land of the living. 'I see. So I take it you think this ghost was responsible for Rev Wilcox's death?'

'It's a spirit that can't rest – can't rest and has to continue taking vengeance until it's finally given peace.' Her voice had become rather lilting and unworldly.

'How would you do that?' asked Andy.

'Exorcism. It's the only way. We need the bishop to come and perform the ritual. The ghost will be laid to rest and all evil banished from the church. Then we shall attain God's peace.' She crossed herself while Andy drew back, looking startled.

'Who is this Mr Eliot?' asked Oldroyd, returning to the earthly practicalities of the investigation.

'Austin Eliot. He comes to church; he has a bookshop down by the river. He knows a lot about history – Knaresborough and the old buildings, stories and stuff.'

'I see.'

'The trouble is, not everyone believes in the ghost. And that makes it worse, Chief Inspector. The more people don't believe in it, the angrier it gets and the more it hates us after what the church did to it in life.'

'Did Rev Wilcox believe in it?' asked Oldroyd.

Saunders shook her head. 'No, she didn't. I tried to persuade her. And now look what's happened.' Oldroyd frowned. 'Anyway,

I'll just clean around the entrance here, if that's OK? If you need me, you know where to come.'

'Thank you, Mrs . . . ?'

'Miss Saunders. I live just round the corner and down the hill from here, near to Donald and Mary Avison.'

'Good. Well, just a quick sweep round and then pop back home.'

'Oh, I . . .' Saunders was about to say more, but Oldroyd and Andy pressed on to the vestry. Their office was warm; the efficient Donald Avison had brought in a portable heater.

'She was a bit weird too, sir. Are they all like this in the Church?' said Andy as he put the kettle on, after both men took off their coats and gloves. 'I wouldn't like to meet her on a dark night in the church, never mind a ghost.'

'Oh, don't be unkind, Andy. I'm sure she's harmless enough. The church has always attracted lots of older single women like that . . . and men, too. It gives them somewhere to belong to.'

'What is it with this ghost thing, though? Does she really believe the murderer was a phantom?'

'It appears so.'

'She says a figure dressed as a monk disappeared near where Rev Wilcox was killed.' Andy held up his hands in disbelief.

'If she did see something, I'd like to know how thoroughly she searched. The person could have been hiding somewhere. Sometimes it's easier not to look too deeply, in case you disprove your own beliefs.' He took a mug of tea from Andy.

'We need to find out more about the story behind this ghost. I'll do the research on that.'

'Do you really think it's important, sir?'

'Not in itself, but it sounds like there was a split in the church between those who believe in it and those who don't, which could have caused aggravation.' He took a drink of his tea. 'I'd like you to

41

search out this homeless hostel that Avison mentioned. We need to track down that man who's been seen around the church. He may turn out to be the perpetrator, but more likely, he may have seen something if he was around yesterday afternoon.'

'OK, sir. To be honest, I'd rather deal with that than some of these church types; they spook me out.'

'Get away with you!' joked Oldroyd, and Andy laughed as he left the church.

～

Back at the rectory there was a somewhat strained silence after Oldroyd and Andy left. No one quite knew what to say next until the bishop spoke.

'Well, I must say I found that reassuring. That chief inspector seems extremely competent and I'm sure he'll get to the bottom of this dreadful business. How do you feel, Jeremy?'

'I agree. Apparently, he has a very good reputation for solving difficult cases. He'll need all his skill on this one; I just can't imagine anyone . . .' Wilcox stopped and turned away, putting his hand to his face.

'Let's not talk about that now,' said the archdeacon. 'It will be more helpful for you to focus on practical things, with our help. Are your daughters coming home?'

'Yes. I'm expecting them tonight.'

'Good. I'm sure you will all support each other. My advice is to let people do things for your family; don't try to be too strong and put on a brave face all the time. You will have to certify the death and arrange the funeral when the police give their permission. None of it is easy, as I'm sure you're aware.'

Wilcox nodded, as he thought about the grieving relatives who had visited Clare over the years, and the funeral services she had conducted.

'As far as the church goes,' said the bishop, 'Robin here is quite capable of standing in the breach in the short term. We can't hold any services, anyway, until the police allow it. I'm looking at who we can draft in to help in the medium term. I think a longish inter-regnum would be appropriate. It would be unseemly to appoint a new rector too quickly after such a tragedy. By the way, Robin, I'm going to preach and preside at the first Sunday communion service the church holds when the ban is lifted. I want to be with the congregation, and minister to them in their grief.'

'Yes, Bishop,' said Robin, quite relieved that he didn't have to lead the first – and no doubt very emotional – service after the rector's death.

'Oh dear, I haven't offered you anything to drink!' said Wilcox.

'Don't worry about that,' said the archdeacon. 'Michael and I will be away soon, though I'm sure Robin will stay here for a while and give you a hand with things.'

'Of course,' said Robin, smiling at Wilcox.

'I'm sure there will be many parishioners wanting to know lots of things, so it would help if you could field some of those calls and visits. They're very exhausting for the bereaved person,' said the bishop, and Robin nodded. 'So, as Patrick said, we'll be off now.' The bishop and the archdeacon both stood up and they each briefly embraced Wilcox who struggled to his feet. 'Don't hesitate to call either of us if you need anything. We'll be working on putting in the support you and Robin will need, and we'll be praying for you both and for the family.'

'Thank you,' replied Wilcox in a weak voice.

'Now, please sit down, we'll see ourselves out,' said the archdeacon.

Wilcox felt exhausted when they'd left. He appreciated the fact that they'd visited him so soon after the awful thing had happened, but they had also reminded him of how many daunting things there were to do. Robin got up.

'Just stay there, Jeremy, I'll get you a drink. I know where everything is. Tea or coffee?'

'Thanks, and coffee please.' As Robin went into the kitchen, Wilcox leaned his head against the back of the chair and closed his eyes. He had to conserve his energy so that he could pick up his daughters at the station later on. If he thought about all that needed to be done, he had a feeling close to panic. It would be much better when they arrived home. Jenny and Fiona were both very capable young women, and he was really going to need them.

Two

Between these two figures stands a shape muffled in a long mantle. This might at first sight be mistaken for a monk . . . for the head is cowled and a knotted cord depends from somewhere above the waist. A slight inspection, however, will lead to a very different conclusion.

From 'The Stalls of Barchester Cathedral',
M. R. James, 1910

There was no relief from the intense cold as Andy walked from the church to the hostel. Although it had stopped snowing for the time being, the sky had become grey and heavy again. He was following Google Maps on his phone to the street that Avison had mentioned. He put up the collar of his overcoat and clapped his gloved hands together as he made his way to the Market Place, passing near to the snow-covered ruins of the castle, a medieval fortification on the highest point of the gorge. His feet scrunched on the soft, cold snow; he was glad he was wearing very stout shoes.

He reached the Market Place to find everything eerily quiet. Noise was muffled by the snow and fewer people than normal were out and about in the cold weather. A van skidded along and came to a halt outside a shop; deliveries were still taking place. Andy passed a pub called Blind Jack's, and wondered vaguely who Blind

Jack was. That was a question for the boss, who had an encyclopedic knowledge of his beloved county.

Andy smiled to himself. Against his expectations as a Londoner, and under the influence of Oldroyd, Andy had come to love Yorkshire and its landscapes and was interested in its history, although he still had difficulties sometimes with strong local accents and dialect words.

On the other side of the Market Place was a very old timber-framed building which claimed to be the oldest chemist's shop in Britain. How many other places claimed that distinction, wondered Andy with another smile. It was like four-poster beds in old inns where Queen Elizabeth had supposedly slept. If all the claims were true, the old girl must have spent most of her life travelling around the country and hardly ever been in London.

Passing out of the Market Place, Andy discovered that Niddgate was an extremely narrow street, barely more than an alleyway or ginnel, he thought, remembering one of the Yorkshire words he'd learned. It was also a dead end. At the bottom was an old building with grimy windows and a door with a strong-looking security lock. A small sign said: 'Knaresborough Men's Hostel', and next to it was a doorbell and intercom. Andy pressed the button, and after a few seconds' delay and some crackling noises a voice said: 'Who's there?'

'Detective Sergeant Carter, West Riding Police. I'm investigating a murder and I'm looking for someone who may have information. I have reason to believe this person may be here.'

'OK. Come up the stairs.' There was a loud buzz, and when Andy pushed at the door it was open. He was immediately faced by a steep flight of steps that took him up to a large room, which was warm and stuffy. There were old sofas around the edge and a number of unkempt men with straggly and dirty hair were laid out asleep on them. A group were sitting at a table and playing dominoes. A door into a side room opened and a tall man in his thirties with a beard and ponytail beckoned to Andy.

'In here, Sergeant.' Andy followed him into the room, which turned out to be a small office. He showed his ID. 'Have a seat. I'm Trevor Wood, the manager here.'

Both men sat down.

'We're a hostel for homeless men run by a charitable trust,' Wood said. 'No money from the government or the council. Dickensian, isn't it, in one of the world's richest countries?' He gave a grim laugh. 'Anyway, I'm sure you're not here to talk politics. You said you were investigating a murder?'

'Yes, at St Anne's. The vicar, Reverend Wilcox, was murdered there yesterday in the late afternoon.'

Wood raised his eyebrows. 'Bloody hell, so that's what all the police cars are about. I noticed them on my way here this morning. And you think someone here knew something about it? Do you mean a homeless person, or a member of staff? I—'

Suddenly, there was the sound of shouting from outside the room. 'Just a minute,' said Wood, and he went quickly through the door which he had left open. Andy could see what was happening. One man in the domino game had got up and was cursing at the others.

'Malcolm, calm down please,' said Wood loudly and firmly, but the man continued to shout and gesticulate. Wood stood between him and the others at the table, who were laughing and jeering. He turned to them sharply. 'Cut that out. I need to calm him down.' He faced Malcolm again. 'Malcolm, sit down and stop shouting now. If you don't, you'll have to go. It's nasty and cold out there.' This seemed to have an effect. Malcolm slumped on to a sofa and stopped swearing, though he continued to glare at the other men. 'Now, just stay there and don't get involved again.'

Malcolm stared at the floor. Wood waited for a moment and then went back into the office. Another man joined the domino game.

Wood sat down again. 'Sorry, Malcolm can't bear to lose; he always accuses someone of cheating. Mental-health problems, of course, like many of them. He's been a bit better recently; I don't know what's got into him today. I don't like to threaten them with expulsion when they've nowhere to go and the weather is as it is, but sometimes it's the only way.'

'It's a homeless man we're looking for,' said Andy. 'Do a lot of them come back to you regularly?'

'Of course. We're supposed to offer temporary help and accommodation, but they've nowhere to go apart from other hostels in Harrogate and Leeds. They try to get from one to the other and go backwards and forwards, just like they did with the casual wards in the old workhouses. Like I said, it's Victorian. There's no affordable rented housing for men like them.'

Andy shook his head. 'Yeah, I can see it's tough. A bloke at the church' – he looked at his notes – 'Donald Avison. Said there's a man been hanging around the churchyard recently. He described him as having long hair and a beard; often smells of drink and can get a bit aggressive. He walks unsteadily; I don't know if that's because of drink.'

'I don't know anybody at the church, but the man he's describing sounds like David Tanner. He had an accident which left him with a limp. I know he goes up to the church a lot, and he has a drink problem which we're trying to help him with.'

'Is he here now?'

'No, I'm afraid not. He wasn't here last night and if he saw police cars up at the church, he would run a mile. He's had problems with the law in the past. I'm afraid he hates you lot.'

'He's not the only one,' said Andy with a grin. 'We get used to it. If he comes in here, please let us know.' He gave Wood a card. 'If he was up at the church yesterday afternoon, he might have seen something. Tell him he's not a suspect.' This was not entirely true, but Andy decided not to say more, otherwise they might really scare this character off.

'OK,' said Wood. 'I'll ask around and see if anyone has seen him.' He escorted Andy to the door. All seemed reasonably calm in the room. One man was singing to himself in a corner. Wood looked towards him thoughtfully. 'They get jumpy up at the church if any homeless people hang around; too dirty and uncouth. I'm not religious, but I thought Christianity was all about caring for others. Here we are struggling along, trying to put a roof over people's heads, and there's that huge building up there empty most of the time.' He shook his head. 'Maybe I'm being unfair, but I don't get it. Anyway, watch it on the stairs, they're steep. You won't be able to do much investigating with a broken leg.'

～

There were few places that Oldroyd would rather visit than a second-hand bookshop. His favourite was one in Skipton, run by a knowledgeable old Yorkshire eccentric called Gilbert Ramsden. He'd passed Nidd Books in Knaresborough in his car, but he'd never been inside. The shop was down on a road that ran by the river. From here you had a good view of the spectacular eighty-foot-high railway viaduct of 1851, designed with castellated walls and piers to blend in with the ruins of Knaresborough Castle. This was the bridge which, viewed from near the castle, featured in many of the classic photographs and paintings of the town.

Oldroyd walked gingerly on the steep footpath down Briggate towards the river. The water was grey and slow-moving. It looked bitterly cold, and snow covered the banks. He wondered if the shop might be closed, but when he reached the low building, part of an old terrace in a jumble of architectural styles, he saw the light was on and a little sign in the door said 'Open'. He went in.

The interior gave Oldroyd a strong sense of déjà vu; it was so similar to Ramsden's shop in Skipton, with its floor-to-ceiling shelves crammed with books and the hint of narrow corridors winding through the building. There was even a man – who he assumed was the owner, Austin Eliot – sitting, like Ramsden did, at a desk by the door.

'Mr Eliot?' asked Oldroyd, shutting the door behind him and feeling glad to be back inside and out of the cold.

'Yes?' replied the man behind the desk. He was somewhat younger than Ramsden – in his early fifties – and powerfully built, with thick and longish hair, still black. He was wearing a tweed jacket and charcoal chino trousers. His eyes were intense and dark. They fixed on the newcomer, who was clearly not a regular customer, with a quizzical expression.

Oldroyd produced his ID. 'Chief Inspector Oldroyd. I'm investigating the murder of the Rev Clare Wilcox at the church on Wednesday afternoon. I understand you are a member of the congregation.'

Eliot's expression darkened. 'Dreadful business; I've been following reports on the radio. Lots of people have been calling me asking if we should go up to the church. I said no, leave it to the police for now. How are Jeremy and the girls?'

'I've spoken to Mr Wilcox twice. He seems to be doing well. The curate, I can't remember his name.'

'Robin? Excellent young man. He'll make a good priest when he gets his own parish.'

'Yes. He's at the rectory now. I think Mr Wilcox's daughters are arriving home tonight.'

'Of course, they're away at university, aren't they? Doesn't seem two minutes since they were schoolgirls.' Eliot shook his head and then seemed to collect himself. 'I'm sorry, Chief Inspector. Please draw that up.' He pointed at an old spindle-back chair in the corner. Oldroyd pulled it to the desk and sat down. 'Clare's death has shocked us all deeply. Of course we want to know who was responsible, but I'm not sure how I can help you.'

'Were you aware of anyone who might have wished her harm?'

'Certainly not. Clare was a lovely woman at a personal level.' Eliot's eyes narrowed and he chose his words carefully. 'There will be some people, Chief Inspector, who will tell you that Clare was not welcomed into the parish by all the congregation at St Anne's.'

'Why was that?'

'Because there is a group, and I have to say I am one of them, that does not really accept that women can be priests. I'm sure you don't want a theological discussion at this point.'

True, thought Oldroyd. He would like to have challenged Eliot on the issue, but now was not the time.

Eliot continued. 'Basically, we don't find any biblical justification for women priests. Christ chose exclusively men as his disciples and St Paul has significant things to say about men being in authority over women. That's it in a nutshell. However, just because we hold those views doesn't mean we're hostile to Clare as a person. She does – did – an excellent job, and I think her performance has challenged the views of some people.'

Oldroyd looked at him thoughtfully. 'Who else is part of this group opposed to women priests?'

Eliot frowned. 'I really don't think it's my place to say, Chief Inspector, I . . .' He was suddenly faced with Oldroyd's piercing grey eyes at their most hawkish.

'This is a murder enquiry, and information of that nature is very important. In this situation you must name names regardless of considerations of privacy and loyalty. I'm sure you're aware that in a case like this the killer can turn out to be the least likely person.'

Eliot gave Oldroyd a sour look. 'There isn't a formal group who meet. I'm simply referring to conversations I've had, views I've heard expressed. There are only two people who I can say for certain share my opinions and I know they won't mind me saying so: that's Donald Avison and Maisie Baxter, the current churchwardens.'

'We've met Mr Avison. He spoke very warmly about Rev Wilcox.'

'Of course he did. As I said, she was excellent in her pastoral role. It's just that when it comes to the sacraments, some of us cannot accept them from a woman. The priest is representing Christ at that moment, and he was a man.'

'So, how do you voice your concerns?'

'We don't go up to receive at St Anne's unless Robin the curate is celebrating, and we go to communion services in other churches.'

'Where the clergy are male?'

'Exactly.'

'Don't you think that was distressing for Rev Wilcox?'

Eliot sighed. 'It may well have been, Chief Inspector, and I regret that. But there are very deep principles at stake here. The elements of bread and wine cannot become the body and blood of Jesus Christ unless they are blessed by a true priest. And I'm afraid, however worthy, that cannot be a woman.'

Oldroyd decided to change the subject. 'What can you tell me about this supposed haunting by a monk? It seems that some people at the church take it seriously. Violet Saunders told me you would be able to tell me more.'

Eliot's face lit up. 'Ah yes, Violet. She's a person of, what shall I say, imagination? But she's correct, you've come to the right place. I've done a lot of research on local history.' He pointed to a bookshelf behind Oldroyd. 'Those are the books on Knaresborough and the surrounding area which are on sale, but I have an additional private collection of rare volumes. If you'll excuse me a moment, I'll get the book I need.'

He got up and mounted a narrow staircase to the room above. There was a lot of creaking in the old floor joists. Oldroyd experienced a second bout of déjà vu as he remembered how Ramsden had loaned him an old volume on early potholing in the dales, which had helped him to solve a case.

Eliot soon returned carrying a heavy volume. He placed it on the desk and Oldroyd saw the title and author: *Hauntings in the Harrogate and Knaresborough Area* by A. A. Murray. Oldroyd smelled the fustiness and saw the yellowing edges of the pages. 'When was this written?' he asked.

'There's no date on it but it was most probably in the 1880s, during the golden age of antiquarian activity. Local records were explored; legends and folklore were collected. Lots of stories which had been handed down orally were written down just in time, before the collective memory was disrupted by twentieth-century life. We don't know how historically accurate many of these narratives are, but I'm sure they all have some basis in truth.'

Oldroyd leafed through the pages and then handed the book back to Eliot. 'So the relevant story is in here?'

'Indeed. Murray, who was a local schoolmaster and historian, calls it "The Monk of St Anne's". He used a lot of original documents, but he could well have embroidered the stories a little. We have no way of knowing how reliable his sources were. It was a superstitious age, but I think something must have been going on.'

Oldroyd felt a little chill. The shop was cold. There was only a small electric heater at the side of Eliot's desk and the door was draughty. But he also felt strangely uneasy, and remembered the figure he'd seen on the road down from Kirkby Underside.

'Go on,' he said.

Eliot sat back in his chair. 'It was in the early fifteenth century – 1406 is the date often given. In those pre-Reformation days, St Anne's had a monastic foundation attached to it. It was the time when there was much controversy in the Church about the Lollards.'

'They were a kind of pre-Protestant group, very critical of the corrupt practices in the Church, weren't they?'

'That's right, and it was discovered that a monk at St Anne's had been reading Lollard texts. Lollardry had been declared a heresy. John Wycliffe, the leader of the movement, came from Yorkshire, but there was never much Lollard activity in this particular area. That's probably why they made such an example of Thomas Rawcliff, or Rowcliff as his name was spelled in some texts. They wanted to stamp it out before it could take hold. Rawcliff was tried in the church by officials from the ecclesiastical courts in York. He claimed that he was only reading the texts to find out what the Lollards believed. I think there's a quote; Murray likes to use the early-fifteenth-century English.' He found the place and read: '"To knowe the extent of this recent perilous heresies that I may not falle into any of Satan's traps." Unfortunately, they didn't believe him and he was condemned to death.

'The normal method of execution for heretics was burning at the stake, but on this occasion he was taken to the edge of the gorge and thrown over on to the rocks below at the edge of the water.' Eliot read again from the text: '"To shew how far he had fallen from grace in the sighte of God." He died of head and neck injuries and his body was thrown into the river.

'Normally, records of these events tell of how contrite the condemned person was and how they asked forgiveness, etc., and died a brave Christian death, but the curious thing is that in this case, Rawcliff was angry and unrepentant. Before they cast him off he insisted he was innocent and that he would not leave the church alone until it acknowledged its crime against him.' Eliot searched for the quote and read in a dramatic voice: "'To the grete dismay of all present he seyde he wolde inhabit the chirche of St. Anne's until the grete wrong done to him was righted. And that others wolde suffer what he did. Saying thus he went to his dethe and to the Lord God Our Father without repentance.'"

'I suppose they were more horrified by that than the fact that a man had been brutally thrown to his death,' reflected Oldroyd.

'Probably, they were brutal times, but according to the records, Rawcliff was as good as his word. People started to suffer violent deaths and the injuries were always the same: trauma to the head, neck and shoulders. The problem was that none of them fell from a great height; they were found in the church or the graveyard and nobody could understand how they had received the injuries.'

A memory flashed into Oldroyd's mind. Tim Groves had said that Rev Wilcox's injuries were consistent with falling from a considerable height, but she hadn't. There was a fairly low wooden ceiling under the tower even if she'd managed to climb up to the top somehow, which didn't seem possible.

Unless . . .

He shook his head. 'Have any such deaths happened recently?' he asked.

'They were mostly in the years following his execution. I suppose he was taking revenge on the people who had executed him.'

'Or people were using it as a cover for getting rid of people they didn't like,' suggested Oldroyd cynically. Nevertheless, this link between the death of Clare Wilcox and that of the monk was a little unnerving.

Eliot laughed. 'Maybe. One of the victims was the abbot who had sent him for trial. But in addition to these strange deaths, there were sightings in the church of a monk dressed in a cowl with the hood up and a rope round the waist. These appearances have been recorded at various times over the centuries, and there was one case of a death in the nineteenth century which some people linked to the ghost.'

'And the appearances are still going on today, according to some people?'

'Indeed. People do report seeing and hearing unusual things in the church.'

'So, what's your view of it all?'

Eliot shrugged. 'I keep an open mind, Chief Inspector. There's not much in the Bible or Christian doctrine about ghosts and hauntings, but Christ himself cast out evil spirits, and we do still occasionally perform exorcisms in the Anglican Church, so maybe there's something going on.'

'Have you ever seen this phantom yourself?'

'I've certainly seen and heard things I can't account for. I was once walking back from a friend's house late at night and passed near the church. There were some odd sorts of faint groans, cries and knocking sounds, which seemed to be coming from inside the building. I looked around and there was no light inside and no sign of anyone.'

'Old buildings move and creak a bit, don't they?'

'They do, but these were very peculiar sounds. I've also occasionally caught glimpses of something which could have been the ghost of the monk; you know, something seems to disappear behind a pillar and you think: What was that? Is there someone there? Was it a trick of the light? But then you can't find anything.'

'You seem very sanguine about it all. But I hear that some members of the congregation are quite frightened and won't go into the church at night.'

Eliot shook his head. 'That's weakness and superstition in my view. We should never be afraid of the forces of darkness, especially in a consecrated building like St Anne's.'

'That didn't seem to protect Rev Wilcox.'

'People have free will to perform evil deeds; we can't prevent that.'

'So you don't think her murder was anything connected to the supernatural?'

'I don't know. She was killed in the church, like many of the apparent victims of the ghost. On the other hand, the church is open and anyone could have gone in and laid in wait for her.'

'OK,' said Oldroyd, and got up from his seat. 'Can I borrow this book? I'd like to read the full version.'

'You're welcome to, Chief Inspector. I'll put it in a bag for you.'

'Thank you. There is one last thing.'

'Yes?'

'Where were you yesterday afternoon between three and five in the afternoon?'

'Easy, Chief Inspector. Every other Wednesday I visit an old lady for tea. It's a befriending scheme run by the church. Mrs Henderson, number two Maple Walk. It's up towards the church.'

'Thank you.'

Oldroyd struggled back up the slippy path to the top of the gorge, thinking that his encounter with Austin Eliot had raised more questions than it had provided answers. As he reached the top, a car came skidding and swerving down the road at high speed.

'Idiot!' muttered Oldroyd to himself, and then looked up at the cold sky and shivered. There was going to be more snow soon.

∾

After Archdeacon Owen left the rectory in Knaresborough, he drove off with a grim expression and went straight back to his house in Harrogate.

His wife was a teacher, and she was still at work when he arrived home. He sat in an armchair in the lounge for a while drumming his fingers on the arm. Then he got out his phone and rang a number.

'Hi, I'm back. It was OK. Jeremy, Michael and Robin were there. It was all about supporting Jeremy and the church. I think Robin will step up and do a good job. It's obviously terrible for Jeremy. His daughters are coming back tonight . . . No, of course no one said anything, why should they? You're being completely paranoid. The whole thing will be forgotten about for a while now and it may even completely fade away. We'll just have to wait and see . . . Well, what else do you think I can do? Be reasonable . . . I know, but you'll just have to sit tight and be patient . . . There's no point making threats, is there? You've made it all absolutely clear to me already . . . Well, I don't think—'

Owen frowned. The other speaker had rung off. He continued to sit in the chair looking out of the large French windows on to the dormant and snow-covered winter garden. If only it were spring and he could get out and do some work there. He enjoyed gardening, and it would take his mind off this awful situation.

After a while he sighed, shook his head and forced himself up. It was his own fault. If there was no distraction outdoors, then maybe he could lose himself in his paperwork. He trudged down the parquet-floored corridor to his study.

~

When Oldroyd arrived back at the church, his hands and feet were numb with cold. He was glad to feel the warmth inside the old building. It seemed there was a heating system here that was better than in many churches. He was also very hungry, and when he got to the vestry office, he was relieved to see that Andy had been shopping and bought some sandwiches and fruit. It was well past their usual lunchtime.

'Well done, my trusty lieutenant,' declared Oldroyd with his familiar flamboyant gusto, taking his coat off and rubbing his hands together as he cheered up at the prospect of food and drink. 'What do I owe you?'

'Oh, just get the next one, sir, it's fine.'

'Ah, cheddar cheese and tomato, lovely. I'm—' There was a knock at the door. 'Damn! You hardly get a minute to call your own in this job.' He went over and opened the door. It was Donald Avison, and a woman dressed in a Barbour jacket, jeans and Hunter wellies. Very 'county', thought Oldroyd.

'Are we disturbing you, Chief Inspector?' said Avison. 'It's quite important.'

'That's fine,' replied Oldroyd. 'We'll make it fairly quick if that's OK, as we're pretty busy.' Oldroyd glanced at Andy, who raised his eyebrows.

The two visitors entered the vestry and everyone sat down. Avison introduced the newcomer, who was Maisie Baxter, the other churchwarden. As she said hello, Oldroyd detected a slight Scottish accent.

There was a pause and then Avison began. 'We've come with information, Chief Inspector. This is not easy, but we've searched our consciences and we feel that we must speak out.'

'Go on.' Oldroyd wasn't sure he liked the sound of this.

Baxter said, 'There is one person in the church who may have harboured a grudge against Rev Wilcox. That person is Olive Bryson, the church treasurer.'

'I see. And on what grounds?' asked Oldroyd.

Baxter glanced at Avison and took a deep breath before continuing.

'We think there may have been a suspicion that she's taken money from the church funds. Certain amounts of money are not accounted for.'

'I presume Rev Wilcox was investigating this?'

'She was, but the issue had not been resolved.'

'Furthermore, Chief Inspector,' said Avison, 'it's recently been discovered that she was disqualified from the role of church treasurer as she ran a business which was declared bankrupt; that contravenes Charity Commission rules.'

'But we want you to know,' added Baxter hurriedly, 'that of course we don't really think that she . . . did it. It's just that we felt it our duty to come forward with this information, as Donald said you were asking about anyone who may have had anything against Rev Wilcox.'

Oldroyd sat back and thought. 'So I take it the police have not been called in on that matter?'

'Oh no,' replied Baxter. 'This has all been very recent.'

And probably one of the issues that Rev Wilcox had mentioned to Alison, thought Oldroyd. He said: 'And what makes you suspect this?' Again, the two parishioners exchanged glances.

Avison replied, 'There was a parochial church council meeting not long ago. Olive had circulated accounts beforehand and these puzzled some people. I won't go into the details, but the income shown for things like church-giving and the summer fete seemed low. It wasn't the first time this has happened while Olive has been treasurer. When someone tentatively asked a question about this, Olive insisted the accounts were accurate. Rev Wilcox seemed to move in very quickly at that point and said she would meet with Olive and go through things with her. Then she moved on swiftly to the next item on the agenda. It was all rather uncomfortable.'

Baxter nodded her head in agreement. 'And it left us feeling that something was going on,' she added. 'So, you see, if Olive realised the Rev Wilcox was going to discover her . . . fraud, if there was one, it would have been much to her advantage if the rector was . . . not there.' Baxter was now warming to her subject and leaned forward. 'You see, Chief Inspector, I think Rev Wilcox wanted to give Olive a chance to explain things in private and to see if matters could be resolved without taking anything further.'

'Yes, I'm sure you're right,' said Oldroyd, smiling at the woman, who clearly saw herself as an amateur detective.

'It would be so typical of her; she was such a compassionate woman and—'

Oldroyd intervened. 'Yes, well, I'm afraid I must stop you there because, as I said, we are very busy. But thank you for telling us this and we will definitely look into it. Please give the address to the sergeant here.'

'You won't tell Olive that we informed you about this, will you?' Baxter looked very anxious as she gave the information to Andy.

'Not in the first instance. If things were to develop, you'd have to make a statement.'

'I see. We'll be on our way then, Chief Inspector,' said Avison, and he and Baxter got up and left quickly.

Oldroyd chuckled. 'Well, the machinations in the church! They fancy themselves as two little sleuths, don't they? Doing their duty as long as it's all kept secret and they don't have to face any trouble.'

'It's like at school when some well-behaved little sneak reported you to the teacher,' said Andy.

'I take it you weren't one of those, then?'

'More like the one that was dobbed in.'

Oldroyd laughed. 'I suppose we shouldn't be too hard on them, they think they're doing the right thing, but bludgeoning the vicar to death God knows how seems a remarkably violent response to being under suspicion about the PCC accounts.'

'We'll still need to follow it up, sir.'

'Of course; you can never be too thorough in an investigation. It could also be an attempt to divert our attention from something else. I always get suspicious when someone starts to point the finger at other people.' Oldroyd opened his sandwich packet and started to eat as Andy put the kettle on. 'How did you get on at the homeless shelter?' asked Oldroyd between mouthfuls. Andy consulted his notes.

'The bloke in charge there, Trevor Wood . . . very helpful. Suggested we look for a man called David Tanner; didn't give me any idea about where he might be at the moment. Maybe the best idea is to wait for him to come back here to the graveyard. Apparently he comes here a lot.'

'The trouble is, he may steer clear if he sees the incident tape and police all over the place.'

'True, sir.' Andy brewed some tea and they both sat drinking and eating apples.

'Steph would be proud of us, eating fruit,' remarked Oldroyd. 'Wasn't there any flapjack or anything?'

'There was, sir, but I thought it better to not, you know?'

'And what happened to the biscuits?'

'I've hidden them away, sir. I thought it would be better for us. If you see me with one, call me out.'

Oldroyd nodded reluctantly. Both detectives had a tendency to put on weight, and Steph had decided to take them in hand by banning fattening food from the office and locking up the biscuits.

'Anyway, how did you get on, sir?'

Oldroyd sipped his tea before replying. 'I went to this old bookshop down by the river. It's run by a man called Austin Eliot. He was very informative; seems to know a lot about the history of the area. We talked about the church and he admitted that he and a few others at St Anne's, including Donald Avison, don't really accept that women can be priests.'

Andy shook his head. 'It's a good job Steph wasn't there, sir. She would have had plenty to say.'

'As would my sister. So it seems there might have been some hostility towards Rev Wilcox on that basis. But I think it's stretching it a bit that any of them would want to harm her. Also, he told me about this ghost business. It goes back to the fifteenth century, when a monk was executed for heresy. They threw him off the cliff into the gorge.'

'Religious people were charming in those days, weren't they, sir?'

'Indeed. Anyway, he vowed to haunt the church and get revenge because of what they did to him.'

'I don't blame him.'

'Quite. Apparently there were some strange deaths after that, where people had severe injuries like the ones suffered by the monk and no one could explain them.'

'It sounds like a good old ghost story to me. I remember watching some of those on telly as a kid; I used to be terrified when I went up to bed. But surely it has no bearing on the case, sir?'

Oldroyd sat back in his chair with his hands behind his head. He was enjoying a little post-lunch rest. 'Not directly, but Rev Wilcox's injuries were similar to the ones the monk and the others allegedly suffered, so maybe someone is trying to suggest a link. It certainly makes for a very chilling story, as you say, and it's an excellent distraction from what is really going on. And as we still don't know what is really going on, you could say that all we have, as yet, is a phantom.'

~

At 4.30 p.m. that same day, Jeremy Wilcox put on his coat and left the rectory for the short walk to Knaresborough station. His daughters were due to arrive on the train from Leeds. The unsheltered edge of the platform was covered in snow, and he waited in the cold with a few people who were probably passengers waiting to board the same train, which went on to York.

The train sounded its horn as it glided over the viaduct and into the station. He scanned the carriages as it came to a stop and he saw his eldest daughter, Jenny, waving at him. She and Fiona got off the train and ran towards him. They were very much alike, with blonde hair like their mother. They were both wearing parka coats with fur-lined collars and jeans. Jenny had prepared for the weather by wearing her Doc Marten boots; Fiona was regretting wearing her running shoes. There was not much of an age gap and they could have been twins. Both clung to him and started to cry. 'Oh, Dad!' said Fiona between sobs. He put an arm round the shoulders of each of the girls, fighting back his own tears.

'I know,' he said. 'Let's get back, it's cold. Can you manage your bags? Be careful, it's slippery.' He carried the case that contained Jenny's flute, as they walked almost in silence back to the rectory. What they were enduring was almost beyond words.

Entering the rectory brought a renewed assault of grief. The three of them had another group hug in the hall. The daughters felt the absence of their mother from the family home keenly. The house was full of things that Clare had collected over the years: a watercolour from France which covered a damp patch on the wall; items of furniture acquired in junk shops; small pieces of ceramics bought from local artists whom she liked to support. Everything reflected her eclectic tastes, and her concern for recycling and the environment and climate change.

Wilcox sat down on the sofa, which was covered with the colourful quilt Clare had made when they were first married.

'I'll make a drink,' said Jenny. She'd always been the more practical of the two.

She went off into the kitchen. Fiona sat on the sofa next to her father. She held his hand for a while and then said, 'I can't imagine what it's been like for you, Dad.'

He shook his head and seemed momentarily incapable of speech.

'What happened? How did you . . . find out?'

Wilcox winced at the painful memory. 'I got back from the surgery and . . . she wasn't here. I was just starting to wonder where she was when Donald Avison arrived and told me what had happened. I think I've been in shock ever since.'

'Of course you have.'

'I had the bishop and the archdeacon round this morning offering support, which was nice. And Robin's been brilliant. He stayed all morning and it was great to have someone here. The worst is when I'm by myself; everything in the house reminds me of her. I couldn't sleep at all last night. The bed was . . . empty.' He was on the verge of tears again.

Jenny came in with a tray containing tea things. She poured out three cups and sat down next to Fiona. 'What have the police said to you? Who on earth could have done it?' she asked.

'I don't think they've any idea. It was probably some random maniac who strayed into the church.'

'What . . . what happened to Mum?' asked Fiona with some difficulty.

Wilcox took in a deep breath. 'She was hit over the head very hard.' Fiona put her hand to her mouth. 'It was brutal and nasty, but I don't think she would have felt much, if anything. She would have lost consciousness from the moment whatever it was hit her.'

'Oh, Mum!' cried Fiona.

'And she was in the church?' asked Jenny, who was shaking a little.

'Yes. Which is strange, and why I think it must have been an interloper. The police, of course, are probing around trying to find people who had a motive for harming her.'

'Mum?' said Fiona. 'Who would want to hurt Mum? She was lovely.' She put her hands to her face and started to cry again.

'I don't know,' said Wilcox.

'Don't worry, Dad. We're here now and we'll help you. We'll all get through it together,' said Jenny as she put her arm round Fiona.

'Thank you,' said Wilcox. He was pleased that his daughters were home, but still uneasy about things that they didn't know. It was impossible to tell them now.

～

Andy accompanied Oldroyd on his visit to interview Olive Bryson. The church treasurer lived not far from the church, in a terraced house on a steep lane down to the river. The weather seemed even colder as the detectives approached the house, and the sky was very dark.

'We're definitely going to get more snow,' observed Oldroyd, frowning up at the black clouds moving slowly and threateningly in from the north. 'We'd better call it a day after this and get home, or we might get snowed in.'

'I think you're right, sir,' replied Andy as he knocked on the door. It was opened by a tall, arty-looking woman wearing skinny jeans and a slouchy cashmere jumper. She had large gold hoop earrings. It was very far from the look that Andy had been expecting in a church treasurer.

She was clearly puzzled but rather pleased by the appearance of two men at her door, and they showed her their ID.

'Olive Bryson?'

'Yes.'

'DCI Oldroyd and Sergeant Carter. We're investigating the murder of the Rev Wilcox and we'd like to ask you some questions.'

'I see. You'd better come in.' She gave them both a big smile.

The detectives followed Bryson into a narrow hallway and through to a small living room. It was decorated and furnished in excellent taste, and included some sumptuous Turkish rugs on the floor. They accepted tea after their freezing walk, and were soon sipping it from very fine crockery.

'I'll come straight to the point,' said Oldroyd as he nibbled on a very fine-quality ginger biscuit coated in dark chocolate. He thought this was justified by the cold weather, and neither Steph nor Deborah were here to stop him. 'I understand that you are church treasurer at St Anne's?'

'That's correct.'

'It has been brought to our attention that there have recently been some irregularities in the accounts you have presented, and that the Rev Wilcox was aware of this.'

Bryson was sitting languorously in a Victorian spoon-back chair with her long legs crossed. She smiled charmingly at Oldroyd and then even more broadly at Andy, appreciating his blond hair and handsome features.

'Well, Chief Inspector,' she said, turning her attention back to Oldroyd, 'you don't hang around, do you?' She paused and her expression turned sour before she continued. 'I don't expect you to tell me who's given you this information, but I can guess it was either Donald Avison or Maisie Baxter, or even both. And no doubt they told you it was their duty to come forward and imply that I might have bumped off the Rev Wilcox because she was about to reveal my indiscretions with church funds.' Oldroyd had to smile at her perspicacity and frankness. 'In my experience, churches are full of pious busybodies like that and they don't make anyone feel welcome who doesn't conform to their idea of what a churchgoer should be like. I'm too arty, you see. I'm also divorced and some-times I smoke outside the church. And,' she continued in a whisper, 'I enjoy the company of men.'

'It doesn't sound as if you fit in there very well, but you still attend.'

'Yes, why not? I have my own style of faith. There are one or two of us who are seen as the rebels; a bit strange, you know, and we don't volunteer for the flower rota, things like that. But the church is for us too.'

'Is it true that you've taken money from the church funds?' asked Oldroyd, abruptly returning to the matter at hand.

'Oh, Chief Inspector!' she replied with mock surprise. 'That's an invitation to incriminate myself. Of course, the answer is no, but I might have borrowed some.'

'I see. And why was that?'

'I run a small fabric and design shop in the town. In the autumn it was going through a difficult time financially, so it was tempting to use some money to tide me over, if you see what I mean, and then pay it back later.'

'To do that, you would have to have had permission from the church.'

'It was naughty not to get that, I know, Chief Inspector, but sometimes I can be very naughty.' She gave Oldroyd an unexpect-edly alluring look.

'Anyway,' he continued, looking away, 'we're not interested in pursuing this at the moment. There's not been an approach to the police and no one has been formally accused of anything. But can I confirm that Rev Wilcox knew about this, how shall I put it, "unauthorised temporary loan"?'

Bryson laughed. 'Very delicately put, Chief Inspector. It's pub-lic knowledge that at the last parochial church council meeting, Rev

Wilcox stated that she was going to meet with me and go through things.'

'And did she?'

'Yes, and we agreed a timetable for me to pay the money back. She was a very compassionate person. It wasn't a large amount and I'd always intended to repay before long, but I was very grateful to her. Of course I apologised for what I'd done and she accepted that. I thought the church was all about forgiveness? You wouldn't know it from the attitudes of some people.'

'So it was all settled amicably?'

'Yes. And anyway, why would I murder Clare, who was doing a wonderful job as a woman in that role? For some paltry amount of money? It's a monstrous idea.'

'Unless she was going to report you to the police. That might have ruined you.'

For the first time, Oldroyd thought he saw a flicker of alarm pass over her face. 'She never threatened to do that, Chief Inspector, as I said.'

'Where were you yesterday afternoon between about three and five o'clock?' asked Andy.

'I tend to close the shop about four in winter, especially when the weather is bad. So at that time I would have been walking back here. It takes about fifteen minutes.'

'Does your route take you past the church?'

'Yes.'

'But you came straight back home?'

'I did, Sergeant.'

'Can anyone corroborate that?'

'I'm afraid not. I live by myself.' She shrugged her shoulders and seemed unconcerned. 'Not by choice.' She glanced at the two men provocatively. 'I'm just waiting to meet a man I can share my life with. I take it you two are accounted for?'

'We are,' replied Oldroyd with a smile, and then continued. 'Do you know of anyone who might have wished to harm Rev Wilcox?'

Bryson sat up, looking serious. 'No. Clare was great. Not everyone in the church liked her, some are not happy with women being priests anyway, but I can't honestly say that I know anyone who would have really wanted to hurt her. I hope you find out who did it. When you do it will certainly test my willingness to forgive.'

'And what do you think about this ghost legend?'

'You mean the vengeful monk? We've all heard the story but I don't know what it's got to do with the case. You surely don't think poor Clare was killed by a ghost?'

'Violet Saunders seems to think so?'

Bryson laughed. 'Oh, poor Violet! She's a dear, but one of life's eccentrics, Chief Inspector!'

Shortly after, Oldroyd and Andy got up to leave. It was nearly six o'clock. Bryson followed them into the hall and opened the door to reveal a snowstorm. Thick white flakes were coming down so heavily that it was a white-out: the houses across the narrow street could barely be seen. A bitter north wind was whirling the snow, and drifts were already forming up against walls.

'Oh dear!' exclaimed Bryson. 'You're both welcome to stay the night here,' she added, laughing and raising her eyebrows.

'That's a very generous offer, but we'll have to get back to the church even if we can't get any further,' replied Oldroyd, and the two detectives set off back up the lane, their feet plodding through the snow.

'Well, sir,' laughed Andy. 'We could have both been in there.'

'I know. Goodness knows what would have happened if we'd stayed. She's certainly not what you think of as the typical churchgoer.'

'If she was, I might start going myself,' said Andy, laughing again.

'Well, I hope Steph doesn't hear you say that,' replied Oldroyd with a chuckle.

About halfway up the lane, Oldroyd stopped and looked around. 'It's beautiful, isn't it?' he said with a voice full of awe. 'Listen, there's all this snow coming down and yet it's nearly silent; just a light pattering noise if you listen hard. And all the noises in the distance are muffled; you can't hear the road or anything. Tomorrow there'll be a wonderful world of white.'

'Marvellous, sir,' replied Andy, who was freezing and keen to get back inside as soon as possible. It didn't seem the right moment for one of his boss's raptures about beautiful things in the land-scape. They weren't wearing boots and they had to struggle through deep snow, and at times almost wade through drifts. Every step was an effort.

'I haven't seen anything like this for years,' said Oldroyd, who was a little out of breath as they reached the church. He was grateful again for his improved level of fitness after Deborah had got him running twice a week. They passed their cars, submerged under mounds of snow, and made it inside into the warmth. Oldroyd's phone went off. It was Deborah.

'Ah, talk of the Devil,' said Oldroyd. 'I was just thinking about you. Andy and I have been fighting through the snow, and I felt much more energetic than I would have done a while ago. And it's all due to running!'

'I'm pleased about that,' said Deborah, who sounded dis-tracted. 'It's serious, Jim.'

'What is?'

'The snow. I'm home and I've got the news on. They're fore-casting it to carry on for hours. The main roads are already starting to be blocked.'

'Really?'

'Yes. You'll have to stay there tonight. Don't even consider driving anywhere; you'll only get stuck or have an accident. I don't think the trains are even running. You could have gone to my place over there, but I've got the key.'

'Right. I'll have a talk to Andy and see what we can do.'

'OK. Call me later.'

'I will.'

Oldroyd turned to Andy, who was also just finishing a phone conversation.

'OK, I won't,' he said. 'Bye.'

'I take it that was Steph telling you not to drive on the snow-bound roads?'

'You're right, sir. It's bad out there, and it looks as if we're stuck here for the night. No buses, no trains or anything.'

'I'm afraid so. I wonder if . . .'

There was a knock and Avison popped his head round the vestry door. 'Sorry to intrude, but I thought I'd just check on you two gentlemen. I take it you're not going to be able to get home tonight?'

'No, we're not,' replied Oldroyd.

Avison came into the room. 'I thought as much. Do you have anywhere to go?'

'Not really.'

'I see. Well, I could ring round to see if anyone has any space in their house, or it's possible you could stay in here. We've got some sleeping bags stored away; they're used by the church youth group when they go camping. I'm sure we can make you comfortable for the night. We can leave the heating on.'

Oldroyd looked at Andy and nodded. They both preferred to stay here rather than go through the palaver of struggling out to someone's house.

'That's very kind. We'll stay here,' said Oldroyd. Avison went off to sort things out while Oldroyd's attention turned to food. 'Now, Andy, I think there's a nice pizza takeaway in the Market Place. Do you fancy a plod over there? It's not far. I'll stay here and get things organised. I'll give you some money.' He felt for his wallet. 'I'm sure you'll find somewhere selling bottles of beer as well.'

The last thing Andy fancied was walking out again into the blizzard, but he always liked to oblige his boss. While he was away, Oldroyd rang Deborah and helped Avison with the sleeping bags. He was quite looking forward to a night in the haunted church. Who knew? It might reveal something useful.

~

Curates at St Anne's were housed in a comfortable semi-detached house across the other side of the church grounds from the rectory, in a modern development. Robin Eastby stood at the front-room window watching the snow cover the small garden like a white blanket.

'Is it still coming down?' asked his wife Christine. She was sitting at a table in the dining end of the open-plan living area, marking books. She was an English teacher at the local comprehensive school.

'It is. I think you'll be getting the day off tomorrow. I can't see how anyone's going to get anywhere if it goes on like this.'

'Great! It's always good to get an extra break. I can catch up with things a bit.'

'Teachers – always on the skive!' he teased.

'Hey, watch it, you! That's rich coming from someone who only works one day a week.'

'Touché!' he laughed. They were both aware of the unkind, inaccurate view of their jobs held by many people.

Robin sat at the table near her. 'Have a rest for a minute, will you? There's something I want to ask you about.'

She put her red pen down and looked over at him. 'What's that, then?'

'It's to do with this dreadful business at the church.'

Suddenly the mood of humorous teasing, which had been a relief, vanished as they both recalled the enormity of what had happened.

'How are you feeling? I'm sure you've done a great job supporting Jeremy today.'

He sighed and ran his hand through his hair. 'It's not that . . . it's . . .' He turned to face her. 'What I'm going to say is confidential, so you mustn't say anything to anyone, OK? I just need to ask you what you think.'

'Of course I won't.'

Robin looked away. 'The police haven't interviewed me yet, but I'm sure they will. They've been asking people if they knew of anyone who would want to harm Clare.'

'Do you know someone?'

'This is the problem. I don't think so, but there was a difficult issue that Clare was about to deal with and it concerned Harvey Ferguson.'

'The organist?'

'Yes. And I'm almost certain he's gay.'

'So what?'

Robin shook his head. 'It's not that easy, especially in a traditional church like this with a number of conservative-minded people. It would be hard enough for someone in the regular congregation to come out as gay, but to be in a prominent position in the church is another matter. And remember, he supervises boys in the choir. A lot of people wouldn't like it.'

'It's the kind of thing that makes me glad I was brought up a Quaker. We're famous for our tolerance.'

'Yes. Anyway, there were some rumblings about this in the church. If you're a single man past a certain age, people get suspicious; and then, apparently, someone saw him with a man in a gay bar in Leeds.'

'What was this person doing there?'

'Exactly. Reeks of hypocrisy, doesn't it? Anyway, Clare wouldn't tell me who had said what to her, but she asked me to be involved and we talked to Harvey together. Clare explained what had been reported to her and made it clear that there was no reason at all to take any action against him. We just felt he should know that things were being said about him.'

'I'll bet he wasn't pleased.'

'No. He was extremely defensive and angry; said his sexuality was entirely his own business and he wouldn't comment on the matter. He then went on to say all sorts of things about St Anne's and the church in general. Most of which I agreed with, actually. But I think Clare was a bit shocked. She asked him whether he really wanted to continue at St Anne's if he felt like that.'

'Really? That doesn't sound like her.'

'I know. She made a mistake, and she felt bad about it later. All she meant was that she genuinely didn't want him to feel like he had to carry on if he felt uncomfortable at St Anne's. But it came across as if she was blaming him and defending the people who were spreading rumours. Of course, that made things worse and he ended up storming out of the room.'

'Oh dear, but surely you don't think he would be a physical threat to her because of that?'

Robin frowned. 'The thing is, if it did come out that he was gay, it would put his livelihood at risk. He's a music teacher at a private school for boys in York. It could cause a lot of problems for him. I think a lot of the parents have very conservative views.'

'That's awful. I feel sorry for him. And he does all that work for the church.'

'I know. The problem is: do I tell the police about this?'

'I see.' Christine thought for a while. 'It's a terrible thing to have to do, but in the circumstances, I think you have to. The police will be very discreet.'

'He'll know I've told them.'

'There's no way round that. Imagine what it would be like if it turned out that he was involved in some way, and you hadn't said anything. I'm sure it won't be him and when this all blows over I'm sure he'll understand why you had to tell the police.'

'Maybe.' He breathed heavily. 'OK then, I'll go to the chief inspector; he seemed a decent bloke, but goodness knows what kind of hornets' nest I'll be stirring up.'

~

Back in the church, Oldroyd and Andy were eating their pizza and settling down for the night. Avison had brought in all sorts of things which church people living nearby had donated or lent: toothbrushes, soap, pieces of cake, towels, pillows, rugs. The church toilets were near the vestry. They had both called their partners to assure them that they would be fine for the night. Outside, the snow continued to fall.

'Wow, we've got a feast here, sir! People have been so generous.'

'Church people are like that: very kind when people are in need, however bigoted and old-fashioned you might think they are. My sister's always set me a wonderful example of thoughtful behaviour.'

Andy laughed. 'Well, I can't disagree with you, sir, on this evidence.' He finished a slice of pizza and swigged from a bottle of beer before continuing. 'But we haven't had time to talk about that woman, Olive Bryson. What did you make of her?'

'Not as much as she seemed to make of us.' Oldroyd had a twinkle in his eye.

'No, but what did you think of her story?'

'It was all very plausible, but we've only her word for it that Rev Wilcox took a lenient view of her stealing the church's money. She may have taken a hard line and demanded that Bryson pay the money back immediately. Maybe Bryson couldn't pay and she knew that the next stage would be the police and financial ruin. In that situation, getting rid of Wilcox was very convenient. It gives her more time to try to raise the money to pay back her "borrowings" before more questions are asked.'

'Also, we don't know exactly how much was involved, do we? She called the sum paltry, but maybe it was quite a lot.'

'Correct, so I'm not prepared to rule her out at this stage. I think we . . .' Oldroyd stopped, put his beer down, got up and went to the door. 'What was that?'

'Sir?'

'I heard a noise. Someone's in the church.' Outside the vestry it was very dim. There was just one light on, back at the entrance. He'd seen Avison flick switches on the wall near the vestry and he groped around, found the panel and flicked a switch. A light came on, illuminating a figure in the aisle. Oldroyd was momentarily startled before he saw that it was Violet Saunders. She was dressed in wellington boots and an old duffle coat. She was kneeling on the floor and putting something down on the cold stone. She screwed her squinting eyes up in the light, got to her feet and looked towards Oldroyd. Andy was peering over his shoulder.

'Ah! Chief Inspector. I heard you were staying in here for the night, so I thought I'd bring some of these to give you protection. It's just a few palm crosses I've kept from last Easter. I'm laying them here and saying a little prayer over each one. It'll keep any ghosts and evil spirits away.'

There was an arrangement of three palm crosses on the floor before the altar. The two detectives were speechless. It was all rather odd and somehow unsettling.

'I also like to sprinkle some herbs that ward off evil.' She took out a small basketwork container and scattered some dried leaves around the crosses. 'There's some rosemary and dill. They're two we've known about for centuries.' She nodded her head.

'I see,' said Oldroyd. 'Well, er . . . thank you.'

'It's no trouble. We need to be constantly on our guard against the forces of evil. It's a proper exorcism this church needs. The spirit will haunt us until we lay it to rest. I've written to the bishop lots of times but he doesn't seem to take me seriously.'

What a surprise, thought Andy.

'I'll be off then,' she said, and made the sign of the cross at Oldroyd and Andy. 'Stay safe and may the Lord be with you.' She turned and shuffled away up the aisle and to the door, pausing to sweep some snow out of the entrance before she left.

'That woman gives me the creeps,' said Andy when they'd returned to the vestry.

'I think she means well. Just one of life's eccentrics.' Oldroyd chuckled, although he also felt the strangeness in the atmosphere, and was starting to wish that they'd been able to make it home after all. 'I don't envy the poor bishop trying to resist her calls for an exorcism.'

'He'd want to exorcise *her* I would think.'

'Yes. Mind you, she's the type of person who was persecuted in the past. Thousands of single older women like that were burnt at the stake for being witches if they dabbled with charms and potions or behaved in strange ways. Anyway . . .' He yawned. 'It's getting late and it's been a long day; probably time we got these sleeping bags sorted out. I'll just go down and lock that church door. We don't want any more interlopers tonight.'

There was just enough light from the vestry to show him the way. He walked past some elaborate Gothic memorial stones and the lines of empty pews. There were dark shadows in every corner and it all made him rather uneasy. He locked the door and returned quickly to the vestry, half expecting to meet Violet Saunders again. Maybe she was a ghost herself. She reminded him of one of the creepy servant figures who hung around in the shadows in some of M. R. James's stories.

The two detectives got themselves comfortable in the sleeping bags, and turned out the lights. The snow was still coming down, but unlike the pattering of a rainstorm, there was nothing to hear.

Oldroyd lay on his back, listening. He always found it difficult to sleep in unfamiliar places, and this was one of the most unusual he'd ever known. It was very quiet, but from small sounds like creaks and tapping, you could somehow sense the acoustics produced by the high ceiling. It was unsettling at night.

He was just nodding off when Andy started to snore. He was getting a taste of what Deborah had to put up with from his snores. Pity Avison hadn't brought them any ear plugs.

Oldroyd couldn't get M. R. James out of his mind. It was the perfect setting for one of his stories, like the terrifying 'The Stalls of Barchester Cathedral', in which a guilty archdeacon was haunted after touching some grotesque wooden carvings with particularly gruesome origins.

He was starting to wonder what he could do about the noise when the snoring gave way to muffled snuffling, and eventually Oldroyd himself got to sleep.

Oldroyd woke later in the night with the impression that he'd heard something. For a moment he wondered where he was and then remembered. He looked at his watch; it was just past midnight. He sat up in his sleeping bag. Everything was quiet apart from Andy, who was snoring again. It was very dark but he'd left a small light on by the toilets in case either of them had to get up in the night. There was just enough illumination for him to see that the vestry door was open, and standing in the doorway looking in at him was a truly ghostly figure. It was dressed in a monk's cowl with a rope around the waist. The hood was up and the face was hidden in the darkness. It was a shock.

Oldroyd drew back and exclaimed, 'What the—'

As soon as he spoke, the figure vanished from the doorway. Oldroyd leaned over and shook Andy. 'Andy, wake up!'

Andy came awake with a tremendous snort. 'Eh? What, sir?'

'It's the phantom; we've had a visitation. It scared the living daylights out of me.'

'What, sir? You mean the monk?' said Andy, looking around with sleepy, screwed-up eyes.

'Yes.' Oldroyd's heart was still beating fast. 'Look, we need to try to follow it.'

Andy slunk back down into his sleeping bag. 'What? Don't you think we can wait until morning, sir?'

Oldroyd looked at his sergeant and saw that Andy's arm was shaking. He had to smile. 'Come on, you big coward; we know these things don't really exist. It's somebody dressed up. We might find something important.' He looked at Andy's terrified face. 'OK, you stay here.'

He got out of his sleeping bag, and in his socks and underpants he ran out into the church. It was so dark that he could make out very little. Despite what he'd said to Andy, he had to keep remind-ing himself that murdering ghosts did not exist. He looked up and down the aisle, towards the west tower and through the choir stalls to the east tower. He found nothing. He thought about putting on his clothes and looking outside. If there were fresh footprints in the snow of someone coming into the church, that might mean that the 'ghost' was more corporeal than phantoms usually were. A glance through the window showed him that there was no point. Snow was still coming down and any footprints would be quickly obliterated. It was very chilly out in the church, and he went back into the warmer vestry.

'Did you see anything, sir?' asked Andy, who was still cowering in his sleeping bag.

'Not out there, but there was definitely the figure of a monk in that doorway. It looked solid enough to me – I certainly couldn't see through it – but it seems to have disappeared "into thin air", as they say. It seems that this monk may be significant in the case after all,' said Oldroyd as he got back into his sleeping bag. 'But I'm not yet sure why.' He turned to Andy and chuckled. 'Wait till they find out at Harrogate HQ that Andy Carter the big bold sergeant is afraid of ghosts.'

'Oh, don't do that to me, sir. It's a weakness of mine. I don't like watching horror films and stuff like that, it freaks me out. Maybe I saw a ghost when I was a kid, but I can't remember it.'

'Never mind. Your secret is safe with me,' replied Oldroyd, and he settled back down to go to sleep.

Three

'I suppose,' he said, as they walked towards the altar-steps together, 'that you're too much used to going about here at night to feel nervous – but you must get a start every now and then, don't you, when a book falls down or a door swings to?'

From 'An Episode of Cathedral History',
M. R. James, 1914

Oldroyd slept surprisingly well for the rest of the night, waking to the noise of the electric kettle. Andy was already up, dressed and making tea. Oldroyd sat up, yawned and rubbed his eyes.

'Morning, sir,' said Andy, who had recovered from his night fears. 'It looks like a nice day – too bright for ghosts I'm pleased to say, but wow is there plenty of snow! I don't know whether I've ever seen as much.'

'Well, you wouldn't, would you, being brought up down there in the soft south?' jested Oldroyd. 'Morning to you, too.'

'Sorry about last night, sir, I really freaked out.'

'Not to worry. It was definitely a person. I wasn't dreaming; it was real enough, though I don't believe it was a spirit. I think we need to find out who knew we were in here last night.'

'You think someone came in deliberately to scare us?'

'Perhaps, but also to confuse us and distract us with spooky goings-on from what's really happening in this case. I think I'll go and take a quick look at the snow.' He went out of the vestry and into the church, which was now flooded with light. He looked out of one of the medieval windows and saw a blue sky, and deep snow covering everything. It was very refreshing after the claustrophobic darkness of the night-time. There were two mounds of snow where their cars were parked.

Returning to the vestry, he crouched down and examined the floor where the figure had stood by the door. There was some grit and dampness, suggesting the 'ghost' might have real feet. But it was inconclusive, as many people must have walked over the same area.

'Look at this, sir, we've even got a toaster and some bread, butter and jam. They thought of everything.'

'Splendid! And thank you for getting breakfast.' Oldroyd pulled on his clothes and drank some tea. Andy shared out the toast and they both sat at the table.

'What's the plan today, then, sir? Are we going to be able to do anything?'

'I don't know.' Oldroyd crunched his toast. 'We've obviously got to try to get out of here. Much as I enjoyed your company overnight in the vestry of a church, despite your snoring, two nights might be stretching it, especially when we had a ghost paying us a visit.'

Andy laughed. 'Well, it's been an adventure, sir. It's certainly broken up the routine a bit, but I wouldn't fancy another night in here either.'

Oldroyd stopped and listened. 'That sounds like someone knocking on the church door. I'll go.' He walked back down to the door and opened it, to be met by a blast of cold air. The sky was now clear, but the cold was intense. Standing outside was the ever-reliable Donald Avison, brandishing a shovel.

'Good morning, Chief Inspector, I trust you passed a reasonable night.'

'We did. And please thank everyone who contributed things to make us comfortable. You've all been very kind.' Oldroyd was not going to mention the monk to anyone at this stage.

'You're welcome. I've just come to tell you that I'm organising a team to help me clear the drive into the church and to dig out your cars. I'm sure you don't want to spend another night here.'

'I was just saying the same to my sergeant. Thanks again.'

'According to the forecast, it's going to be dry today, so hopefully the roads will be cleared as the day goes on. A lot of people are snowed in so I think I'll get plenty of volunteers. I'll be back with some more provisions later on.'

'Before you go, can I ask you who knew that we were staying in the church last night?'

Avison looked puzzled. 'Well, quite a few. I sent an email round explaining the situation and asking for help to make you comfortable, so most of the regulars in church knew. Why do you ask?'

'I was just curious about how many people gave assistance.'

'Quite a number; we're a thoughtful group of people, I think.'

'Indeed you are.' Oldroyd thanked him again and Avison went off, trudging determinedly through the snow.

Oldroyd returned to the vestry.

'It was our trusty supporter Corporal Avison,' joked Oldroyd. 'He's going to arrange for the snow to be cleared out there, so we should be able to get home tonight. I asked him who knew we were here last night, but quite a lot of church people were informed so it wasn't particularly helpful.'

'Except that whoever is playing this game with the monk's costume must have a church connection.'

'Good thinking, Andy. That should rule out a random killer. Not that I ever thought that this murder was random. The killer and the monk could be two separate people, even accomplices, but I think it's unlikely. No, Clare Wilcox was killed by someone she knew and it's likely that that person was a member of this church. Now, let's sit down and work out what we can do today. One good thing is that the weather will delay the reporters getting out here, so I won't have to hold a press conference yet. I ought to report back to DCS Walker. He was on a management training day yesterday with Matthew Watkins at some hotel near Wetherby, and presumably he's holed up there now. He won't be pleased.'

Oldroyd got on well with his boss, Superintendent Tom Walker. The superintendent was in his sixties and had spent most of his career as a detective out in the field. He wasn't really happy in a senior management role. He shared Oldroyd's love of Yorkshire and had similar views on policing. Walker also hated the young-ish, fast-tracked chief constable of West Riding Police, Matthew Watkins, decrying him as a man who espoused managerialism and business culture in all its jargon-ridden excesses.

'We'll also have another look round the church and see if we can find any clues as to how the murder was committed. We'd better call our partners now and tell them we're OK after a night in a haunted church.' He winked at Andy and took out his phone to call Deborah.

'You're right there, sir,' replied Andy with a smile. He'd been texting Steph since he got up, but knew his boss fell back on more traditional methods of communication.

～

The snow was causing difficulties all over Yorkshire. In Harrogate, at the Spencer Road Surgery, Sylvia Addison, the practice manager, had walked into work to find that staffing levels were much reduced. Two doctors and one practice nurse who lived nearby like her were there, but Jeremy Wilcox and another nurse, Julie Harrison, were unable to get to Harrogate. Addison hadn't expected Wilcox to come in anyway in the circumstances, and it was convenient that Harrison was absent too.

The day was probably going to be relatively quiet, with people cancelling non-urgent appointments, so she had the opportunity to resolve her dilemma. Addison sat down at her desk and turned the problem over in her mind yet again. The murder of Clare Wilcox had been a shock to everyone at the practice, but especially for her. She felt she had information that she needed to tell the police, but to contact them felt sneaky and disloyal and what she knew probably had no bearing on Clare Wilcox's death. Nevertheless, she just had to do it; there was no point procrastinating any longer. She picked up her phone and called Harrogate Police Station.

❧

'Thank goodness you've called, Jim; it's so good to hear a voice of sanity.' Tom Walker sounded genuinely pleased to hear from Oldroyd. 'I'm locked up here with a bunch of lunatics; can't understand a word they're talking about. It's all "visioning", "reassessing", "future proofing", "using the XYZ model" or whatever. Watkins is in his element: prancing about cracking lame jokes like a failed stand-up comic, and introducing all these damned charlatans from management consultancy firms who speak in bloody acronyms half the time. We listen to these goons blathering on for a while, then we go into these things called "break-out groups". "Break out"!? I'd like to break out of the whole bloody thing and get back to do some proper work! Then, yesterday, just as I thought it was all over and I was ready to drive home, we found we couldn't leave because of the snow and we had to spend another bloody night here! God knows how much it's all going to cost, and then he'll be slashing our budgets.

'Anyway, how are you getting on? You went over to Knaresborough to investigate that murder in the church, didn't you? What's the world coming to, eh? Is nowhere sacred anymore?'

Oldroyd had listened patiently to Walker's rant and took his opportunity to get a word in. 'Well, Tom, we're snowed in here too. Andy Carter and I had to spend the night in the church. The locals were very helpful; gave us sleeping bags and food. I thought I'd just check in with you, although we've not really got going properly yet and it's a bit of a puzzler how the poor woman was killed.'

'It'll be right up your street then; you specialise in cases like that.'

'There might be a ghost involved.'

'A what?'

Oldroyd explained about the legend of the monk and how some in the congregation took it seriously.

'Good Lord, whatever next?' said Walker, and Oldroyd could picture him frowning and stroking his moustache.

'Don't worry, Tom, it won't distract us from identifying our key goals before establishing an investigative paradigm.'

'Eh!? Oh, get away, you old bugger – you're having me on! I can't be doing with that sort of guff from you too.'

Oldroyd laughed. 'I can assure you we'll be doing some real detective work, like interviewing people and assessing the evidence.'

'I'm very glad to hear it. I'll catch up with you when we're both back in Harrogate. Bye.' Walker rang off.

Oldroyd chuckled to himself. Walker was a good boss to have, despite his tendency to indulge in rants against modernity in general and Watkins in particular. He allowed Oldroyd a lot of freedom in his investigations, and Oldroyd knew there was a very warm heart underneath the gruff exterior.

'OK, let's have a look round, Andy.'

They walked over to the old west tower, to the spot where Clare Wilcox's body had been found. It was still taped off.

'So, this is the place she was hit,' said Oldroyd, almost to himself. He looked around the floor and then to the wooden ceiling in the tower, which was about twenty feet up. It seemed to be constructed out of wide floorboards.

'I wonder what's above that?'

'Just the rest of the tower, sir, I would think. Do you think that ceiling was put in to conserve heat?'

'Yes, there's probably another one in the other tower.' Oldroyd peered up into the tower and shook his head. 'There must be a way up there.'

'Is there any point, sir? Nothing came through there, did it? Otherwise the ceiling would have been smashed. If there was a way up there it might have been demolished when it was no longer necessary.'

'Yes, when the new tower was built. You could be right.' He walked around the three sides of the tower base, the fourth side being open to the church interior. 'Now that's interesting.' He'd stopped by the wall with the archway going through to the storeroom, close to where the body had been found. Two tall and sturdily built cupboards made of dark wood were fastened to the wall. They were both locked.

'Probably full of bibles and hymn books,' he said, and turned his attention to the wall. He discovered some holes going up in a line, and the remnants of fixings. He stroked his chin. 'It looks as if something was once fastened to this wall. A long time ago.' He looked at the floor, around where the body was found. 'I take it everything's been left as it was discovered?'

'Yes, sir. We haven't allowed that woman to clean the floor yet.' Andy grinned.

'Good.' Oldroyd knelt down and examined something. 'These look like bird droppings.' He looked up at the wooden ceiling. 'I'll bet there are plenty of pigeons and other birds in that tower, but how would the droppings get down to the ground? They can't get through that ceiling.'

'Don't birds get inside churches, sir? They fly around a bit confused, and eventually find their way out.'

'True, they have been known to make nests inside sometimes.' Oldroyd stood up. 'Anyway, show me the boiler room.'

They walked to the east tower. Andy opened a small door in the stone wall, switched on a light and they descended into the dusty gloom. There was a huge and rusting monster of an old coal-fired boiler with enormous metal pipes going up into the ceiling. Next to it was a large, modern oil-fired boiler sprouting newer, copper pipes. Bits of wood and pieces of piping littered the dirty floor.

After a brief glance round, Oldroyd went over to a ram-shackle-looking door which presumably led to the outside, and spent some time prodding and poking. He tried the handle but it was locked. He called to Andy. 'Now, this is interesting, come over here.' Andy joined him. 'Look at this. The door appears to be boarded up, but these planks have been carefully cut through so that the door will open, even though that looks impossible from a distance.' He pointed to the fine, scarcely visible saw cuts. 'I think this is how our friend the monk gets in and out of the church. They must have a key for this door. It's the first sign of some kind of planning. Let's get out of here, it's a bit claustrophobic.'

Just as they got to the top of the staircase, Oldroyd's phone went off.

'I'll take this, you get back to the vestry.'

Oldroyd answered the phone. It was an officer from Harrogate HQ giving him Sylvia Addison's number to ring.

'She was very insistent that she wanted to speak to the officer in charge of the investigation into the murder of Clare Wilcox, sir. Said she has information which might be important.'

'OK, give me the number.'

He dialled it immediately and Sylvia Addison answered. She sounded nervous.

'Is that Chief Inspector Oldroyd?'

'Yes. What can I do for you?'

'Oh, well . . . I . . . there's something I need to tell you. I'm practice manager at the Spencer Road Surgery in Harrogate, which is where Jeremy Wilcox works.'

'I see.'

'And . . . it's . . . I'll just come to the point. He's been having an affair recently with one of the practice nurses; her name is Julie Harrison.'

'Do you have any proof of this?'

'A number of people here at the practice have seen them together, and they were caught in, shall I say, a compromising manner in a consulting room. I feel terrible telling you this, but in the circumstances I felt I had to report it.'

'I understand. So, are you suggesting he had a motive to kill his wife?'

'Maybe, but I don't believe he did it.'

'Did he ever express any hostility to his wife?'

'No. He always spoke warmly about her. My impression was that he felt very guilty about what he was doing. It was all very furtive, and he's not been himself since it began; he's been morose and quiet.'

'As far as you know, has anyone else revealed what was going on? Has it gone beyond the people in the practice?'

'I don't know; I don't think so.'

'Could it have got back to his wife?'

'It's unlikely, but I can't be sure.'

'OK. Can I ask you about Wednesday afternoon? Dr Wilcox told us that he was at the surgery until the late afternoon and then went home. Can you confirm that?'

'This is the point which worries me. He was at the surgery, but he left quite early, at about three thirty. Julie wasn't here, so I wonder if he went off to meet her somewhere? But I understand Clare Wilcox was murdered later than that, so he may have been able to get back to Harrogate in time to . . . Oh, it's so awful!'

'Yes, I understand. Let me reassure you, you've done the right thing. We'll need to speak to the woman involved if you can provide contact details, and we may need a statement from you at some point.'

'Yes. I need to go now if that's OK?'

'Certainly. Thank you for calling.'

Oldroyd ended the call feeling sorry for the woman, who had done her duty but still felt like a sneak and a busybody. However, it was a potentially interesting lead. They would have to return to the bereaved husband as soon as possible. Maybe his grief was not as genuine as it had appeared.

Oldroyd returned to the vestry and found Robin Eastby waiting beside Andy. Here was another person tormented by the need to report a situation, and who felt they were betraying someone in doing so.

Eastby explained his concerns about Harvey Ferguson and how it was possible that his sexuality could have provided a motive. The curate looked deeply troubled.

'Please be very discreet, Chief Inspector. Things like this can cause terrible feelings in a church community like ours. As I told my wife, Harvey is bound to know that it's me who's informed on him, and I may not ever be able to repair my relationship with him after this. And what if it turns out that he's not gay?' He threw up his hands in a gesture of despair.

'OK,' said Oldroyd. 'I can see how difficult this is for you. We will obviously have to follow this up, but I assure you we will tread very carefully.'

Eastby seemed relieved at this, and breathed out. 'Thank you, Chief Inspector. I appreciate that a lot.' He got up from his chair. 'I'd better be getting on now. I'm going to see how Jeremy is. His daughters arrived back yesterday afternoon, so I think he may be feeling less isolated.'

'Good,' said Oldroyd. 'Can you tell him we'll be over to see him again sometime today?'

'I will.'

'There's just one more thing I'd like to ask you before you go.'

'Yes?'

'What do you make of the story about the monk who's supposed to haunt this church?'

Eastby laughed. 'Well, it makes a nice story if you like that kind of thing, but I don't believe in things like that. It's superstition, not faith – the kind of thing they believed in a different era.'

'Mr Avison was saying the same, but do a lot of the congregation here believe in it? Might some of them think that Rev Wilcox's death could be due to the monk?'

'Well, I hope not. I've not really been here long enough to get an idea about how many people give some credibility to the story. I suppose some of the older parishioners whose families have lived here for generations will have had the story passed down to them. Things are more vivid and tend to retain some power if you were told about them as a child.'

'That's true. Thank you again.'

Eastby left and Oldroyd turned to Andy. 'Well, what a morning so far! We haven't even left the church and two leads have emerged.'

He told Andy about his conversation with Sylvia Addison.

'So the doctor's knocking off one of the practice nurses?'

'Yes, as you so elegantly put it.'

'And he could have wanted his wife out of the way?'

'That's the idea, but let's not jump to conclusions. He had a very narrow opportunity on the day of the murder and I think, if he is involved, he must have had an accomplice. But that often turns out to be the case, doesn't it, in many of the crimes we've seen?'

'Yes, sir, and at least we've got some real things to work with now and not just a ghost.'

'True,' replied Oldroyd with a grin.

～

Alison Oldroyd was still in shock and feeling rather lonely in the vicarage at Kirkby Underside. She had become used to living by herself since her husband died, but Clare's death, combined with this deep snow, meant she was unable to get out of the village, and that was having a bad effect on her mood.

She'd already fielded a number of phone calls from concerned parishioners asking if she needed anything, so she was not short of provisions. But there was no one in the parish that she felt she could speak to about how she was feeling. She would have driven over to see her brother and Deborah, or into Leeds where she had old friends, but that wasn't possible in this weather. And the phone was a poor substitute for proper contact. So here she was, marooned in a white sea of snow. Normally she would have enjoyed the snowy landscape, but today it seemed oppressive.

She sat in the armchair in her study and looked out of the window at her large, unkempt garden, now covered in snow. It was the same chair she had been in when Clare rang on that fateful afternoon. It had only been two days ago, but it seemed far longer. The memory brought tears to her eyes. Not only was it such a personal loss for her, but she'd also had such high hopes for Clare, who she believed would have been an outstanding bishop and another step forward in the ongoing battle for gender equality in the Church. She had a mentor's pride in the younger woman, who'd been her curate here in Kirkby Underside. She'd taught Clare a lot in that time, and they'd grown close.

She sighed. This was a stern test of her faith. She turned over in her mind the dark and difficult questions surrounding the intractable problems of Evil, Free Will and the God of Love. The brutal murder of a woman like Clare seemed so opposite to what God must intend for the world and for the Church. How could you make sense of it? She sat and thought and prayed for a long time in silence.

She finally got up to make a drink, and began to think again about who could possibly be responsible for Clare's death. This was as difficult a problem as the theological issues she'd been struggling with. Despite what her brother had said about the likelihood of the murder being planned, she still thought it could have been a disturbed person who got into the church. Perhaps Clare had stumbled upon them and this person had turned violent . . . a random encounter which had ended tragically. But if it was a parishioner who had reason for Clare to be out of the way, her brother would find out who. What on earth would the press say about something like that? She could see the sensational headline now: 'Murder at St Anne's: The Killer in the Congregation'.

There was another alternative which she couldn't get out of her mind, although she knew Jim thought this was far-fetched. Clare was such an obvious target for the misogynists in the Church, and she knew there were some strange and fanatical people involved in very unpleasant campaigns, but would any of them go as far as to kill someone like Clare? If they had, it was a very dark moment in the history of the Church of England. And other people might be at risk.

~

Oldroyd and Andy wrapped themselves up and finally ventured out of the church in the early afternoon. They discovered a team of people at work in the church grounds, shovelling snow and clearing paths. The cars had reappeared from their covering of snow, their colours standing out vividly against the dominating white. Avison was there now, wielding a snow shifter, and he paused to speak to them.

'You should be able to get home tonight. There's no more snow forecast and the roads are being cleared. It'll be frosty later if this sky remains clear, but I imagine the gritters will be out so you shouldn't have a problem if you stay on the main roads.'

'Many thanks,' said Oldroyd, and he felt like saluting the man for his military efficiency.

He and Andy walked across the grounds to where they could see into the gorge. 'Just look at that!' exclaimed Oldroyd. Before them was a beautiful winter landscape illuminated by the slanting January sun. Snow clung to the branches of the tall trees lining the gorge, and the river was crystal clear and reflected the blue sky. Snow was also piled on the terracotta roofs of the cottages at either side of the steep roads leading down to the river.

'Beautiful, sir.'

'It really is, isn't it? They say with global warming it won't be long before winters will be snow-free. It'll be a great shame not to see a beautiful scene like this any more. Anyway, let's get on. We should catch Ferguson at home in this weather, then we'll have to return to the rectory.'

It was a long trudge through the centre of town to where Ferguson lived. Shops had made a big effort and were finally able to open up and conduct business as usual. This included a fish and chip shop from which wonderful smells were wafting down the street.

They arrived at a Victorian terrace of handsome brick houses with bay windows on the edge of town. Harvey Ferguson answered the door. He was a portly man in his late thirties with a balding head, a round red face and a wide smile. The smile disappeared when he learned that Oldroyd and Andy were detectives.

'Well, you'd better come in, gentlemen.'

He showed them into the front room, overlooking the street at one end and a courtyard garden at the other. It had a waxed wooden floor with a couple of expensive-looking oriental rugs laid across it. Deborah would like this, thought Oldroyd; she often joked about the dull beige carpets in the Harrogate flat. At the street end was a piano, a music stand and a saxophone next to it. They all sat down on two brightly coloured velvet sofas. 'As you can see, I'm a musical man. I'm a music teacher in York but I can't get in to work today; the roads are impassable. I'm sure you already know that I'm also the organist and choirmaster at St Anne's.'

'We did,' replied Oldroyd. 'But thank you for confirming it. And I'm sure you know we're here because we're investigating the murder of Rev Wilcox.'

'Yes, I thought as much. How can I help you?'

'How would you describe your relationship with Rev Wilcox?'

Ferguson hesitated. 'Good. I think she's done an excellent job since she came and I'm all in favour of women priests. I don't think that goes for everyone at St Anne's, though.'

96

'So we understand.' Oldroyd looked at Ferguson closely. The man was tapping his foot nervously, as though he knew what might be coming next. 'We also understand that there was something of a dispute, shall we call it, between yourself and Rev Wilcox regarding your sexuality?'

Ferguson's brow furrowed and he took a deep breath. 'Clearly, Robin Eastby's been talking to you.' Oldroyd fixed Ferguson with his fierce grey eyes.

'Yes, he has, but in the circumstances he had no choice. We have been asking everyone who knew Rev Wilcox, and that will include you, to tell us about any enemies she might have had or anyone who might have had a reason to harm her. I don't think Rev Eastby believes you were the killer, but he was duty-bound to tell us what he did. It's important that you accept that in the context of this, a murder enquiry, and don't react in the wrong way. Is that clear?'

Ferguson nodded, but looked angry and sullen.

'So, tell us what happened.'

Ferguson shrugged. 'I'm sure Eastby's told you everything. They called me to a meeting.'

'Yes.'

'They said that things were being said at St Anne's about me being gay.'

'And are you?'

Ferguson flinched. 'Is that really relevant to your investigation?'

'Yes. We need to get everything very clear and out in the open between us. This interview is confidential in all aspects unless there is material which is relevant to the case and has to go to court.'

'OK. Well, the answer is yes, but I don't have a partner.'

'Is it true that you visit gay bars in Leeds?' asked Andy.

'Yes. I try to be very discreet about it. People might be surprised about that in this day and age but there's still a lot of homophobia around, particularly in the places I live and work.'

'You mean the church and your school,' said Oldroyd.

'Exactly. For some people, if you're gay that means you're almost certainly a paedophile, and I spend a lot of time at work and in the church with young boys.'

'You don't have any paedophile tendencies?'

Ferguson looked taken aback. 'My God, you're very blunt, Chief Inspector.'

'I have to be, and I find it's better not to skirt around subjects.'

'The answer is definitely not, which is why I was so angry when Robin and Clare called me in.'

'Did they accuse you of anything?'

'No . . . no. I wasn't really angry with them. It was more the church . . . and society, generally. Why can't a man like me do the things I do without being under suspicion? I'm no more likely to abuse boys than a heterosexual man is. But no, we have to listen to the pernicious gossip of bigots and homophobes; those who've never accepted gay people in society and the Church.' Ferguson's face had gone redder and his tone was angrier. 'Of course, she wouldn't tell me who had made a complaint or raised it as an issue.'

'Were you afraid of losing your job as well as your position in the church?'

'Yes, you're on a tightrope all the time. The same thing applies as in the church; you'll get parents mumbling about not wanting a gay teacher in the school, working with boys, regardless of what the law says about discrimination.'

'They couldn't sack you, could they?'

'No, but they could make it very uncomfortable for me. That's why I and so many other people don't come out. It's the whispering and awkwardness; the sense that you may be a threat, that you're different, especially when you're working with young people like I do. Some people still think being gay is like an illness which might be passed on to the young. It's bloody medieval.'

'Obviously you feel very strongly about this and I can appreciate that. We take homophobia and homophobic attacks very seriously.'

Ferguson frowned but said nothing. He was clearly unconvinced by Oldroyd's reassurance.

'So, the meeting with the clerics didn't go well?' continued Oldroyd.

'No. As I say, I got very angry. I understood why they were speaking to me, but at the end of the day I didn't think my sexuality was any of their damn business, and I said a lot of things about homophobia in the Church which I don't regret saying because they're true.'

'Did you feel they were supportive?'

'Well, up to a point. I don't doubt that they are sympathetic on a personal level. But it's all very well people in authority saying they will support you, but would they when push comes to shove? When parishioners at church or parents at a school start to say they're unhappy? Somehow I doubt it.'

'Did you leave the meeting in a rage?'

'Yes, I did. Clare made this remark about, was I happy to continue in the church if I felt as I did? And I thought: victim blaming again – why should I leave the church? What about those who would like to drive me out? Why didn't she talk to them about their attitudes? I'd just had enough, and I stormed out. I'm sorry about that now because I don't think she meant it in an unkind way, but there we are.'

'So you weren't nursing a grudge against her?'

'Good heavens, no. She was only doing her job and maintaining a confidence. I thought Clare was great.'

'It's going to be much easier for you now she's gone, isn't it? It's less likely that any action will be taken against you.'

Ferguson laughed. 'I'm not sure about that. No doubt there will still be people who have it in for me, and the next rector may be less sympathetic to people like me. So if you're implying that I had a motive for getting rid of Clare, I don't think that works.'

'Where were you on Wednesday afternoon?'

Ferguson grimaced. 'Blast it! On a normal afternoon I would have been at school with plenty of witnesses. But we have Wednesday afternoons free, and the boys play games. I was in York doing some shopping but I can't prove it I'm afraid. I got home at about six o'clock. Nobody else here to prove that either.'

'I see. So did you know of anyone who might wish Rev Wilcox harm?'

Ferguson shook his head. 'No. The only negative feeling towards her came from those who can't accept women as priests: people like Donald Avison, Maisie Baxter, Austin Eliot and maybe a few others; I don't know any more names. But they were very clear and honest with Clare about their feelings and I never witnessed any hostility.'

Oldroyd got up and Andy followed. 'OK, thank you for your time, Mr Ferguson.'

Ferguson showed them out, feeling a certain amount of relief. His lack of alibi was a problem, but he didn't think they would consider him a major suspect. As far as his sexuality went, he had allies who would help him to keep it all quiet in the future.

~

'I have to say, sir, he doesn't look like a bloke who could have inflicted the injuries we saw on that woman. He's too podgy, for one thing,' said Andy, as the detectives struggled through the snow-drifts and back to the town centre. It was slow and exhausting; the snow was almost knee deep in places on the pavement.

Oldroyd laughed. 'Yes, I agree, but of course he could have had an accomplice. He may be trying to conceal something and was frightened that it would come out.'

'It would be helpful to know who made the complaint about his sexuality, wouldn't it?'

'It would.'

'You'd think that person might have been Ferguson's target rather than Wilcox.'

'Maybe that's why Rev Wilcox wouldn't say who it was. Unfortunately, it looks as if she's taken that information to the grave with her.'

'Won't that person complain again, sir?'

'Probably, but not for a while after all this. We're at that difficult stage where there are a number of potential leads but we don't know which ones are going to prove to be dead ends.' He stopped for a rest, panting. 'It's bloody hard going through all this, isn't it? I wish I had my rubber boots; my feet are going to be wet through.'

'And mine, sir, but not far to the rectory now.'

~

At the rectory, the atmosphere was subdued after the outbursts of grief from the night before. Jeremy Wilcox and his daughters had had a late breakfast. None of them had slept well and they spent the rest of the morning sitting in the lounge together. They tried to avoid the terrible subject which loomed over everything by engaging in small talk. Wilcox asked his daughters about their terms so far at university, and they asked him about the surgery. As yet, none of them could face the terrible practical tasks which they knew they would have to complete together: registering the death, planning the funeral, sorting out all the things belonging to the wife and mother.

The doorbell sounded, startling everybody in the tense atmosphere.

'I'll go,' said Fiona.

'I don't want to talk to anyone,' said her father, shaking his head. 'Just explain, will you? They're very well-meaning but . . .'

'Of course, Dad.'

Wilcox heard voices at the door and then his daughter came back. 'It's the police,' she said. He was surprised; he hadn't expected the police to return so quickly.

'OK, show them in.'

The detectives came in. Oldroyd introduced himself and Andy to Fiona and Jenny but then continued, 'I think it's going to be better if we talk to you alone.'

Wilcox looked uncomfortable. 'Oh, but . . .'

'That's OK, Dad,' said Jenny, and the two women went out.

There was silence for a few moments. Wilcox had a sense of foreboding.

In typical fashion, Oldroyd got straight to the point. 'We've had a call from Sylvia Addison, your practice manager. She reports that it is well known in the practice that you've been conducting an affair with one of the nurses.' Wilcox sighed and looked down. 'I'm sorry to have to raise this, but I'm sure you can see that this is relevant to our investigation. Is it true?'

Wilcox was exhausted; there was no fight in him. 'Yes, it is true; please don't tell my daughters. I want to tell them in my own way and in my own time. But I didn't kill my wife to be with my lover. The affair was nothing as serious as that. I still loved Clare. It was just . . .' He shook his head.

'You were obviously trying to keep it a secret. Is that why you lied to us about your whereabouts on the afternoon of your wife's murder?'

Wilcox's voice was weak. 'Yes. While my wife was being murdered, I was with Julie at her house while her husband was at work.' He started to cry. 'How do you think I feel, Chief Inspector? The guilt about what I did is almost as bad as the grief of losing Clare. If I'd come home earlier that day instead of . . .' He shook his head. 'I might have saved her.' He put his head in his hands and groaned in agony. 'Oh God!'

Oldroyd waited for a moment. 'We won't say anything to your daughters at this stage, but you will have to confirm the name and address of your lover so she can support your alibi. How long have you been seeing her?'

'About six months. Clare's always worked very hard. Being a vicar is very demanding, whatever people think. We hardly had any time together. I felt sidelined; I felt she wasn't interested in me any more, and Julie is so vivacious. She came on very strong.' He stopped and shrugged his shoulders, as if to indicate *what more can I say?*

'Would you say your relationship was strong up to that point?'

'If you mean had I had other affairs before, the answer is no. This was the only one and I'm so sorry about it.' His face looked anguished.

A bit late for that now, thought Oldroyd. But he had some sympathy for the man. His feelings seemed genuine. It had to be truly horrible, to be tormented by grief and guilt at the same time.

'OK. I've said this so often to people: it's best to be straight and honest with the police. We usually find things out in the end, and then all you've done is brought suspicion on yourself.'

Wilcox nodded. 'Yes, I realise that and I apologise, but I didn't kill Clare.'

'Yes, well, we'll leave it there. We'll need a statement from you when you can manage it, and we'll also need to speak to your practice manager again, and to Julie. In the meantime, there's no need for anything we've talked about to go any further.'

'Thank you.'

'I assume you're getting plenty of support from your family and people in the church?'

'I am, Chief Inspector. Don't worry about me.'

The detectives left and Wilcox's daughters came back in.

'Dad, you've been crying; what was all that about?' asked Fiona.

'Oh, nothing. I get emotional when they ask me about your mum. Don't worry.'

They both looked at him with concern, and he sighed and closed his eyes. How was he ever going to tell them about what he'd done?

~

When Oldroyd and Andy left the rectory it was nearly one o'clock, so they stopped at a near-empty pub on the way back for a pint and some food. There was a roaring fire in a small snug bar, and the two detectives made themselves comfortable with their glasses of amber-coloured bitter. They took the opportunity to review the case as they tucked into two hot beef sandwiches.

'He was in a right state, wasn't he, sir?' said Andy, referring to Wilcox. 'But cheating on your wife like that. Well . . .' He shook his head and took another bite of his sandwich.

'The question is,' replied Oldroyd, 'do we think he could be the killer?'

'It's a common motive, isn't it: getting rid of the unwanted partner?' replied Andy. 'But I can't imagine him doing it somehow. If he was involved, he must have had an accomplice.'

'Who did the dirty work. How often have we seen that?' Oldroyd took a drink and finished his half-pint. He would have dearly loved another but that was not permissible while on duty and then driving home. 'Can you imagine the scandal in the church if it was discovered that the rector's husband was conducting an adulterous affair?'

'Not as bad as the scandal if it came out that he'd murdered his wife, sir.'

'No indeed. I wonder if he thought that, if she could be murdered in a mysterious way and he could get away with it – the dream of a lot of killers – then he could quietly fade away and in time continue his new relationship legitimately and without suspicion.'

'What a bastard if that was the plan! But I didn't detect any depths of cunning and ruthlessness in him, did you, sir?'

'No. He seems genuinely cut up – or it's a class act. So, in addition to him, the people with motives are Olive Bryson, the treasurer, and Harvey Ferguson, the organist and choirmaster.'

'I've still got to track down this homeless bloke, sir; he might have seen something even if he wasn't the killer himself.'

'Yes. Difficult in this weather. He's probably made his way back to the shelter.'

'Yes, I'll have to go down there again.'

'What do you think about the suspects, then?'

Andy was used to these testing questions from his boss and appreciated them. Oldroyd was not the kind of superior who just used you to do the donkey work. He expected you to be thinking about the case, and you felt you were being trained.

'I can't say I'm particularly convinced by any of them at the moment, sir. The motives are real, but are any of them enough to make someone commit murder? Also, we haven't yet solved the problem of how. I think when we know that, we might have a better idea of who it might be.'

Oldroyd grinned at Andy. It was a sensible and calm assessment. He remembered how gung-ho Andy had sometimes been when he'd first arrived in Yorkshire from the Met. Oldroyd regarded the younger detective and his partner, Steph, as protégés. He was pleased with how they were doing, and they often had very useful insights into things. 'Good. I agree with you, and the first thing I need to do when I get back is to see if Avison has a key to that old cupboard. My sister thinks the motive could be something to do with resentment about women in the ministry.'

'Really, sir? I knew the Church was behind the times, but surely not that bad?'

'No, I tend to agree; if we can't uncover some more motives and some more likely-looking suspects, we'll have to fall back on the random-intruder theory, though how she was murdered is . . .' He shook his head. 'Anyway . . . let's get going. This is on me.'

After Oldroyd paid the bill, they continued their walk back to the church, crossing the Market Place.

'By the way, sir, who was Blind Jack?' Andy pointed at the pub of that name in the corner of the square.

'He was a local man in the eighteenth century, one of the first people to build proper roads, despite being blind. Look, that's him.' Oldroyd pointed to a bronze statue of a man sitting on a bench and holding a surveyor's wheel. 'It's amazing what difficulties people can overcome, isn't it? It's a good metaphor for us actually. We go blind into all these cases and stumble around for a while before we start to see things clearly.'

'You're right, sir.' Andy smiled. His boss loved little flights of fancy like this, as well as the occasional big dramatic gesture. It hadn't surprised him when he learned that Oldroyd had studied literature at university.

They crossed the railway by the station, near the little signal box which had a pretty covering of snow on its roof. The railway lines were clear across the famous viaduct; the snow plough must have been through, thought Oldroyd. The station, however, was deserted.

All the paths and the parking area around the church were now cleared and the cars stood gleaming against the snow. Some kind person had clearly wiped them over with a wash leather after the snow had been removed. As Oldroyd entered the church, he was startled by a voice.

'Ah, Chief Inspector.' He glanced to his left. It was Violet Saunders, lurking just at the side of the door. She had a duster in her hand and was wearing the same duffle coat and wellington boots as yesterday. 'I'm glad I've seen you. Did you pass a peaceful night in here?' Her bright little eyes behind her glasses showed her eagerness for information.

Oldroyd frowned at her. She always seemed to pop up when you least expected. He decided to humour her and told her about the figure that had appeared in the night. She listened intently and then nodded her head.

'Yes, well, I'm not surprised, Chief Inspector. Was it about midnight that you saw it?'

'Yes, as a matter of fact.'

'Just the time for it to make a visitation. That spirit is very active at the moment – as we know, with poor Rev Wilcox.' She crossed herself and gazed up to the medieval ceiling. 'It won't be still until we put it to rest, you know, but at least it didn't attack you last night. It was the palm crosses and the herbs that gave protection. I'm going to leave them there until your work in the church has finished.'

A thought occurred to Oldroyd. 'You said you've seen this figure dressed as a monk?'

'Oh yes,' she said portentously.

'And you said it disappeared?'

'It did, Chief Inspector, because walls—'

'Yes, you told me that, but can you remember which wall it disappeared into?'

'No, it just seemed to dissolve into the dark. I'll never forget it, Chief Inspector. Anyway, I hope you have a restful night. Things are very disturbed at the moment.' She looked up to the heavens. 'That's why all this snow has come. Are you staying here again?'

'No, I think we'll make it back home.'

'I see. Well, you both take care. I'll be around tomorrow as usual.'

'Thank you,' said Oldroyd with a smile. He was intrigued by her combination of Christianity and some kind of folklorish paganism.

He joined Andy in the vestry.

'What did she want, sir?' asked Andy as he finished texting Steph.

'She was just reassuring us that we will remain in her protection until our work is over.'

'Bloody hell, did she chant a few spells?'

'Now, now, no need for that; I think she's very well-meaning, if rather otherworldly. She says the ghost disappeared into the dark.' He sat down, looking thoughtful. 'I must ask Avison about a key for that outside door in the boiler room. Clearly, this ghost has a key for it.'

There was a knock and Avison put his head round the door. 'Good Lord!' exclaimed Oldroyd. 'Well, I would say talk of the Devil, but you're more like a ministering angel; always here when we need you.'

Avison smiled. 'I saw you arrive back – my house is just by the church entrance – so I thought I'd come and see if you needed anything.'

'No thanks, we're fine. And please, thank everyone again for all their support . . . and for shifting the snow.'

'You're welcome.'

'Actually, there is a way you can help. Is there a key for that external door in the boiler room?'

Avison seemed surprised. 'It's a door which isn't used any more. It would have been there originally for coal deliveries, I would think. It's boarded up now, to stop vandals getting in. But I have a big bunch of old keys which we can try.'

Oldroyd looked thoughtful. 'Tell me, was that east tower built later than the west tower and the main church?'

'Yes, Chief Inspector. That was an early Victorian addition. They built the tower and installed a new clock, bells and the heating system. You can still see the huge radiators in the church.'

'Do you know why they built a new tower?'

'The records say it was because the old woodwork and masonry in the west tower was unsound. The Victorians enjoyed building and making their mark. I think they did a good job matching the east tower to the medieval style of the west, although it's higher and grander.'

'Yes. So, before that there would have been bells up in the old west tower, and a clock?'

'Yes, but there's no record of what happened to them.' At this point, Avison looked uncharacteristically nervous, as if he wanted to ask something but was reluctant.

'Er, did you speak to Olive Bryson?' he finally asked.

'We did, but obviously I can't tell you anything about it.'

'No, no, I understand. Well, I'll just nip back home and get that bunch of keys.'

'Do you still consider him a suspect, sir?' asked Andy when Avison had left.

'Of course; his attentiveness could be a good way to monitor our behaviour. He has a good knowledge of the church, and he's not a supporter of women priests. He's also tried to implicate someone else. So, although I can't really see a convincing motive for him to turn to murder, he fits the bill in many ways.'

'What about that woman he came with? Maisie Baxter?'

'Oh, you mean, do they form a deadly duo of church officials, feared throughout downtown Knaresborough?' Oldroyd laughed at this image and held up his hands. 'Who knows? But it seems unlikely. This is one of those cases where the suspects are going to have to be dug out patiently, not like that case with the writer in Harrogate. There were I don't know how many people who wanted him dead, remember.'

'Yeah.' Andy sighed, and yawned. 'I feel exhausted, sir. It's tough walking through snow, isn't it? And it was a bit of a rough night. I'll be glad to get back home and have a shower and stuff.' He rubbed at his unshaven chin.

'Yes, me too. It's the cold as well; it takes energy out of you. We'll just hang on 'til he comes back with those keys, and after we've had a look, we'll get off. I don't think there's going to be much more we can do today.'

∽

When Violet Saunders left the church, she walked slowly and carefully along the partially cleared but still icy paths towards her small cottage, which stood on another of the steep paths that led down to the river. There was a short, thin garden at the front, and a path leading to the door. At the back of the house, there was a bigger garden. She had a glint in her eye and a sinister, knowing smile on her face. She opened the door and was met by a chorus of meows from her three hungry cats.

'All right, all right, my darlings. Get down, Ginger; Mary, stop scratching the skirting; be patient like little Solomon here.' She went through into a small kitchen-diner and got out the cat food. Plants of various sizes filled every available space.

While the cats ate, she made a cup of tea and sat down in an armchair, smiling again as she thought of those gullible policemen. She was sure she'd persuaded them that she was a loony old woman who believed in ghosts and dabbled in superstitions and herbal cures. She laughed to herself as she thought about it. The truth was, she didn't believe in the ghost of the monk at all. And she had a good idea after talking to the chief inspector about who the killer might be. She'd had her suspicions from the beginning, and since then she'd been conducting her own investigation. If she played her cards right, she could use her knowledge to her advantage. It was time to make a call.

'Hello . . . Yes, that's right, it's Violet. What do I want? Well, just to say that I have an idea who the monk in the church is . . . What do I mean? The so-called ghost of the monk of course. If you'd been with me watching from my hiding place in the dark last night, you would have seen someone approach the church and leave about an hour later. It was during that time that the chief inspector saw the monk. It was easy to put two and two together and I got a good sight of you from behind the bush. It confirmed what I thought. I've seen you before in the church dressed as the monk . . . No, you didn't see me. Nobody ever does unless I attract their attention. I can curl up in a corner but I'm watching all the time. Congratulations on getting into the church and out again. I think you've got some secret way in, down in that old boiler house. I don't know what you've been doing in the church on these visits, but I've heard you making noises in there at night. I told the police I thought it was the spirit of the monk.'

She laughed.

'They think I'm a batty old woman but I'm sure they would be interested in what I've got to say . . . Prove it? I don't need to. Once the police have got a lead on you, they'll follow it up until they get the evidence they want . . . No, I'm not saying you killed Rev Wilcox, but how would you explain to them what you were doing there and why you dress up as a monk? Whatever the reason was, it's all very suspicious, isn't it . . . ? I was hoping we could come to some agreement so that things don't become unpleasant for you . . . Yes, we can meet up. In a public place of course, and not in Knaresborough . . . OK, but get back to me soon.'

She ended the call with a nasty smirk on her face. Ginger the cat jumped on to her lap. 'Not yet, Ginger,' she said as she got up and the cat fell back to the floor. 'We just need to make sure we're safe tonight.'

The light was beginning to fade. The fronds and trailers on her plants cast shadows on the walls. She went round the house checking that all the doors and windows were locked. After all, not only was there a killer about, but she had a good idea who it was. And they knew she knew.

~

Late in the afternoon, Avison returned to the church with a big bunch of keys jangling together on a large iron hoop.

'There're lots of possibilities here, Chief Inspector.' He laughed. 'Half of them don't appear to be in use any more, but no one wants to throw a key away in case it's needed at some point.'

They walked along the length of the deserted church and down the short staircase into the boiler room. Oldroyd pointed out that the door seemed to have been used and doctored to suggest it was still boarded up. None of Avison's keys worked.

'I think this lock may well have been changed, Chief Inspector,' Avison said. 'It looks quite new. You're very observant, I must say.'

'You have to be in this job. So, if this lock has been changed, the people best positioned to do that would be the churchwardens?'

'Yes, Chief Inspector. They would have had the key for the original lock. But I must protest my innocence.' Avison smiled, not looking unduly worried.

'Who were the churchwardens before yourself and Mrs Baxter?'

Avison shook his head. 'I doubt this is going to help, Chief Inspector. There are always two churchwardens at a time. Over the years quite a number of people have taken on the role.' He thought for a moment. 'I could sort out a list for you.'

'That would be helpful. And those keys have been passed on from person to person?'

'Yes.'

'OK. Thank you for bringing those keys . . . and remember to say nothing. We need to keep this entrance to the church a secret.'

'Certainly, Chief Inspector.' Avison left.

Once he was gone, Oldroyd chuckled. 'Have you noticed, he takes orders from me as if I'm his commanding officer in the army,' he said, as he and Andy walked back to the vestry.

'I'm sure that's how he sees you, sir. You have a natural air of authority about you.'

'Thank you.' Oldroyd laughed.

❧

When they got back to their vestry office, Oldroyd sat down.

'So, I think we know how the monk gets in; he doesn't float through the walls. But what happened then? We're being invited to believe he's the murderer, but how? Clare Wilcox was hit with something. She didn't have a spell cast on her or anything like that.'

He thought for a while. Then he yawned, stretched and got up.

'Right, we're knocking off now, as my grandad would have said. We're not going to get any further with it today.' They collected their things and walked down to the church entrance. 'Tomorrow you call in at Harrogate and get a DC to help us. DCS Walker should be back, so clear it with him. We need to start taking formal statements and checking alibis. I feel things are starting to move, but I don't know where they'll take us.'

'Right, sir. It's been an odd couple of days, hasn't it? Though I think we've managed to do a lot in the circumstances.'

'We have.'

They went through the door and the cold hit them. The sky was clear and the moon shone between the still branches of the tall trees in the churchyard. The flagstones were already a bit slippery, and frost had begun to sparkle on the covering of snow. It was beautiful and invigorating but also a little sinister. Oldroyd was glad he didn't have to spend another night in the church, and not just for reasons of comfort.

~

'Ah, the wanderer returns at last!' called Deborah as she heard Oldroyd coming into the flat in Harrogate, and she went to meet him and gave him a kiss and a hug.

'It's freezing out there,' said Oldroyd, rubbing his hands. 'It took ages to get back; the gritters are out, and there are hold-ups because cars have slid across the road and blocked it.'

'Never mind, come in and get warm. I've stayed here most of the day and I've not been out apart from a walk on the Stray. That was very hard going; it was almost knee deep in snow in places.'

'Tell me about it. Andy and I had to struggle up and down the hills of Knaresborough going to interview people.'

'Oh, poor you! I'll bet it looked pretty in the snow looking over the gorge.'

'It did.'

'Tea's nearly ready. I've made a nice veg crumble with a cheesy topping. You can't beat some hearty root vegetables at this time of year: carrots, parsnips, swede, butternut squash.'

'It sounds lovely,' said Oldroyd, thinking how he longed for steak and kidney pie with chips.

'Let's just have a glass of wine while it finishes off and you can tell me more about what's going on in Knaresborough.' She went to the kitchen, and returned with two glasses of red before joining him on the sofa. 'Right, come on then. It's such a fascinating case that you didn't even come home last night.' She took a drink and her eyes sparkled at him mischievously.

Oldroyd sat back and luxuriated in being back home and able to relax. 'I think you know the outline; it must have been on the news, but I've missed it all.'

'There was a brief mention on the local news, but it's mostly been about the snowfall and chaos on the roads.'

'Yes, there are going to be some lurid headlines when the press are able to get to us. I'm expecting them tomorrow. I've had lots of texts and calls from reporters, but I don't reply. I haven't the time to deal with them individually; they can all attend the press conference.'

'Have you any idea yet about who did it?'

'Not really, but I think we've established that the killer was flesh and blood and not spirit.' He told her about the door to the boiler house.

'How intriguing!'

'Yes, and there are some people with juicy motives. If it turns out that one of them was the murderer, the headlines will be even more sensational.'

'Even more intriguing. I can see why you enjoyed staying the night there. Anyway, I know you're not having an affair with Andy Carter even though you spent the night with him. That would generate more glaring headlines, wouldn't it? "Chief Inspector Oldroyd and Detective Sergeant Affair in Church Vestry".'

Oldroyd chuckled. '"Last night the inspector's partner was unavailable for comment . . ."'

'She would be too speechless to say anything,' said Deborah, in convulsions of laughter.

They ate the veg crumble and had a very relaxing evening watching a film. When they finally got to bed, Oldroyd lay there appreciating the softness and comfort. He was decidedly a person who would never take to 'roughing it'.

'So, what's on tomorrow?' asked Deborah as she yawned.

'Carry on probing until we get the breakthrough. We've also got to work out how she was killed.' He lay down and switched off his bedside light. The answer to that, he was increasingly sure, lay somewhere in that west tower.

Four

'Have you ever seen an old brass in a church with a figure of a person in a shroud? It is bunched together at the top of the head in a curious way. Something like that was sticking up out of the earth in a spot of the churchyard which John Poole knew very well. He darted into his bed and lay there very still indeed.'

From 'There Was a Man Dwelt By a Churchyard',
M. R. James, 1924

'Here's your coffee, you lucky so and so.'

It was Saturday morning at the flat in Leeds. Steph was off duty, while Andy had to go to work and continue with the investigation in Knaresborough. He was up and dressed while Steph was having a lie-in. He put the mug down on her bedside table. She sat up in bed, yawned and picked up the mug.

'Never mind, you'll score I don't know how many points with the boss. He couldn't manage without you.'

He leaned over the bed and kissed her. 'Maybe, but I'd much rather be staying here with you.'

She pushed him away with a laugh. 'No time for that, I'm afraid. You need to get over to Knaresborough, and I'm going to do some shopping and have some lunch at that nice Italian café near Leeds Bridge.' She got up and went into the bathroom.

'No need to rub it in.' He grabbed his coat. 'I hope the roads are better today,' he called to her as he heard the shower come on.

'Last night the weather forecast said it would be dry today and a little warmer. Bye!' she called back to him.

~

Andy got his car from the garage complex beneath their flat and drove out of a relatively quiet, early weekend morning in Leeds. The snowfall had not been as bad in Leeds as in the Harrogate and Knaresborough area, and the roads and streets were slushy but clear. He passed now-familiar buildings like the Corn Exchange, Leeds Trinity and the Playhouse. He felt comfortable in Leeds. It was obviously not London in terms of city life, but it was a vibrant place and not too large to feel a bit homely. He loved the country areas of Yorkshire, but at heart he was a city person.

He called in at Harrogate HQ as requested, picking up DC Robinson, who had assisted Oldroyd and his team on a number of past investigations.

'Morning, Sarge,' he said, grinning, as he got into the car. 'Still a bit nippy, isn't it?'

'Morning! Yes, but it's not as bad as yesterday. It was bloody freezing over there, and I've never seen as much snow.'

'Right, I hear you were cut off and had to spend the night with Oldroyd in the vestry of the church.'

'That's right.'

'So, let us into the secret.'

'What's that?'

'Does the boss snore?' Robinson collapsed in laughter and Andy had to laugh too.

'I was so knackered I went straight off to sleep so I didn't hear anything. He said I snored quite loudly.' Robinson laughed again. 'And something else: he woke up in the night and saw a ghost.'

'Eh? Who did? The boss?'

'Yep, the ghost of a monk who was executed in the Middle Ages and some people over there think that this monk could have done the murder. The boss said this phantom was in the doorway of the vestry looking at us.'

'What? You're not serious.'

'I am, and this is why I'm taking you over there today. We need someone to stay in the church tonight and keep watch in case this ghost comes back. The boss wants someone else to corroborate what he saw, you know.'

'Yes, but . . .' Andy turned to look at Robinson, whose face was deadly serious and pale. Andy burst out laughing. 'Oh, Sarge!' exclaimed Robinson, realising the joke.

'Your face. I never thought you'd be someone who was scared of ghosts. Don't worry, the boss did see the figure of a monk, but we're not leaving you there tonight.'

'Bloody hell! I'm glad I wasn't there last night then. My dad used to tell us ghost stories when I was a kid and sometimes I was so scared I had to hide under the sheets when he left. Even worse was when my brother used to hide under the bed after the story and make spooky noises. I've been a bit uneasy about stuff like that since then.'

'Never mind, we'll get you home before it's dark,' Andy continued, laughing, 'and I'll let you into a secret: it freaked me out, too. I stayed in the vestry when he went out to investigate.'

'I don't blame you, Sarge. Well, that makes two softies.'

'We won't be alone,' said Andy. 'There are lots of people who would be uneasy in an old building at night; they just wouldn't want to admit it.'

The fields and the hillsides were still covered in white. When they arrived at the church, Andy noticed that the wooden seats had been cleared, and as he got out of the car, Andy saw a bearded figure sitting on one in the middle of the churchyard. He called out: 'Are you David Tanner? I'm Sergeant Carter from West Riding Police. Can we have a word with you, please?'

Before Andy had finished, the man was up and running off, staggering a little. He had left his bottle by the seat.

'Quick!' Andy said to Robinson. 'We need to question him. There's an alleyway he'll be making for; I'll sprint round and head him off and you stay at this end. Then he's trapped.'

'OK, Sarge!'

Andy ran off as fast as he could on the damp and slushy paths down through the main entrance. He swerved left and towards the alley. As predicted, when Tanner saw Andy, he headed back up the alley only to be confronted by Robinson. Tanner cowered in the alleyway as if he expected to be attacked.

'Get off me, ah've done nowt. Bloody coppers, yer never leave me alone.'

'We're not going to touch you. Just come back with us into the church. It's warm in there. We just want to ask you if you saw anything on Wednesday.'

Tanner scowled at him. He had blue eyes beneath a shock of dirty black hair and above his thick beard. He exuded a strong smell of alcohol.

'Where?'

'In the churchyard. Just come with us, OK? I'll make you a drink and there'll be some biscuits. We're not arresting you.'

Tanner said nothing, but allowed himself to be led back into the church where they were met by Oldroyd, who sensed straight away that this was a situation needing gentle handling. Andy introduced him to Tanner and went off to make the man a drink. Oldroyd, Robinson and Tanner sat in the pews near the entrance.

Oldroyd smiled as he spoke. 'We're investigating a murder; someone was killed here on Wednesday afternoon.'

A look of alarm came on to Tanner's face and he stood up. 'It wan't me!'

'No, we're not saying that. Please sit down. We just want you to help us. You come here into the churchyard a lot, don't you?'

Tanner still looked deeply suspicious. 'What if ah do? Folk can come in 'ere when they want, can't they?'

'Yes, of course. Were you here late on Wednesday afternoon?'

Tanner frowned and didn't reply. He cast shifty glances at Oldroyd and Robinson.

'What if ah wa'?' Andy arrived with a mug of tea and a couple of biscuits taken from the packet he'd hidden. 'Ta,' said Tanner.

Oldroyd continued. 'If you were here, we want to know if you saw anybody go into the church or come out. It would be about half past four in the afternoon and dark when they went in.'

Tanner finally seemed to accept that they were not hostile towards him. He drank his tea, munched a biscuit and reached out to take two more.

'That wa' t'day before t'snow, wan't it?'

'Yes,' replied Oldroyd.

Andy was having to listen very hard, as he often had to when someone spoke in the 'broad' Yorkshire accent.

Tanner nodded. 'Ah wa' sittin' where ah usually sit on that bench and it were gettin' dark. Ah wa' 'bout to go to th'ostel. Ah don't like sittin' in there all day. Ah like fresh air. Anyway, ah saw a woman comin' across from that big house so ah hid behind one o' them big gravestones. Them church people don't like me hangin' around 'ere. That bloke wi' t'tache has told me off a few times.' Oldroyd and Andy smiled as they recognised Avison in the

121

description. 'She went into t'church. There were a light on some-where. Ah sat watching a minute or so to see if anybody else came and then ah heard a great big thudding noise. Ah didn't know what it wa'. Then t'light went out. Ah thought, bloody 'ell, what's goin' on in there? Then sumdy came out dressed in like a sack wi' a big hood over their face, and walked down towards th'alley. Ah stayed hiding behind t'gravestone and after a bit ah went back to th'ostel.'

'Thank you, that's a very clear account and you've backed up what we thought happened. So you couldn't see the person?'

'Not with that hood on.'

'Have you told anyone about what you saw?'

Tanner laughed and shook his head. 'Not likely. Ah din't want to get involved in whatever wa' goin' on. It looked a bit of a funny business to me. Then ah heard sumdy wa' killed and ah thought: Dave, yer keep out of it. Nobody believes what folk like you say. They might fit you up for it. Anyway, ah've told yer now.'

'Yes, and thank you again. We won't be fitting you up for it, as you say. Here, take this for helping us.' Oldroyd took a ten-pound note out of his pocket and gave it to an astonished Tanner. 'Not all coppers are bad, you see. If you think of anything else, let us know.'

Tanner looked dazed but he smiled; broadly this time, showing discoloured teeth. 'Ta' was all he said before taking a couple more biscuits and leaving the church, with his shuffling and limping gait.

'I hope he doesn't spend it all on alcohol,' reflected Oldroyd.

'Not much chance of that, sir,' said Andy.

'Maybe not, but I always find a little inducement goes a long way with people who don't trust the police. We've probably got an ally there now, and who knows when that might come in handy?'

'You might be right, sir, and anyway, to be fair, what do we do when we get home after a hard day?'

'Have a drink. And all his days are hard. Anyway, better get on.'

Back in the vestry, Oldroyd went through the tasks to be done. 'We need to get started on statement-taking and checking some alibis. I've drawn up a list. Messages are being sent to all members of the congregation for whom we have contact details, asking them to come forward if they have any information about Rev Wilcox and what happened. Avison's been very helpful again. This is the day we can expect the press invasion, so I've sent out word that I'll be holding a briefing in the church later this morning. I also told Avison to tell everyone to be wary of the media. They'll be going around trying to get information about Rev Wilcox and the church, and the best thing is to say nothing and avoid risking what you say being distorted.'

'OK, sir, we'll get on to it.'

Oldroyd was left alone. He rested for a while in preparation for the press conference. They were always energy-sapping. Then he went for a walk down to the west tower and had yet another look at the murder scene. There was something here he was missing, but what was it?

❧

Bishop Michael Palmer and Archdeacon Patrick Owen met to discuss the crisis at St Anne's in the diocesan headquarters, which was lodged in a Regency building in the town centre, near the ruins of the castle. It was an odd place, full of large rooms with a faded grandeur that were full of soulless modern IT equipment and furniture.

They conversed in a small private office over mugs of tea.

'I think we've done what we can in the circumstances,' said the bishop. 'I'm going to St Edmund's tomorrow, which is where I expect a lot of the congregation from St Anne's will worship. Paul Trent, the vicar, is expecting people. I'm going to say a few words to try to bring some comfort.'

'Good idea,' said the archdeacon. 'Peter, who handles the media, has been besieged by the press. He's doing a sterling job of fielding all the questions and comments. Some of them are quite nasty, he tells me.'

'Really? Well, what can we expect if, as a society, we patronise the kind of newspapers who simply pursue sensationalist stories? They love it all the more if there's any scandal or drama to do with the Church. Depicting us as a bunch of hypocrites telling the rest of society how to live while falling down ourselves.'

The archdeacon looked rather uncomfortable at this point. 'Yes,' he replied after a pause. 'There appears to be a certain determination amongst some of the media to almost deliberately misconstrue what Christianity is about and to make it appear ridiculous.'

'I fear some of us in the Church tend to make it easy for them,' said the bishop rather bluntly and without elaborating. He went on to consider some more of the ramifications of Rev Wilcox's death. 'I've been in touch with the archbishop. He's devastated of course, like we all are, and now he has to consider what's going to happen in Kendal. He's bitterly disappointed; he wanted Clare in that role. Thought she was the ideal person to move the Church forward in that area.'

'Who do you think may be suggested to replace her?'

'I don't know, but I hope it will be a woman. The Church badly needs more women in leadership roles.'

'I agree,' said the archdeacon, 'but there's still a lot of resistance to this modernising process. I've heard rumours that some people think Clare was killed by a person who is fanatically opposed to women priests.'

'Good heavens! That sounds more like some lurid article in one of the tabloids. I hope that ridiculous idea doesn't reach them.'

'Absolutely.'

'To get back to practicalities, keep a watch on Robin, won't you? It's quite a responsibility for someone so young, especially as St Anne's is now in shock.'

'I will, don't worry. As soon as the police allow it, I'll go through the calendar with him and work out a roster for the services, and we'll start to look ahead to what's going to happen in Lent. I think this year the whole programme for Lent should be led by the other churches in that deanery. We can't expect St Anne's to do anything extra. Easter is going to be a challenge even if we have another person in by then.'

'Yes, I agree. I'm going to be there myself, at least on Easter Sunday, which will be a big, emotional time. They'll remember previous Easter Days when Clare was with them. I've spoken to people here at the office about arranging for some counselling to be available for the parishioners over the next few weeks. It's such a terrible thing to deal with: not only is your priest murdered, but she's murdered in the church. How will they feel about that building now? It's wonderful architecturally, but will they ever be able to forget what happened in there? It's going to take some time.'

'Yes. In the long run, we may need to think about more change. It might be better if Robin moves on and a new rector and curate team take over. You know, a fresh start.'

'But at the moment, he and the rest of the church are going through this together, and that sense of solidarity is important. Anyway,' the bishop concluded, 'I need to go now, I've got more meetings lined up. That's basically what we do most of the time in these jobs, isn't it?' he said with a rueful smile and went off, leaving the archdeacon feeling relieved that the meeting was over, but still guilty about what he was concealing.

It was time he rang a certain person. He wished again that he'd never got into this situation, and he had to summon all his willpower to dial the number.

'It's me . . . No, nothing to report. I don't know why you think there should be . . . Yes, the police will have been through Clare's papers and computer files, but I don't think she will have put anything on record. Anyway, it's not the police you're worried about, is it? I don't think any police officer would let anything slip. I think you're being paranoid again . . . I know, but when this is all over, we might get a better atmosphere in the church and the whole thing will be forgotten . . . Yes, I hope so too . . . Just keep your nerve and try to stay calm. I'm doing what I can . . . Well, there's no need to threaten me again like that! I'd better go.'

He ended the call, feeling a surge of self-loathing. At a time when the Church needed morally upright, exemplary leaders, here he was involved in grubby plotting for his own self-preservation and keeping it secret from everyone. If the newspapers he'd been referring to earlier knew about this, it would confirm their view of the Church. He put his head in his hands and could have wept.

～

Olive Bryson had decided not to open up her shop until the afternoon. The pavements were in such a bad condition that few people would be venturing out in the early morning. However, she was fed up of being in the house so she decided to walk up to the Market Place for coffee in her favourite little café, which also served sourdough bread with avocado. The traffic was moving on the main roads, but the smaller streets were still largely snowbound, with vehicles making slow and skiddy progress over the snowy surface.

Inside the café it was warm, the windows were steamed up and the floor was wet from the snow brought in on people's boots. It was crowded and the atmosphere was very cheery, filled with the smells of brewing coffee and wet Labrador. She immediately noticed Harvey Ferguson at a table by himself and went over.

'Harvey.'

'Ah, Olive.'

'Mind if I join you?'

'Not at all. It's nice to see you.'

Olive sat down and ordered a skinny latte and a slice of stem-ginger cake from the waitress.

Harvey, usually talkative, was very subdued. He was writing in a notebook and sipping from an Americano. His face looked rather strained.

'You're the first person from church I've spoken to since Thursday,' said Olive. 'It's shocking, isn't it?' Harvey stopped writing and put his notebook away. She noticed that his hand was shaking a little.

'Yes, yes, it is.' He looked straight at her. 'Have the police been to see you?' Olive didn't appear to expect this question.

'Well, yes, they have actually. They wanted to know about that money business with the parochial church council. They thought I might have a motive to murder Clare. I think I talked them out of it; I can't think they imagine that I would kill Clare for a few hundred pounds and my reputation, but you never know with the police.'

'Right.' He leaned forward conspiratorially and lowered his voice, which became intense. 'Between you and me, they've been to see me too. I can't go into details but you can probably work out what it's about.' Olive was the only person in the church in whom he'd confided about his sexuality. They'd known each other for a while and felt a kinship in being different from most of the congregation. Olive was tolerant and broad-minded, so Harvey felt safe in her company.

'Oh, that's terrible. But what has that to do with Clare's murder?'

'I can't say much, but a complaint about me came to Clare, and I had a bit of a row with her. It wasn't her fault, I know, but I'm just completely sick of it. The Church is sixty years behind the rest of society.'

'I agree.'

'So they think I might have had a motive too, wanting to keep things secret, you know. But don't worry, I can look after myself and I've got an ally who will protect me.' He nodded and smiled. 'I was just making some notes about it.'

'OK, good,' said Olive. She privately thought Harvey sounded a bit intense and paranoid about the situation, but she could hardly blame him. Her latte and cake arrived, and she took a sip. 'I don't suppose you know who it was who made the complaint against you?' she said, tackling the cake with a cake fork.

'Clare wouldn't say, but let's face it, it could be any of dozens of people in that church. I sometimes wonder why I stay.'

'So do I, but why should we allow them to drive us out? The church is for us too, as I told the chief inspector. Who on earth would do the music if you left? They're very lucky to have you.'

'Thanks.'

She took another drink of her coffee. 'I can't imagine what the church is going to be like after this. I don't envy Robin, having to keep the ship afloat. Maybe it will stir people out of their complacency. I think a lot of people go to church to escape from the real world into one where everyone is nice to each other, at least on the surface. Now the brutality of which the world is capable has entered the church and desecrated the sanctuary. That's going to be very hard to deal with for some people.'

'So, you think it might force people to engage with the world a bit more directly?'

'I would hope so.'

'That's optimistic and I hope you're right, but I can't say I share your view.' He finished his coffee and looked at his watch. There was a rather harried expression on his face. 'Anyway, I must be off. It's been nice to see you.'

'Yes, take care, Harvey.' Olive watched him leave and had a feeling of foreboding. She sensed he was in a dark place and hoped he wouldn't be overwhelmed by it.

~

On the way back from the café, Olive bumped into Austin Eliot, who was carrying a shopping bag.

'Hello,' she said. 'The St Anne's people are out in force today; I've just had coffee with Harvey Ferguson.' Eliot flashed her a smile, which she enjoyed. He was a man she'd always admired even though he made no secret of his conservative views on church matters.

'Got to make the effort. I've got nothing left in the house to eat.' Eliot lived alone in a handsome cottage not far from his shop. He seemed to have plenty of money, which she doubted came solely from selling books. She would like to know what he'd done before he came to Knaresborough. It seemed he'd retired to here from somewhere in the south, as he didn't have a local accent. Altogether he was a very eligible and intriguing man, but he gave little away.

'I see. Well, I think most of the shops are open. How are you after all that's happened?'

'Nice of you to ask. It's terrible, isn't it? I thought Clare was wonderful; I mean, I know we had disagreements and I'm sorry it caused her pain, but she was marvellous as a preacher and pastor. It's just that . . .'

'I know.'

'I told the police that—'

'Have the police been to see you?'

'Yes. On Thursday, the day after the murder. The chief inspector was very interested in the legend of the monk and I loaned him a book about it. He was also asking about people in the church who are opposed to women priests. I was quite frank about my position, and that of people like Donald and Maisie. Why would anyone think that we would murder someone like Clare just because we had a theological difference? It's really quite insulting; I wish I'd said so at the time but he was a very amiable chap. I suppose that's how they lull you into revealing things.'

'They have to follow up all the clues and talk to anyone who might have had any hostility towards the victim, and therefore a motive to kill them. They've been to see me too.'

'What on earth for?'

'You know, about that money business and the parochial church council.'

Eliot was outraged. 'They think you might have killed her over that trifling amount? What kind of people do they think we are?'

'I know, Austin, but someone killed her, didn't they?'

'It was more likely to be someone who wandered into the church and got into an argument with Clare, someone who had nothing to do with the church.'

Olive shrugged. 'Possibly. Anyway, it's getting cold standing here. I'll see you soon. It's time I paid you a visit at the shop; I haven't browsed in there for a while. The problem is we both run shops, so we work at the same time.'

'Not to worry, I'll arrange a private viewing for you and a glass of wine afterwards.'

'Oh, that would be nice.' Olive went on her way with a little glow of excitement. That was something to look forward to.

~

The Rev James Oldroyd looked with an amused smile at the congregation sitting in the church pews before him, as he stood slightly raised up above them by the altar. At least that's how Oldroyd was imagining the situation. The reality was that the 'congregation' was a group of reporters eager for news about the sensational murder of a female vicar in her own church. Apparently, she was good-looking too, which made the story even hotter.

They held voice recorders and notebooks rather than bibles and hymn books. Oldroyd was very experienced in handling these occasions and the types of questions he knew he would receive. He always began with a statement of the main facts, which acted as a kind of baseline and helped to prevent too much speculation.

'The body of Rev Clare Wilcox, the rector of St Anne's, was found at about five thirty p.m. on Wednesday evening by Mr Donald Avison, churchwarden here at St Anne's. She had been bludgeoned to death. The last person to speak to her was her friend Rev Alison Oldroyd by telephone, at about three thirty p.m. We have a witness who saw Rev Wilcox enter the church at about four thirty, and this witness also saw someone leave the church about half an hour later. The face of the person was concealed by a hood.'

Oldroyd was careful to avoid mentioning the monk's habit. He didn't want to get into ghosts; that would send them off into wild fantasies and ridiculous theories.

'That is just about the sum of what we know at the moment. Clearly the progress of the investigation has been hampered by the weather. My message to you is as usual: that anyone with any information about this crime should come forward, particularly if they have any idea of who the person was who was seen coming out of the church. That person is clearly the main suspect.'

'Is it true that it was a frenzied attack, Chief Inspector?' A favourite phrase of the tabloids, 'frenzied attack', thought Oldroyd.

'I wouldn't say frenzied, but it was brutal and carried out in a manner, and with a weapon, about which we're still unclear. We hope the person who came out of the church saw something if they're not the murderer themselves.'

'We've heard this church is haunted.' This from a gruff, bald-headed, gum-chewing tabloid reporter who was very familiar from other investigations.

I suppose it's too much to ask that they wouldn't be on to this, Oldroyd thought.

'So have I – which old church doesn't have stories about ghosts? I don't see such stories as having any connection with this terrible crime or our investigation. As I said to my detective sergeant, we can't arrest a phantom.'

This produced some laughter, which he hoped would discourage any more questions on that topic.

'It's not often a vicar gets murdered in their own church, is it, Chief Inspector?'

'No,' replied Oldroyd, frowning and wondering where the question was leading.

'So, do you think something strange and dark may have been going on here? Something which the vicar stumbled on and so she had to be silenced?'

'I'm not sure exactly what you mean, but if it's something like devil worship, naked orgies or pagan sacrifice, we've found no evidence for things of that nature and they're not top of my list of possible motives. I think you'll agree, such things would be remarkable in an Anglican church in Knaresborough.' This produced more laughter.

'You said just now that you're not clear how she was bludgeoned, although a lot of force was used. If that's the case, can you completely rule out some kind of supernatural agency? Maybe this was a judgement on the church for the kinds of things going on here. The kind of things you mentioned.'

Here we go, thought Oldroyd. As he'd predicted, and despite his efforts to stop it, they were going off into sensationalist fantasy. None of them believed it of course, but they were looking to create great headlines: 'Was Glamorous Vicar Killed by Avenging Angel?' 'What Exactly Went on at Murder Church in Quiet Market Town?' 'God's Judgement: Did Vicar Take the Rap for Goings-on in Church?' He needed to come down hard.

'I must emphasise that what you're suggesting is pure speculation and very unhelpful. If we focus people's attention on ghosts, ghoulies and depraved goings-on, they're less likely to remember something important from the real world. I urge you not to proceed with any damaging stories of that kind. An actual person or persons committed this murder, and we are going to catch them. Also, there is no evidence that the congregation at this church is anything other than a respectable group of people.'

This seemed to do the trick; the direction of questioning changed. It was like keeping a rowdy class of children in order.

'You said person or persons, do you believe more than one person was involved?' This was a much more sensible question.

'We believe this murder to have been well planned, although we are not ruling out the possibility that it was a random act of some kind. The church was open at the time of the murder, so anyone could have walked in. If it was planned, there's always the chance that more than one person was involved, even if only one person committed the actual killing. I would ask people to think about whether they know of anyone who may have been in the area of the church on the afternoon and evening in question.'

'Is anyone else at risk, Chief Inspector?'

'Always a difficult one to answer. Although we don't have any direct evidence of the presence of a killer who may strike at random,

I would still advise people in the neighbourhood to take extra care, as there is clearly a dangerous person at large.'

'And this murder-weapon business, what's the problem there?'

'Well, the victim sustained very serious injuries and we're not sure how they were inflicted. It is clear that she was murdered in the church rather than brought to it already dead, and we are continuing our investigation into exactly how. You can be sure we will not be looking for evil satanic forces.' Further laughter followed.

'This other vicar you mentioned: Alison Oldroyd. Any relation, Chief Inspector?'

'Yes, she's my sister, and she was a friend of the deceased.'

This caused a bit of a ripple.

'So, you have a special interest in solving this one?'

'No more than normal, and I would ask you not to bring my sister into this. She's not directly involved. It just so happened that the deceased spoke to her on the phone not long before she was killed.'

This seemed to satisfy them, and shortly after this question, Oldroyd brought the conference to an end.

The reporters wandered slowly out of the church photographing everything, especially the west-tower area where the crime scene was still taped off and guarded by police constables. After the last one had left, Oldroyd was studying the west tower again when he was startled by a voice behind him.

'They've trailed in a lot of dirt and water, Chief Inspector. I'd better get to work with my mop.' It was Violet Saunders again. How did she manage to keep popping up from nowhere? It was almost enough to make you think that supernatural forces were indeed at work.

'Yes, I'm sorry about that, there was nowhere else to take them I'm afraid.'

'Not to worry, I'll soon have it clean again. They are an ungodly bunch of people, but it will be easier to clean their dirt than to cleanse this church of the evil spirit which has taken possession.'

Oldroyd nodded, not wanting to get involved in that subject again. But even he missed the little gleam in her eye, and the very slight suggestion of a smile.

~

Alison was too tired to speak to any more of her parishioners, who were grieving over the death of their beloved former curate. She needed to get out of the lonely rectory at Kirkby Underside, and so she accepted an invitation to dine with Jim and Deborah at their Harrogate flat. She decided to drive over to Knaresborough for the day, and maybe call on Clare's husband, Jeremy, before returning to Harrogate in the evening.

As she drove down the same hill her brother had a few days before, through the same wintry landscape, she thought about Clare. It was hard to believe that she would never see her again; a person of such talent and charisma who had so much to contribute. At times like this, faith seemed to offer no protection against the bleak, senseless waste of death. Why had God allowed one of his best servants to be torn away from life like that? Now all of Clare's potential was lost. Alison knew the theological answers, but in the rawness of grief they seemed to offer no consolation.

When she arrived in Knaresborough, she drove straight to the rectory, only to find that the Wilcoxes were out. She didn't want to go anywhere near the church at the moment; it would be too painful and she didn't want to get in the way of Jim's investigation. She went to a café in the Market Place and then decided to have a walk. She had brought some boots so she could deal with the snowy streets. She remembered that there was a second-hand bookshop down near the river in which she had occasionally browsed, so she headed for that, enjoying the views of the snowy gorge.

When she arrived, the shop was closed. She was having no luck today. She looked at the small window display. There was a photograph of the owner receiving an award of some kind for best local bookshop or something. Seeing his photograph reminded her of something. Had she seen his picture somewhere else? As she looked, the door opened, and the owner appeared.

'I wasn't going to open today due to the weather, but I saw you from the window upstairs and you're welcome to come in if you like.'

Alison smiled. 'Well, that's very kind, thank you,' she said and went inside.

'Is there any particular subject you're interested in?' asked Eliot, who was dressed in his tweed jacket and chinos.

'I like to have a look at books on theology, if you have a section on that.'

'We have indeed. I'm a member of the church. I worship at St Anne's.'

'Oh, I see. This is a terrible time for you all. It must be devastating to the parishioners.'

'Indeed.'

'I knew Clare very well. It's a terrible loss.'

'How did you know her?'

'She was my curate before she came here. I'm the vicar at Kirkby Underside, you know, between here and Leeds.'

Alison saw his expression turn cold.

'You must be Alison Oldroyd. Clare used to mention you.'

'That's right.'

'I'm Austin Eliot – pleased to meet you.' They shook hands.

'Clare was a wonderful priest; the people up there loved her,' continued Alison.

'She was very good in her pastoral role, but some of us will not accept a woman as celebrant, as I'm sure you're aware.' Alison looked at him closely. Was this one of the people who had made things difficult for Clare? She was in no mood to accept any hostility towards the female priesthood.

'I understand your views, but the decisions to ordain woman and to consecrate them as bishops were taken by the Church as a whole, so it is surely right to progress them.'

Eliot came back. 'I would take issue there. If the Church departs from biblical teaching, then we have a right to dissent and . . .'

A polite but vigorous theological debate followed, and ended with neither side having conceded any ground.

'It's been a pleasure debating with you,' said Eliot with a smile.

'And with you. I shall have to return to see if I can change your views.'

Eliot laughed. 'Not much chance of that I'm afraid.'

'Well, you never know.' Alison always enjoyed a good discussion, and left feeling less despondent. She returned to the rectory to find that the Wilcoxes were now at home. She had lunch with them and they spent some time talking about Clare, the kind of person she'd been and the great potential she'd had to do good in the Church and forward the cause of women. It ended in tears all round, but at least they all had positive memories of their wife, mother and friend.

~

After Alison's visit, the Wilcoxes wanted to get out of the house again. Before it was dark, they put on their coats and boots and went for a walk, wending their way down to the river on the sloping streets and avoiding the church.

The town was beautiful in its winter garb. Roofs were laden with snow, and fine dustings clung to the branches of the trees like icing sugar. The river was partially frozen and a few rowing boats which had been left out were stuck in the ice near the river's edge.

However, the beauty passed them by. They were all preoccupied with the death of their wife and mother, and the need to start to think about the practical issues involved. Wilcox himself had resolutely refused to say anything yet about registering the death or planning the funeral service.

'Do you remember how we used to go rowing on those boats with your mum in summer?' he said.

'Yes,' replied Jenny. 'Sometimes we took a picnic and moored the boat in the fields opposite Conyngham Hall. Then we looked for bullheads and crayfish under the stones.'

'Mum used to really enjoy that. It was always great spending time with all of us together when we were little. She took some persuading to come out though sometimes, didn't she? A bit of a workaholic.'

'Yes, very dedicated,' said Wilcox. Her overworking was what had led to him and her spending so little time together, then drawing apart and then the subsequent affair. He couldn't talk to his daughters about it. Instead, he started to ask them about their time at university. He didn't want to face the subject he knew they wanted him to consider. Jenny and Fiona exchanged a glance, which meant they'd decided that it was time to prompt him.

'Dad,' said Jenny after a while. 'Don't you think it's time to start to think a little bit about Mum's funeral? I know it's hard, but we've got to see the undertaker early next week and you need to tell him what you want. We can help you.'

Wilcox stopped walking, took a deep breath and screwed up his eyes. He seemed to be about to cry, but he shook his head.

'You're right,' he replied. 'I've been avoiding it I know. It's just so hard and . . . I'm . . . I'm still in shock.'

Jenny put her arm through his. 'I know, Dad; it's really hard, but you need to do it. We've got today and tomorrow to think about it. Then on Monday we'll go into Harrogate to register the death and then we'll go to the undertaker's on Tuesday morning. You'll feel so much better when it's done.'

Wilcox walked on slowly. They reached a lane with cottages by the river. A group of swans and ducks were crowded into a small area of water free from ice. 'So, what about the funeral service then?' he asked.

'Fiona and I would like to speak for the eulogy,' said Jenny.

'Good, good. I'm sure I couldn't . . .'

'No one expects you to say anything, Dad.'

'As for the hymns and prayers, I just don't know. I . . .' He stopped again, looking shaky. He leaned against the garden wall of one of the cottages as the strength seemed to go out of him.

'Look, Dad, that café along there by the river is open, I can see people inside. Let's go in there and have a coffee, then we can sit in a warm place and write our ideas down. I've got a notebook,' said Fiona.

'OK, that's a good idea,' replied Wilcox, and his daughters exchanged a glance and a smile.

Inside the café, they slowly put together an order of service and discussed, with occasional tearfulness, what Fiona and Jenny were going to say.

'I think I would like Alison to conduct the service. I'm sure Robin won't mind,' said Wilcox once they'd planned the outline of the funeral.

'That would be great; her and Mum got on really well. She was Mum's mentor, wasn't she? She's lovely,' said Jenny.

'Yes, she shared your mum's views about a lot of things in the Church, and your mum learned a lot from her,' said Wilcox.

'What about afterwards, Dad?' asked Fiona. 'Shall we just invite people back to the rectory? It's big enough, isn't it?'

'Yes. I don't want to go anywhere else.' Wilcox slumped back in his chair. Any kind of physical or mental effort seemed to exhaust him after a short time.

Fiona had written everything down in her notebook. 'Well, we've got a lot done. Don't you feel better, Dad?'

Wilcox agreed that he did. What he felt bad about was the confession he still had to make to them about his behaviour. He knew that the longer he left it, the worse it would be, but maybe after the funeral would be a better time than now; then it wouldn't be long before his daughters went back to university. It seemed a coward's way out, but it was all he could face at the moment. He couldn't bear to lose their favour as he dealt with this disabling grief.

~

Andy and DC Robinson were coordinating statement-taking by detective constables from the Knaresborough station, and checking on alibis from the list of potential suspects. It was the first time, due to the weather, that the police had been able to show a significant presence in the town, which was still reeling from the awful events of Wednesday. There were very few people around, partly due to the weather, but also because of the fear generated by such a terrible attack.

While they were doing this, Oldroyd took a long walk by the river at the bottom of the gorge. The snow had been cleared from the main paths and he enjoyed the quiet winter scene, so different from the bustle in the town during the summer tourist season when it was full of families on day trips and the river was packed with rowing boats. The river was frozen near the bank, but ran clear and icy-cold midstream and reflected the blue of the sky.

Knaresborough was an ancient place, and it struck Oldroyd how many eccentric and unusual things had accumulated along the Nidd Gorge over the centuries. There was Mother Shipton's Cave, where the prophetess Ursula Soothtell had reputedly been born in the fifteenth century. Near the cave was an extraordinary petrifying well, which he had enjoyed visiting as a boy. The water dripping from a low cliff was so full of minerals that objects hung underneath, such as boots and kettles, were calcified in a matter of months. Further along was an eighteenth-century house partially built into the rock, and an early fifteenth-century chapel that had been entirely carved out of the rock. The exterior of the chapel looked like something out of Tolkien. Furthest downstream was a man-made cave that had belonged to Sir Robert of Knaresborough, a religious hermit reputedly visited by King John in the twelfth century.

Oldroyd found it pleasant to contemplate these curiosities without the throng of tourists. Along with the ruined medieval castle and the dramatic railway viaduct, these were the famous heritage sites of the town and the legends and stories that had built up around some of them. He found himself wondering how many other things had been left over time, and lost to public knowledge. And, as so often with Oldroyd, his train of thought brought him back to the case at hand as he took one of the steep narrow lanes back towards the church. There was something in that west tower where Clare Wilcox had been killed which was hidden from view – something that had been forgotten about for a long time until someone had found it and decided to use it for sinister purposes.

~

Andy and Robinson spent the afternoon following up some alibis. Robinson called on Mrs Henderson to confirm Eliot's alibi, and then went to the Avisons' house to speak to Donald's wife.

Meanwhile, Andy drove out to the Jenny Fields estate, which was the home of Julie Harrison, the nurse at Wilcox's medical practice and his lover. A rudimentary effort had been made to clear the snow from the roads that circled within the estate, but Andy still found himself skidding and sliding a little as he drove to the address.

It was a small semi-detached house in an area of open-front gardens without fences or hedges. The door was opened by a young woman with long hair who looked about thirty.

'Yes?'

Andy produced his ID. 'Julie Harrison?' She nodded. 'I'm Detective Sergeant Carter, I'm involved in the investigation into the death of Clare Wilcox. I need to ask you a few questions.'

Her eyes widened in alarm and she quickly glanced around at the street and the adjacent houses. 'Come in,' she said, and quickly shut the door when Andy had stepped inside. 'Thank goodness you're not in a marked car, I don't want the neighbours to know the police have been.' She showed Andy into a rather cramped through-lounge with large French windows looking out on to a small back garden surrounded by wooden fencing. They both sat down.

'Why is that?' asked Andy.

'Because I know why you're here and I don't want anything to get back to my partner. He's at work.'

'OK, so, to get straight on to things, you are having an affair with Jeremy Wilcox and he was here with you on Wednesday afternoon at the time his wife was murdered?'

'He was,' she said quietly, as if the walls had ears or were so thin that people might hear the conversation next door.

'How long has this affair been going on?'

She frowned and her face looked strained. 'Why do you need to know that?'

You've got yourself into something you never expected, thought Andy. 'The wife of a man who was conducting an affair has been murdered, so naturally Mr Wilcox and yourself fall into the category of people who had a motive.' It was very direct; Andy wanted to scare her into telling the truth. 'With his wife out of the way, you could leave your partner and be with Wilcox.'

'No, it wasn't like that. We've only been meeting up for a few months. We . . .' She broke down in tears and Andy wondered if he'd been too brutal. He waited for her to continue. 'We were just getting frustrated with our partners who worked all the time. My partner, Dave, has his own business as a kitchen fitter and he's always out, working or doing estimates. Clare was constantly involved in church work. Jeremy and I used to talk about it and sort of commiserate with each other.' She dabbed her eyes with a tissue. 'Then one thing led to another, as they say.' She tried to look defiantly at Andy. 'But we never intended to leave our partners; it was just . . . I suppose, some consolation. We both felt neglected. It's definitely over after this.'

Andy wasn't completely convinced. 'Did Wilcox promise you anything? A good life together, maybe? It would have been a big step up for you to be a doctor's wife, wouldn't it?'

'That's ridiculous; things like that never came into it. I know you'll be cynical, but it was all about being with another person who understood.' She looked at Andy again. 'Anyway, Jeremy's a lot older than me. Do you think I would want to hitch myself to a man whose daughters are not much younger than me?'

'That doesn't stop a lot of people. But OK, we'll leave it there for the moment.'

'How did you find out about me and Jeremy?' she asked as she was showing Andy out.

'I can't divulge our sources of information.'

'Don't worry, I know; it was that bloody Sylvia Addison. She's a nasty little snooper. I'm not going back to that surgery after this. I'll get a job somewhere else.' Her anger subsided and she looked concerned. 'How is Jeremy? Have you seen him?'

'Yes. I think he's managing in the circumstances. His daughters are at home with him.'

'Oh good. He's close to them. I feel powerless to do anything.' She shrugged. 'But that's the way it is.' She gave Andy a pleading look. 'I would be grateful if you could keep all this a secret. I don't want Dave to find out, especially now it's over and I can put it behind me.'

'We never make information about a case public unless there's a good reason for doing so. I don't see that there would be a reason here, if what you've told me is true.'

'Thank you,' she said. When she closed the door after Andy, she gave a big sigh of relief.

~

When Andy and Robinson got back to the church, they found Oldroyd sitting in the vestry, resting after his walk and deep in thought.

'Pretty good afternoon's work I think, sir,' said Andy, 'but we didn't turn up anything startling. We've got the written statements and we've checked alibis. Robinson went to Mrs Henderson, who backed up Austin Eliot's story that he visited her that afternoon.'

'The problem was, sir,' said Robinson, 'she was a bit vague about the time he left, but thought it was after five o'clock. She's very old and, I imagine, a bit forgetful, so I don't think it's a watertight alibi to be honest, but even so he wouldn't have much time to organise the attack. I then went to check on Avison's alibi and his wife confirmed he was at home on Wednesday until he went out at about five thirty to lock up the church. That was, of course, when he found the body,' said Robinson.

'I went out to interview Wilcox's lover, Julie Harrison. She confirmed that they were together that afternoon,' said Andy. 'I pushed her a bit on both of them having a motive to kill Wilcox's wife. She got quite emotional about it. I have to say I find it difficult to see her as a suspect, though I could be wrong. She could be a very accomplished actress.'

'Hmm,' mused Oldroyd. 'So we've got two people, Avison and Eliot, who are only really suspects because they don't like women priests – and they have alibis, but one's not reliable. Of the other three with motives: Wilcox and his lover could be covering for each other, Bryson was coming back from her shop, and Ferguson claims to have been in York, but nobody can corroborate their stories. It doesn't leave us with a leading suspect, does it? And those are only the people we know about. How's the investigation of Clare Wilcox's computer files, papers, phone and everything going? Has it turned up any other suspects?'

'No, sir. They've been working on it all at Harrogate, but they've not reported anything significant.'

'OK.' Oldroyd sighed, and shook his head. 'The motives we've got aren't very strong. And we've still got to explain how the hell it was done and how this bloody monk fits into it all.'

'Yeah, it's frustrating, sir. But if I had to pick one suspect, it would be Ferguson. He had the most to lose and he's angry about the situation. Another person we haven't really considered is that weird woman, Violet Saunders.'

'What would be her motive?'

'Who knows? She's got some strange ideas and she's very creepy. I can just imagine her hiding away in the church when Clare Wilcox came in.'

Oldroyd grunted. Far-fetched ideas were always a sign of desperation. In any case, events were shortly to put a brutal end to Andy's theory.

～

Later that afternoon, Robin Eastby was trying to relax in the curate's house. Christine had gone off to do the weekly supermarket shop, leaving him to try to recover a little from the exhausting trauma of the last few days.

He tried to read the Saturday *Guardian* but found it difficult to concentrate, so he got up and looked out over the snow-covered garden. He enjoyed gardening, and he tried to work out which bump in the snow represented which shrub. When this snow melted, he hoped there would be the first signs of snowdrops forcing their way through the icy ground.

He could see the upper part of the west tower of the church topped with snow and looking beautiful against the blue sky. Eastby was also interested in buildings, and had once considered becoming an architect. He found St Anne's a fascinating example of eclectic ecclesiastical architecture, with different parts of the building in styles from different periods. His interest in church architecture had begun when he was a student at Mirfield, the Anglo-Catholic theological college in West Yorkshire. He looked back on his time there with great fondness. Many things about its practice and teaching had affected him deeply.

He went to the bookshelves which were in an alcove by the fireplace, and took out a detailed history of St Anne's. It had been written some time ago by a local expert, Gerald Thompson, but it remained the definitive book. It contained a large amount of historical detail about events in the church, as well as the design of the building and its evolution over the years. It was sumptuously illustrated. Eastby sat down and leafed through the pages, enjoying the images of windows, stained glass and the unusual pair of towers. He found it very soothing.

He knew that the responsibility now coming to him was an opportunity to create a good impression and make progress in the Church hierarchy. He knew the bishop and the archdeacon would be watching him, and he hoped to become the vicar of a large church in the diocese before too long, maybe even St Anne's if he worked hard. And who knew? Some day he could succeed them in their jobs. His mind came back to the death of Rev Wilcox. He was sorry about that, but after all, and here a strange smile came on to his face, every cloud had a silver lining.

He closed the book and replaced it, just as he heard the car arrive back. He went out to help Christine bring in the shopping bags.

'That wasn't easy,' she said as she lugged a couple of bags into the kitchen with Eastby beside her carrying two more. 'The car park was in chaos; half the spaces were full of piles of snow and cars were slipping and sliding all over the place. I'm dying for a cup of tea.'

The bags were left to one side as Eastby put on the kettle.

'How are you feeling?' asked Christine as she took off her coat.

'OK. I've been thinking about the next few months. I'm going to rise to the challenge and show them I can do it.'

'Oh good, that's positive,' replied Christine, although she was a little surprised at his tone.

'This is my big chance and I'm going to take it.'

She looked at him closely. 'Are you OK?'

'Yes – why?'

'It just doesn't sound like you to talk about ambitions at a . . . well, at a time like this, when everyone's bereaved. Don't you think it's a bit insensitive?'

He sighed. 'I suppose you're right, sorry. I don't know what came over me. I suppose it's made me realise that I do aspire to get on in the church and here's an opportunity opening up.'

'But all in good time, Robin, surely?'

'Of course.' He looked at his watch and at the developing dusk outside. 'Look, I'll help you unpack the shopping and then I've got to pop out for a while. I said I'd visit one or two parishioners who are taking it badly, and there's no service at St Anne's tomorrow. I'll make tea when I get back.'

'OK.'

When he'd left, Christine sat down for a moment. She felt unsettled. She'd never heard Robin talk like that before, sounding so hard and ambitious. Was it the shock of what he'd been through? Or was she seeing a side of him she'd not seen before? If so, it was a side she didn't like.

~

Oldroyd arrived home that night feeling discontented. His mind was spinning with information, but nothing was coming together. It was the worst point in a case like this: lots of work done, but little to show for it. At least Alison was coming for tea tonight, so he would have the company of two of his favourite women in the world – the third being his daughter, Louise, who was working in London.

When he got to the flat, he saw that Alison's car was already parked outside. It was now very cold again, and he walked gingerly up the path on which the frost sparkled. Inside, his mood was lifted immediately by the warmth and by the presence of Alison and Deborah.

'Oh, Jim, you look tired,' said Deborah. 'Come and sit down and have a glass of wine.' He gave both women a hug and a kiss and sat down on the sofa next to Alison. Deborah went into the kitchen.

'She's right,' said Alison, looking at him. 'This is a nasty case, isn't it? And I imagine it's getting to you.'

'It certainly is, and we're not getting on particularly well. We have some suspects but not one that really stands out and we don't know how the poor woman was killed. How are you?'

Alison sighed. 'I was quite busy yesterday when people had dug themselves out of the snow; lots of parishioners calling round to talk to me about Clare. They've taken it very hard in Kirkby Underside. They remember her as a wonderful curate and she was – so warm and approachable but also very efficient and a deep thinker. She was so multi-talented and had so much more to contribute. Now she's gone. It's tragic.'

'That's the essence of tragedy isn't it: loss?' Oldroyd had studied English at Oxford and liked to use examples from literature. 'Think of Macbeth and Othello; their greatness and potential are destroyed due to the choices they make in those plays: Macbeth to commit murder for his own gain and Othello to listen to Iago and not to trust Desdemona.'

'And the potential of Lady Macbeth and Desdemona,' added Alison, 'particularly the latter, who is a virtuous and blameless woman, much like Clare actually.'

'Of course,' agreed Oldroyd. He sensed the strong feminist in his sister was outraged by this crime. 'Do you still see Clare as a victim of misogyny? We don't even know for sure that it was a man who killed her.'

Alison took a deep breath, and he could feel her anger. 'No, Jim, but it's highly likely to be a man, isn't it? So yet again, a talented woman who is threatening the male establishment is cut down. I know you'll think I'm imposing meanings on the murder, and the actual motive, when you find it, will probably be much more trivial, but I'm afraid that's how it feels to me, and to a lot of women in and out of the Church who have sent me messages.'

'I know,' said Oldroyd, 'but I have to be very careful to take it a step at a time and not to jump to conclusions.'

Alison gave him a smile, because she knew he always tried very hard to understand the feminist position.

'On this point,' she said, 'I'd had enough of counselling parishioners, so I decided to spend a bit of time in Knaresborough today and I ended up in that bookshop down by the river. It was closed, but the owner—'

'Austin Eliot?'

'Oh, you know the place?'

'Yes, and I'll bet he engaged in a discussion with you about women in the Church.'

'He certainly did. I was in there for a couple of hours. He's an Anglo-Catholic, very High Church; can't accept that a woman can celebrate communion. He was very polite about it, but it didn't go down well with me, especially in the circumstances, as you can imagine.'

'I can,' said Oldroyd with a smile.

'You see what kind of hostility we still face.'

'Yes. He's open and honest about it, but it's still really objectionable. I went into his shop to find out about this business with the ghost of the monk and he was very helpful. He knew all about the legend but then he got started on women in the ministry. I thought about you at the time. It would be nice to think that men like him were a minority.'

'It's ready!' announced Deborah at this point, bringing an end to the discussion. Alison and Oldroyd went through to the kitchen-diner.

All three of Oldroyd's favourite women were vegetarian, and he willingly gave up meat when he ate with them. Deborah had made a delicious and hearty vegetable casserole which she served with home-baked bread. It was just right for this cold winter season. They made a point of not talking about the case during the meal, and conversation turned to the younger members of the family; to what Louise and Robert, Oldroyd's daughter and son, were doing, and to Deborah's offspring in London and America.

'How's Louise doing on her course, Jim?' Louise was studying some kind of social-work conversion course in London.

'Fine. No news is good news with Louise. I haven't heard from her for a little while, but I think she's OK. The same goes for Robert and Andrea. Little Rosie's three now, can you believe it?'

'Good heavens! It's a shame they're not closer. I think I've only seen Rosie once.'

'They seem to be quite content. We're going down to see them soon. Deborah hasn't met them yet.'

'No, I'm looking forward to it,' said Deborah. 'Richard's in California with his partner, June, making a pile of money working for an engineering company. Jane's in London following in my footsteps, training to be a psychotherapist.'

'That's good,' said Alison. 'They all seem to be doing well. It's so good to get some positive news in this awful time. No grandchildren yet, then?'

'All in good time I suppose, but it would be nice,' said Deborah. Oldroyd felt a pang. He didn't think he'd done that good a job of being a parent, and his marriage had broken down. Was he doing any better as a grandparent? The fact was that his son and family lived in Birmingham, and he only rarely saw his little granddaughter.

'I'm lucky to be a great-aunt,' said Alison, laughing. 'It's great fun.' Alison's husband David had died of cancer several years ago, but his sister had grandchildren who were not too far away, in Sheffield. 'I went down just before Christmas to go with them to the children's play. They always invite me. We had a marvellous time; they did a version of *The Lion, the Witch and the Wardrobe*. The kids were fascinated by how the children in the story went through the wardrobe into another world. When we got back to Celia's house, they were opening cupboards and trying to get inside them.'

Deborah laughed, but Oldroyd looked distracted. Deborah recognised the signs.

'Jim,' she said in an ominous tone, 'we said no work during tea. Wherever your mind has gone, bring it back to now and tell me if you want tea or coffee.'

'Oh! Coffee please,' he said with a smile. He suddenly felt more optimistic about the case. At least he had something new to explore the following day.

~

Earlier, as the light was fading and the cold intensifying, Violet Saunders arrived back home. She had been shopping in the town centre. It had been a bit of a struggle because the streets had become increasingly slippery as frost formed on the pavements. She'd wanted to be home before the light failed completely. She didn't feel safe being outside after dark in her current situation. She was still waiting to hear from her blackmail victim. She reflected on how church was always such fertile ground for picking up bits of gossip and scandal, and she smiled rather unpleasantly as she opened the door and was once again met by the sound of her cats.

'There, there, darlings. Mummy's home.' She looked at the hungry miaowing creatures as they brushed up against her legs, but there were only two. 'Where's Solomon? It's not like him to be missing when I get back. He's usually ready for his tea as well. What have you done with him, darlings?' She went through to the kitchen but there was still no sign of the cat. 'Solomon!' she called. 'It's teatime.' There was still no response, so she took the kettle to fill it at the sink, which was by a window overlooking the back garden. She glanced into the garden, where her attention was caught by something moving.

'Solomon! What on earth are you doing?' The little cat, barely more than a kitten, was sitting by a lilac tree in the snow. It looked as if there was something tied to its collar. Saunders put the kettle down and unlocked the back door. She called the cat but it didn't move and just miaowed at her. Luckily Saunders hadn't yet taken off her boots and so she walked quickly towards the cat. She saw that it was tied to the lilac tree by a length of cord. 'Oh, Solomon, what's going on, you poor thing. Who did this? I—' She was entirely focused on the cat and the light was poor. She didn't see the low tripwire strung across the path, fell full-length and heavily on to the ground. She was badly winded, but before she could even make an attempt to get up, a figure appeared from behind a shrub and struck a severe blow to the back of her head. It stooped over the body for a moment, and then released the cat before making a quick escape over a fence into the back lane.

After a while, Ginger and Mary appeared in the garden and came to sniff and paw at the prostrate body of their mistress. Blood had stained the snow a dark red. The cats made tentative miaows. It didn't seem as if they were going to be fed after all. Little Solomon had gone inside where it was warmer, with the cord still fastened to his collar.

Five

'. . . there was someone or something on the watch outside
my door the whole night. I almost fancy there were two.
It wasn't only the faint noises I heard from time to time
all through the dark hours but there was the smell – the
hideous smell of mould.'

From 'The Treasure of Abbot Thomas',
M. R. James, 1904

Oldroyd strode past the familiar sounds and sights of police presence at a murder scene: crackling radios, blue and white tape, and
police constables on duty to prevent intruders contaminating the
scene. It was a cold, overcast morning.

Oldroyd spoke briefly in the house to a sergeant from the
Knaresborough station. The body of Violet Saunders had remained
undiscovered in her garden all night. Neighbours had become concerned about the persistent miaowing of cats who were also seen on
the top of the garden fence. It was noticed that the back door was
open, and on investigation the victim was discovered. The police
were called, and the cats were fed.

Oldroyd found Tim Groves in the garden, finishing his exam-
ination of the body.

'Ah, Jim,' he said. 'This time it was definitely a blunt instrument, probably a hammer. She's been dead about fifteen hours or so I'd say. I don't think it takes Sherlock Holmes or even you to work out what happened.' Oldroyd smiled. He always enjoyed Tim's dry humour. 'One of the cats was found with a length of cord attached to its collar. I reckon the killer tied that poor cat to a tree, which is visible from the house. She comes in and sees it from the back window there.' He pointed. 'She comes out to get the cat and falls over that tripwire.' He pointed again to the length of wire stretched tautly across the path. 'There are abrasions to the knees, legs and arms as a result of the fall. The assailant then attacks her, and probably escapes over there into the back lane, having first released the cat. Killers can be sentimental about animals, can't they? Like the rest of us.'

Oldroyd clapped. 'Well done, Tim! I'll be off then, as you seem to have solved it.' He pretended to start to walk back to the house and then stopped and turned. 'Ah, there's just the little matter of who the assailant was!'

'Well, you can't expect me to tell you everything,' replied Groves, laughing, before returning to the serious questions. 'I don't know whether you think these two crimes are connected; there's nothing in particular to link them, but two savage murders in less than a week in a place like Knaresborough is not exactly usual, is it?'

'No, and I'm working on the assumption that the same person or persons are responsible. Clearly whatever method they used to kill Clare Wilcox in the church was not available to them here. We need to find what connects the victims.'

'Did you get any further in working out what could have killed the first victim?'

'Not yet, though I'm beginning to have some vague ideas.'

'Let me know when you've worked it out. I'd love to know what the first murder weapon was. I'll leave you to it. It is Sunday after all. It's supposed to be the day of rest.' Oldroyd smiled at this comment too. They both knew that, in their senior positions, they were on call twenty-four hours a day if a serious situation developed.

As Groves began to collect his things together and remove his plastic gloves, Andy arrived with DC Robinson.

'Morning, sir,' Andy said. 'I'd just called in at Harrogate to see if they'd got any further with their analysis of Clare Wilcox's computer and phone when I got the message.'

'Yes, I'm afraid it's the end of your theory about Violet Saunders being responsible. She's been murdered in her back garden.'

'Bloody hell! The media circus are going to love this, aren't they?'

Oldroyd winced. 'Yes, I'm afraid they are. We need to prepare ourselves for another onslaught today.' He glanced around the garden and towards the house. 'We might as well go back to the church. Robinson, come back later and see if the SOCOs find anything. I don't think they will; the killer almost certainly never went into the house. There may be some footprints amongst the bushes, but I don't think they'll tell us much.'

'Sir.'

The detectives set off back up to the church.

'I take it we're assuming the same killer is at work here, sir?' asked Andy.

'Yes. As Tim Groves said, two murders like this in Knaresborough is very unusual.'

'Why do you think Saunders was the second victim? She could have been an accomplice, couldn't she? And they fell out about something?'

Oldroyd shrugged. This new development was a setback: it made things more urgent – there was a high chance that the killer might strike again – but also more puzzling. 'I doubt it, Andy, but

I suspect that she might have known things. She had that furtive ability to always be around and somehow to remain invisible. I suspect she was a lot sharper and more practical than her eccentric manner suggested. I think she was very adept at listening and observing, always on the lookout for useful information.'

'You mean she might have known who the killer was, and maybe blackmailed them?'

'That's my hunch, but it's no more than that at the moment. This killer was clearly prepared to strike again for whatever reason, so it could mean other people are at risk. We're going to have to move fast. The next thing is to look again at the tower area. I have another hunch, which I hope is right because we're badly in need of a break in this case. We need to call on Avison; his house is in this street, isn't it?'

'Yes, sir, just up here on the right,' said Robinson.

When Andy knocked on the door, Avison answered, looking surprised. 'Oh, Sergeant, Chief Inspector. I was hoping to see you. What's going on down at Violet Saunders's house? The police arrived there early. I was going to go down there but I don't like to pry.'

'I'm afraid Violet Saunders has been murdered.'

'What?!' He looked genuinely shocked. 'Do you think it's the same killer?'

'Very likely, I would say. Now, look, things are getting more urgent. We need your bunch of keys again. We want to get into those large cupboards under the tower.'

'The cupboards?'

'It could be very important.'

Avison thought for a moment. 'One of them is where we store hymn books and I have a key for that. But I've never seen the other cupboard opened in the ten years I've been here. No one's ever asked me about it, so I presume no one has anything stored in there. It may not have been used for many years. However, we can certainly try the big bunch of keys again.'

'Good. Can you bring them up to the church now?'

'Certainly.' The detectives waited for Avison, and soon they were all inside the church and once again standing under the west tower. Although it was Sunday, the church was deserted as all services were suspended for the moment.

'So, this is the key for the hymn-book cupboard.' Avison opened one of the cupboards to reveal a pile of musty-smelling books. 'Now, let's try some of these on this other cupboard.'

He studied the large number of keys on the iron ring. They were of various shapes and sizes and some of them were very old. He tried several before one finally turned, and Avison opened the door.

'Funny,' he said. 'It opened very smoothly, almost as if it's been in regular use.' Inside, it was completely empty and there were no shelves. 'Sorry, Chief Inspector. I don't know what you were expecting.'

'Probably exactly this,' replied Oldroyd, as he stepped into the cupboard. He fiddled around at the back for a moment. 'Ah, yes,' he said at last, as he pressed on some kind of catch and the back panel of the cupboard swung inwards.

Andy smiled. Finding secret doors and compartments was one of his boss's specialities.

Immediately behind the panel was a very old-looking door which was also locked. The lock, however, looked quite modern.

'Damn,' said Oldroyd. 'Can you try opening this?'

Avison tried, but none of his keys worked. It was tantalising.

'OK,' said Oldroyd with a sigh of frustration. 'Clearly the same person who fitted the lock to the boiler room door has been at work here too. We need to get help. I'd prefer not to break it down; we don't know what else we might bring down with it. Mr Avison, if you could recommend a locksmith to Detective Constable Robinson here. Robinson, call that locksmith and then go back to the crime scene and see what's happening.'

'Sir.'

Avison and Robinson left, and Oldroyd and Andy went to the vestry. Andy put the kettle on.

'I think we might be finally getting somewhere in the mystery of how Clare Wilcox was killed, and if we can get inside that door it may also give us some clues as to who the killer is.'

'Maybe we'll find the ghost of the monk, sir,' jested Andy.

'You could be right in this sense: the person who's dressing up as the monk is behind all this. They are very real, and clearly have an evil mind, so we'll have to be careful. I was put on to this when Deborah mentioned *The Lion, the Witch and the Wardrobe*, in which the children go through the wardrobe into Narnia. I was suspicious of that locked cupboard; it seemed big enough to be concealing something behind it, and so it proved.'

'I hope we don't find ourselves in a different world, sir. Steph will never forgive me for being involved in such a fascinating case while she's stuck in the office in Harrogate.'

'Not a different world, Andy, but maybe back in time. I have an idea that we'll find something dangerous from a previous age, though what, exactly, I'm not sure.'

∼

Violet Saunders lived in the same area of the town as a number of St Anne's people, including Olive Bryson, Donald Avison and Maisie Baxter. Baxter's house was very close, and she saw the early-morning police activity around the cottage and a number of police cars parked outside. She walked across and spoke to a police constable on duty by the gate, but he would give no information. She joined a group of bystanders, many of whom she knew. One of them, who must have spoken to a neighbour of the victim, confirmed that Violet had been found dead and seemingly murdered.

'Apparently she was lured out of the house by the sight of her cat tied to a tree. That's what they said. There's some lunatic on the loose. Where are they going to strike next?'

Baxter shook her head and said nothing.

'Maisie?' Baxter turned her head. It was Olive Bryson. 'I thought it was you. I heard the sirens a while ago and I could see the blue lights flashing. What's going on?'

'It's Violet; people are saying she's been murdered.'

'What?'

'Yes. I'm waiting to see if the chief inspector or his sergeant appears, then I can ask them. I think they will remember me. I went to see them with Donald.'

'Where is Donald? I thought he might be here.'

'I don't know. He's been helping the police a lot, so he could be with them.'

Olive looked across at the police and SOCOs coming and going down the path to the cottage door.

'What on earth's going on, Maisie? How can this be happening to us at St Anne's?'

Baxter turned and gave her a strange look. 'Maybe it's a judgement, Olive.'

'On what?'

'Things going on at the church. Things that don't please God.'

'What on earth do you mean? What things?'

Baxter didn't answer. She shook her head and walked off.

❧

There was a knock on the vestry door.

'Ah, that could be him now.' Oldroyd had been waiting impatiently for the locksmith to arrive. He opened the door to reveal a man in overalls holding a case.

'Chief Inspector Oldroyd? They said I'd find you here.'

'Yes, hello. This way please.'

Andy and the locksmith followed Oldroyd to the still-open cupboard under the west tower, and through the false back to the old door in the wall. It didn't take the locksmith long to open this. The door opened to the right, and immediately on the left was a very steep and narrow stone staircase.

'Just a standard mortice lock. I would say it's been fitted within the last few years. It's by no means as old as this lot.' He pointed to the ancient timbers of the door and to the medieval stonework.

'Thanks,' said Oldroyd. 'Send your bill to Harrogate police station.'

After the locksmith left, Oldroyd said, 'Someone has indeed been busy in this church. Just as Avison said.'

'I still think it could be Avison, sir.'

'Maybe. Send a message to Robinson to come to the church and deal with any enquiries, and tell anyone who comes in wanting to see us that we'll be back shortly. He's not to let anyone in. And you'd better shut that cupboard door so no one can follow us.'

'Sir.' Andy felt like he really was in some children's fantasy story as he closed the cupboard door. He texted Robinson and then re-joined his boss in this adventure.

'Right, let's see what we can find. I've brought a torch with me. It's going to be difficult to see up there.'

Oldroyd switched on the torch and went slowly up the staircase, which was barely wide enough for one person. Andy followed. They were climbing a dark and dusty cavity between an inner and an outer wall of the ancient squat tower. At the top of the staircase, they reached a wooden platform. They seemed to be midway between the corners of the tower. Just to their left was a very thick and rusty round iron bar, which emerged from the outer wall and continued through the gap and into the inner wall. To their right was a large opening in the inner wall, and blackness.

'Careful here, this probably opens into the tower space and we're fairly high up. What the . . .' Something flew out of the hole and past his face, making him stumble.

'Steady on, sir.' Andy gripped his boss by the shoulder.

'That was a blasted bat!' Oldroyd cursed. 'I see they have them up here, even though this tower doesn't have a belfry any more.' He moved the torch around. They were indeed looking down into the empty space inside the tower. They were about three-quarters of the way up. It was very draughty and cold. Below, they could see the other side of the wooden ceiling, covered in dirt and bird droppings. From where they stood, a rickety-looking wooden ladder fastened to the wall went down to that ceiling. Nearby, they could also see where the thick iron rod came through the inner wall for a few feet and then stopped. Attached to it at right angles was an enormously long, but narrow, flat piece of thick metal with a heavy-looking ball attached to the end. It was tied securely to a metal hook close to where they stood.

'Of course,' said Oldroyd. 'I should have known.'

'What is it, sir?' asked Andy, fascinated by this strange place.

'That,' replied Oldroyd, pointing at the long piece of metal, 'is the murder weapon.'

'What?'

'It's the pendulum of the old church clock, which was once fixed to this tower. It swung down inside here and was attached to the clock mechanism via that rod. The tower isn't very high and the pendulum must have reached nearly to the ground. It would have been encased in a wooden structure so that no one down below could have been hit by it. On the wall below you can see some of the holes where the wood was fastened to the wall. When a new clock was built in the east tower, it looks as if nobody could be bothered to remove this pendulum; it would have been quite a job. So they secured it high up to the wall as if it were at the top of its swing, and built that wooden ceiling to seal the tower space off. The staircase up to here fell into disuse and was forgotten.'

'The murderer unfastened this thing and dropped it down?'

'I think so.'

'But, sir, surely it would have hit the wooden ceiling.'

'I think that's where that ladder comes in. We need to get this properly investigated, but I imagine that ceiling must be hinged so that a section can be pulled over, leaving space for the pendulum to swing.'

'So anyone standing at the bottom is going to be smashed by this as it swings down?'

'Yes; the protective casing is no longer there. Rev Wilcox was standing directly in line by that archway into the storeroom, which wasn't there when this clock was operating. She would have taken the full force on her left side, producing exactly the injuries we saw. Then, I presume, the killer, still holding the long fastening rope, pulled the pendulum back up, and tied it in position again on the hook. Look, a pulley's been fitted to make that job easier.' There was indeed a large metal pulley fastened to the wall which the rope went through. 'Then they went back down the ladder to shut the flap in the ceiling and everything was concealed again.'

'Bloody hell, sir, that would take some hard work, and a lot of planning.'

'I know. I think we can now finally say for sure that the murderer was not a stranger who just wandered into the church.' He shone the torch up and down again. 'The problem is, though: how did whoever it is manage to do all this work? The joinery involved in constructing the hinge in the ceiling, if I'm right, and also the door at the back of the cupboard. It would have taken a long time, and been extremely noisy.'

'Hold on, sir. Didn't Saunders say she'd heard noises in the church? Maybe that's what she heard and not a ghost.'

'You're right. Austin Eliot said the same thing. We need to ask around if anyone else has heard noises in the church at night, because that is when our killer was doing their preparations. But I wonder . . .' He looked at the metal pulley again. 'You know, that pulley isn't new, in fact it's pretty old. It might have been greased recently, but it's been here a long time. Hmm, it's time I did some more research. Come on, we'd better go down.'

They descended the stone staircase and went back through the secret door, the panel in the cupboard, and the cupboard door back into the church. DS Robinson was standing by the door and was surprised to see them.

'Sir? Sarge? Where've you been?'

'You wouldn't believe us if we told you.' Oldroyd laughed. 'Right, you can carry on with what you were doing before, we're fine now.'

Robinson left looking very puzzled.

'OK,' said Oldroyd on the way back to the vestry. 'We need an investigation of everything up there and a full report. You'd better get on to Harrogate and get them to send a team over.'

'Sir.'

'I don't think this takes us much further forward in terms of who's responsible for all this,' said Oldroyd.

'Surely it must be someone who knows a lot about the history of the church, sir,' suggested Andy.

'Yes, but most of the people we've spoken to could have that knowledge or have access to it. Austin Eliot was very upfront about his expertise, but that doesn't mean other people aren't also knowledgeable but are just keeping quiet. I'm increasingly thinking that more than one person could be involved.'

'Right.'

'Unfortunately, I'm going to have to speak to the media again today. They won't be as well behaved as last time. This is a big story now. It might be unfair to say they love a series of killings, but that's the way it seems sometimes; it means they get a long-running story and can build up the tension. It sells newspapers. And as I haven't much to tell them in terms of who the killer is, there'll be no manner of speculation about their identity.'

~

In the sad life of David Tanner, Sunday was just a day like any other. He remembered from his childhood how the family would sit down to Sunday dinner together, but that was before his father started hitting his mother, the family split up and he and his brother went into care. He'd started drinking in his teens and it had plagued his life since then, until he was no longer able to sustain a job or a relationship.

He hated sitting in the hostel all day. He wanted to be out in the fresh air. All the jobs he'd had were on farms or in gardens. It was harder in winter when it was cold, and there were fewer people around who might give him something. He had a well-trodden route around the town, including various warm doorways where he could shelter for a while before he was moved on.

As he trudged around the town trying to keep warm, he thought about that chief inspector who'd given him the money. He'd hidden that money, and was desperately trying not to spend it on drink. He wanted to give himself a fresh start. Maybe someday he could train to be a joiner like his father, who'd taught him a bit before the family broke down. If he could remember something else about that weird monk-thing he'd seen in the churchyard, the chief inspector might give him some more money. It would have to be the truth though. If he made anything up, they would find out and then he would be in real trouble.

He sat down under the wide eaves of an old building near the Market Place. He put out his begging cup and leaned against a wall. What else could he remember of that incident in the churchyard? He played it through in his mind as he'd described it to the police officers. As he was thinking, a woman with a hooded winter coat was walking past and stopped. She put a fifty-pence piece in the cup.

'Thanks, love,' he said, then remembered something. Although he'd not seen the face of the monk figure, he'd seen their hair, though he couldn't make out the colour. Long hair, which was visible at the sides of the hood. Hair like that woman who'd just given him the money. So the monk was likely to be a woman!

He smiled to himself. The chief inspector would definitely like to hear that. And it might earn him a nice reward. He picked up his cup and headed in his slow, lurching way towards the church.

~

At the second press conference in the church, Oldroyd felt less like a vicar with a congregation than a teacher with a large and unruly class. The story was now a sensation, and he could predict the latest headlines: 'Another Church Murder in Sleepy Market Town', 'Has the Ghost Struck Again?' 'Would You Worship in This Church?' or even: 'What Do They Worship in This Church?'

There was a clamour amongst the assembled reporters, who were much bigger in number than last time. Oldroyd had to use all his skills to control the situation. Grim-faced, he began with his usual outline of what had happened and then started to field questions.

'Chief Inspector! Are the two crimes related? Who might be next?'

'Could we please have calm and order?' he requested as the shouting continued, and he waited until there was near quiet. 'We do believe that it is likely but not certain that the murder of Violet Saunders was related to that of Rev Wilcox. They knew each other through their involvement with this church, but we're not aware of any connection between them as yet. It is highly unlikely that two members of the same church should be murdered in a similar way – and by "similar", I mean that both crimes were planned, neither was a random, spontaneous attack.'

'Was the second victim killed in the same way as the first?'

'With a savage blow, yes. I said to you before that there was something unexplained about the nature of the attack on Rev Wilcox, but I don't propose to make any further comment on that at the moment.' Oldroyd wanted to keep their exploration of the west tower a secret, so as not to alert the killer.

'We've heard this latest victim cleaned the church and was in there quite a lot. Do you think she saw the first murder and knew more than was good for her?'

This was a good question and quite close to Oldroyd's own theory. 'I don't think she was a witness to that murder. But she was the kind of person who picked up a lot of information about the church and the people in it.'

'Blackmail!' someone called out.

'That could be the motive for the murder, but we still need to investigate other possibilities. Now,' he moved on swiftly, preventing more questions for the moment, 'yet again I need to ask for anyone with information about the circumstances of this crime to come forward. They may have seen something suspicious around the area of the murder scene yesterday in the late afternoon or early evening. Maybe they knew the victim had enemies – had they witnessed an argument or anything like that?'

'Do you think the killer will strike again, Chief Inspector?'

'It would be foolish of me to give false assurances now that two people have been killed. It is still my view that this is not the work of a random killer, but everyone needs to take extra care and should report anything suspicious. And by the way, I hope this terrible attack in the victim's garden, which involved a nasty tripwire, will put an end to any idea that the perpetrator is some kind of ghost. I doubt that supernatural killers need to set physical traps for their victims, nor hit them on the head with a hammer – which is most likely what happened here.'

He felt quite drained when it was over. Andy arrived back and joined him in the vestry.

'Right, sir, there's a full team coming and they're going to go over that tower. They're going to fingerprint everything and look for any other evidence as to who might have been going up there. I've also asked them to look at the locks, pulleys and all the mechanisms, to see if we can find out more about that pendulum business.'

'Excellent. I think I've seen the press off for the time being. Let's have a little update, I'll put the kettle on.'

They sat down with their cups of coffee.

'So, who are our suspects?' began Oldroyd, who characteristically sat back with his eyes shut and his hands behind his head when they were reviewing a case and things were still far from clear.

Andy consulted his notes. He always liked to make a written record. 'I'm going to start with Avison, sir. He's been very helpful. But as we said, that could be a bluff. Helping us helps him keep track of what we've been doing. He's a churchwarden, so he has access to things. Maybe he had a key to that door in the tower but he just didn't tell us. He's also likely to have a good knowledge of the church and its buildings.'

'The problem is we don't really have a motive except his opposition to women priests, and he has an alibi for the first murder – unless his wife is lying. Another thing is that he knows we're on to the secret door into the tower. So that will scare him off if he is the murderer.'

'Does that really matter, sir? I can't imagine the killer trying to use that method again. There are too many of us all over the church.'

'No, you're right. What I'm beginning to think is that the killer may have only intended to kill Rev Wilcox, and the whole ghostly monk business was designed to throw us off the scent. I suspect that now, if we're right about the blackmail theory, they've had to kill Saunders to keep her quiet, and that is worrying. Now that the initial plan has gone awry and their cover as a ghost has been blown, they may become reckless. There may be other people they would like to get rid of.'

'Won't they try to lie low, sir? They've got away with it so far; why take another risk?'

'It depends on the motives and their state of mind. I wouldn't be surprised if they strike again.' He shook his head. 'So, who else have we got?'

Andy consulted his list. 'Jeremy Wilcox, the husband; he was conducting an affair so he might have wanted rid of his wife. Julie Harrison, his lover, had the same motive. And they cover each other for their alibis, so I suppose it's conceivable that one or both of them could have gone to the church that day and murdered Rev Wilcox, and then Violet Saunders found out.'

Oldroyd frowned. 'It just doesn't hang together for me. Wilcox seems genuinely wrecked by grief. He would have to be a skilled actor, and you said the same about Julie Harrison. It's also difficult to imagine either of them knowing about the concealed staircase and preparing everything in that tower.'

'There may have been another person involved.'

'Then we're getting into the area of conspiracies, and you know what I think about those. Murders of this kind are rarely committed by groups of people. Who's next?'

'Harvey Ferguson, the organist and choirmaster. He struck me as the person with the most anger about the situation, and he seemed desperate to keep his sexuality a secret. I think he might be capable of violence if he was really provoked, and he has no alibi for that evening.'

'There is a powerful motive there, but I couldn't see him doing it all himself. By the way, we'll need to go back to all these people and see what their alibis are for the time of the Saunders murder.'

'Right, sir. I'll get Robinson on to it. Then there's Olive Bryson, who had "borrowed" the church's money, as she put it. No alibi, but I can't see her killing the rector over that amount unless she's concealing something.'

'There's Austin Eliot, the bookshop owner,' continued Oldroyd. 'He made no attempt to conceal his opposition to women priests and he certainly knows the church. You said his alibi was a bit shaky.'

'Yes.'

'I don't know. He was so upfront about his views; I didn't feel he had anything to hide. As yet, no one else has appeared as a suspect. The only other person who's featured in the investigation is the curate. What's his name again?'

Andy consulted his notebook. 'Robin Eastby.'

'Yes, but we've no reason to suspect him.' Oldroyd got up. 'OK. No one's leaping out at me as the prime suspect. We'll just have to carry on and . . .' He stopped, because there was the sound of angry raised voices coming from the church entrance. He looked at Andy, and they both ran down the aisle towards the door.

The constable on duty was confronting an angry David Tanner, who was shouting at him: 'Let me into t'bloody church. Ah've got summat to tell that inspector bloke.'

'Which inspector? You can't come in here, it's a crime scene.'

Oldroyd appeared and intervened before things got out of hand. 'OK, I've got it. I know this man.' The constable looked extremely surprised, but was glad to yield to his superior. 'What do you want, David?'

Vindicated, Tanner sneered at the constable before turning to Oldroyd and Andy. 'Ah've remembered summat else, yer know, about that monk in t'churchyard.'

'OK.' Oldroyd sounded a little sceptical. 'You'd better come in then.' Tanner gave the constable another look of contempt, and followed the detectives into the church. 'Will you do the honours again, Andy?'

'OK, sir,' replied the ever-willing sergeant with a smile, and went off to make some tea. Oldroyd sat again with Tanner in the pews. He was relieved to find that the man didn't smell of alcohol this time. Maybe he hadn't spent all the money on drink after all.

'So, what have you got to tell me?'

Tanner paused. He was going to make this sound dramatic, and then Oldroyd would be impressed.

'Well, this afternoon ah wor in a doorway with me cup and a nice woman stopped and put some brass in. Ah noticed she had long 'air, like, and ah suddenly remembered: that monk did. Ah mean, when they walked past, ah saw some 'air coming out o' t'side o' that 'ood thing.'

'I see.'

'So, ah think it wa' a woman, dressed up like a monk.' Tanner stopped after this climactic revelation. 'What do yer think o' that then?'

Oldroyd smiled. 'Thank you very much. That is useful. Is there anything else you remember?' He took a ten-pound note out of his wallet.

'Aye, well, thanks. Ah don't think there's owt else.'

'OK, stay and have your tea. I'm pleased to see you've not been drinking today.'

'No.' He looked proud of himself. 'Trevor at th'ostel's a good bloke, he's got me to cut down on t'booze.'

'Good. Well, follow his advice and things will look up for you.'

'Aye.'

Paying a man like this out of his own pocket for information was irregular, but Oldroyd felt that Tanner had the potential to improve his life, and he wanted to help.

Andy arrived with the tea and biscuits. The detectives left Tanner to eat and drink under the watchful and still-wary eye of the duty constable.

'What did he have to say, sir?' asked Andy as they returned to the vestry.

'Not a lot, but then again it's sometimes the little details which prove to be so important. He noticed that the monk figure had long hair, and so he thinks that means it must be a woman. Not that that's necessarily the case, of course – a wig could have been part of the disguise – but it's certainly making me think.'

Oldroyd sat down and drummed his fingers on the little table. It was a frustrating point in the case.

'We need to do more research into the backgrounds of these suspects, and see what it throws up. I don't think any of them are native to the town and they've moved here in the last five to ten years. We can get Steph on to it and see what she can uncover. And first thing in the morning, I need to go to the library.'

'Right, sir,' replied Andy, who, after a few years' experience, had learned it was easier not to question his boss's methods, even if they seemed unorthodox.

~

The news of the second murder added to the distress of the Wilcox family. Robin Eastby attended the service at St Edmund's, the other Anglican church in the town, and then went round to the St Anne's rectory to see how they were coping with yet more horror. Jenny opened the door when he knocked, and seemed relieved to see him.

'Thank you for calling, it's just dreadful. We're just sitting in here and don't know what to say to each other.' She led him into the living room, where her father and sister were sitting in silence. There was a pot of coffee on the table and she poured him a cup. Wilcox greeted him in a weak voice.

'Robin, nice of you to come. Have you been to St Edmund's?'

'Yes.'

'How was it?'

'It was very solemn; some very nice things were said about Clare and a lot of people send their best wishes to you.'

'That's good of them.'

'Of course, everything's been made worse by the dreadful news this morning.'

Wilcox shook his head and closed his eyes, as if this extra trauma was too much even to contemplate.

'What the hell's going on, Robin?' asked Fiona. 'Is Knaresborough going mad or what?'

'I don't know about Knaresborough as a whole, but someone seems to have gone over the edge. I can't believe there would be two murderers in the town at the same time.'

'Have you spoken to the police?' asked Jenny.

'No, not yet, but I'm sure they'll be round before too long, as Violet was another St Anne's parishioner with a role in the church.'

'I know it's an unkind thing to say, but that woman always gave me the creeps,' said Fiona. 'Whenever you went into the church, she seemed to be lurking around and watching everything. She used to come right up to you and go on about ghosts and spirits and stuff! I was frightened of her when we first came here.'

'I don't think your mum found her easy to deal with,' said Wilcox. 'But she wasn't the only person in that category in the church.'

'No, I'm sure you're right,' said Robin. 'There are difficult people in all communities and organisations.'

'But somehow you expect more from the church, don't you?' said Fiona. 'I know it's not fair and you're going to say we're all flawed and sinners and so on, but if the churches are preaching to us about how to behave, then people expect believers to show a good example, don't they?'

'Yes,' replied Robin. 'That's true. But it's also true that church-goers and the clergy are the same as everyone else. They don't have any special powers to avoid doing wrong. And there are people around, particularly in the media, who love it when a cleric is found stealing money or conducting an affair.'

Wilcox shifted uneasily. 'Well, they'll have plenty to go on if this killer turns out to be a member of the church. Horrible as it is – it has to be though, doesn't it? It must be someone we know.'

Robin looked very uncomfortable. 'Yes, and that's the most chilling thing of all.'

That evening, Oldroyd and Deborah were relaxing in his Harrogate flat, listening to some chamber music. Beethoven's String Quartet, Op. 59, No. 1 was playing, a vintage performance by the Quartetto Italiano. Oldroyd loved the warmth and spaciousness of this piece which took you on a journey, like many Beethoven compositions, through emotions from sadness and playfulness to euphoria. It was just the kind of music to distract you from the stresses in your life, which also diminished in comparison with the angst suffered by a musical genius going deaf.

Since the beginning of their relationship, Oldroyd had encouraged Deborah to listen to classical music with him, and she sat quietly until the final triumphant chords at the end of the final movement.

'Well, gosh, that was an odyssey,' she observed, sitting back in her armchair. 'How on earth did he manage to pack so much into one piece? And how did they manage to play it?! It sounded fiendishly difficult.'

'It takes years and years of practice. That quartet were together for the best part of thirty-five years and there was even a period when they used to play from memory without musical scores, which is just mind-boggling.' He stretched and yawned. 'Well, that was wonderful. Do you fancy a drink?'

'No. I'm OK, thanks.' She yawned too. 'Oh, this weather makes you tired, doesn't it? What time is it? I'm nearly ready for bed. I was going to play you some Ella but I'm not in the mood now.' Deborah was a jazz fan and loved Ella Fitzgerald. The quid pro quo of her listening to classical was Oldroyd sampling jazz.

'It's only ten o'clock, but it's a dark winter's night and I could play you a Beethoven piano trio called "Ghost". The slow movement is a spooky piece of music.'

'Not at this time of night; you know ghost stories make me nervous.'

'What, you, the great rational analyst of the human mind?' teased Oldroyd.

'We all have our primitive fears, Jim. I think mine go back to my grandparents, who lived in a rambling old house in one of those villages in the hills around Halifax.'

'It wasn't Northowram, was it?'

'No, it was somewhere near Norland. Why?'

'Northowram was the birthplace of John Christie, the famous serial killer. That would have increased the spookiness, wouldn't it?'

'Oh God! I didn't know that. That wasn't far away.'

'So, what was it about this house?'

'It was very old and there were lots of stories about it being haunted. My grandfather used to tell us about it when we were kids, and then we were too scared to go upstairs. It was supposed to be the ghost of a lady who leaned over people while they were in bed. The ghost shimmered blue, and had been seen on the stairs as well as in the bedrooms. Maybe she'd been a nurse or something. Things like that make a big impression when you're young and they tend to stay with you.'

'Yes, well, you wouldn't like it in St Anne's. It's very M. R. James in there. It was pretty scary when that monk figure was standing in the doorway that night when Andy Carter and I stayed in the vestry.'

'Yes, you said.' Deborah shuddered.

'Of course, we know it's a real person trying to distract us from what's really going on. And you don't believe in ghosts now, do you?' asked Oldroyd.

'No, but I'm not dogmatic about these things. There's clearly plenty about the universe that we don't know. Some people believe that terrible events can leave behind some kind of mark on the fabric of time and space, and that's what ghosts and hauntings are.'

'Yes, I've heard that theory.'

'So it's not surprising that churches and cathedrals often get the reputation for being haunted, given the awful things that have happened in the history of religion. Didn't you say that this monk was put to death because he was a heretic or something?'

'That's right.'

'It's incredible how religious beliefs can sometimes motivate people to do hideous things, isn't it?' There was no reply. 'Jim? Oh, you haven't gone off on one again, have you?' She yawned again. 'Well, I'm off to bed. Don't stay up thinking about it, or you'll never get to sleep; and don't play a violin like Sherlock Holmes did when he had a difficult case, or I'll never get to sleep.'

'OK,' replied Oldroyd, distractedly. He was thinking how what Deborah had just been saying was true, and that there was an aspect of the case to which he'd not given enough attention.

∼

Oldroyd and Deborah were not the only people listening to classical music on a dark Sunday night. Harvey Ferguson was sitting in his front room, which was cosy in the lamplight. He was drinking whisky and trying to relax as he listened to the complex structures of Bach's 'The Art of Fugue' played on the organ. He found it fascinating and otherworldly.

So, that busybody Violet Saunders was dead. He found it very difficult to feel anything about that, other than relief. He'd never trusted her; she was always sniffing around for tasty morsels of information and gossip, like a nasty little grey mouse that seemed to appear from nowhere in the church. He was sure that she'd been on to him as far as his sexuality went, and she would probably have used that information against him at some point. Well, not any more.

He sipped his whisky and tried to concentrate on the Bach, but it was difficult. There was so much going on at the moment. One thing he knew was that he was heartily sick of concealing the truth about himself from people for whom he had no real respect, but who had authority over him. When he got depressed about this, he made an effort to imagine what it must have been like for men like himself in previous generations, when homosexual acts were still against the law and it was impossible to come out in almost every job and profession. Things were clearly much better now, but in the socially conservative places he spent most of his time, it often didn't feel that way.

The phone rang. It was Olive Bryson. 'Hello, Harvey. How are you?'

'I'm fine, Olive. Thank you for being concerned.' He turned the organ music down.

'I was a bit worried about you yesterday. You seemed very anxious.'

'Aren't we all at the moment? And it looks like the killer has struck again.'

'Yes, she lived quite close to me and I heard all the noise early this morning and went up to see what was going on. It was awful.'

'I'll bet.'

'Did you go to St Edmund's this morning?'

'No. I've had enough of anything churchy at the moment.' Ferguson sipped his whisky again.

'I went, just to show solidarity with everyone.'

'Good for you.'

'It was a bit intense, you know? The subject no one can really mention. Everyone was very nice, but I have to admit it was a bit of a chilling thought that the killer could be in the congregation. I wonder if some of the St Edmund's people thought that too. That there was a murderer from St Anne's in their midst.'

'Maybe it was someone from their congregation – you never know,' observed Ferguson with grim humour.

'I almost wish it was, but that's a wicked thought.' Bryson laughed and then became serious again. 'Harvey, I really want you to be careful. This killer is still on the loose.'

'Why? Do you think I'm more in danger than anyone else?'

'I'm not saying that but . . . all those of us who are . . . alone, have to take extra care. Look at Violet.'

'You mean those of us who are different, who don't conform to the image of the nice, orthodox, respectable Anglican. That goes for you too.'

'Maybe you're right. I don't know why, but I sense there's still a threat to us out there.'

'I'm not so sure. I think Violet Saunders probably found out something about the killer and was silenced.'

'Harvey, you make it sound so brutal, like some gangland killing.'

'It is brutal; everyone's extra-shocked because this is taking place in a church community, where things like this are not meant to happen. Anyway, I've already told you: don't worry about me. I can take care of myself and I've got people on my side.'

Bryson sighed. 'OK, well, let's meet up at the café again soon.'

'Fine.' A time was arranged, and the call ended. Ferguson returned to his whisky and his organ music. Despite his show of confidence to Bryson, he remained in a difficult place and didn't know what was going to happen next.

$$\sim$$

'Second Murder Rocks Sleepy Market Town', 'Latest Victim in Church Murders Believed in the Ghost', 'Police Baffled by Second Murder in Knaresborough'.

These were some of the headlines Oldroyd noticed in the Monday morning papers as he stopped in at a newsagent on his way to Harrogate police HQ. It was a cold, overcast day. Dirty snow was piled on the verges as cars drove past on the gritted roads. He continued on his way with a grim expression on his face. The reporters had clearly been hard at work talking to any locals who were prepared to speak. Once the media had built up a level of hysteria, the police came under pressure to find the solution, which sometimes led to wrongful arrests and even convictions.

When he arrived at HQ, Oldroyd went straight up to see Tom Walker, who looked pleased to see him.

'Ah, morning, Jim! I'm glad to be back here, I can tell you.' Walker sat behind his desk with his glasses on, looking – despite what he'd just said – uncomfortable and out of place. He had never really adjusted to the bureaucratic desk work involved in his senior position. Oldroyd always felt that Walker envied him as a detective still working on cases.

'So, what the hell's going on in Knaresborough?' asked Walker. 'Two people connected to the church bumped off? It's the kind of thing the press love, isn't it? I see they're getting their teeth into it this morning. There's nothing they like better than to see the police struggling, as if they could do any better in solving these cases.' He snorted with contempt. Walker hated the press almost as much as he hated his boss, Matthew Watkins.

'Anyway, how are you getting on with it? You know who'll be jumping up and down if it drags on.'

Oldroyd knew the answer but said nothing.

'He wouldn't have an idea himself, of course. I'm not sure how much real police work he's ever done. If it didn't involve doing a PowerPoint presentation, he'd be clueless.' Oldroyd decided to step in before Walker's rant about Watkins developed into an unstoppable flow.

'It's a tough one, Tom.'

'Don't worry, you'll crack it given time – if we can keep the press and that idiot off your back. Don't worry about Watkins. If he starts getting jumpy, I know how to handle him, though I wish I could say the same for the press. So, what leads have you got?'

'We've ruled out the random killer, and we've had some help from a homeless man who frequented the churchyard. I'm sure the two murders are connected; I think it's likely that the second victim knew something so she was silenced.'

Walker shook his head. 'Good God, it sounds like the Sicilian mafia rather than an Anglican church in Knaresborough!'

'I know. Anyway, you'll be pleased to know we've also discounted the ghost of the monk as the perpetrator.'

'Thank goodness for that.' Walker laughed.

'Yes. I told Andy Carter that we couldn't arrest a phantom, and anyway, no prison would be able to hold one, would it?'

'No.' Walker laughed again. Oldroyd had succeeded in lightening the old boy's mood.

'We've also discovered how the first murder was done,' continued Oldroyd, and he explained the business of the secret staircase and the pendulum. 'So it looks like someone who knew about the church and its history. Unfortunately, that still leaves us with a lot of suspects.'

'I see. Well, it's a weird carry on, isn't it? So I won't keep you. Have you got all the help you need?'

'Andy Carter as usual, and DC Robinson. I'm going to get Stephanie Johnson involved in doing some research.'

'Good. You've got the best people. Off you go then, as long as you can reassure me that I won't be getting a visitation from that ghost.' He chuckled.

'Not from a ghost, Tom, but you might get contacted by a bishop or even an archbishop if we don't find the answer soon.'

Walker laughed again. 'OK, I think I can cope with that.'

Oldroyd went back down to the general office to talk to Steph. He found her at a workstation doing routine tasks. She was glad. When Oldroyd was active on a case, there was always the chance of more interesting work.

'Morning, sir,' she said with a smile. 'How's it going over in Knaresborough?'

'I'm sure Andy's kept you informed. I'm pleased to say that you now have the privilege of being involved.'

'It's an honour, sir. What do you want me to do?' Steph loved Oldroyd's wit and the banter that went on between them.

'Background checks, which could be really important. I'm going to send you a list of people who are suspects in this case, and I want you to see what you can find out about them. We're a bit stuck and I think the answer could well lie in the past. I know it's desk work, and you prefer to be out in the field, but you could uncover something vital. I want someone doing this who I know will do a thorough job.'

'That's fine, sir; you can rely on me.'

∼

Jeremy Wilcox woke late from uneasy dreams back into his nightmare. What had happened came crashing back into his consciousness as he opened his eyes in the dark room. He shut them again and lay still, wanting neither to return to sleep nor to get out of bed. He felt the strangeness of being alone in this large bed. Clare had usually been up first, and he would hear her downstairs and the sound of the news on Radio 4. Those routines had gone forever.

After a few minutes, he heard footsteps on the stairs and Jenny knocked on the door, opened it and peeped inside.

'Dad? Are you awake? I've got a cup of tea for you.'

'Thanks! Come in!'

Jenny came quietly into the room and put the cup on his bed-side table. Wilcox sat up in bed and switched his lamp on.

'Is it light yet? What time is it?' he asked, yawning.

'It's half past eight, but the clouds are so heavy it still seems like the middle of the night. All the cars have their lights on,' said Jenny, who sat on the edge of the bed.

'I suppose it's only to be expected at this time of year,' Wilcox replied as he sipped his tea.

'Sylvia Addison rang from the surgery. I told her you were still asleep. She asked how you were. She doesn't expect you'll be going back to work at all this week, and she told me to tell you that everything is covered. She would like to speak to you at the end of the week if that's OK?'

'Good, that's very kind of her.' Wilcox was genuinely grateful, but he was also pretty sure that it was Addison who had informed the police about his affair with Julie. He'd suspected that she knew, but he'd always got on well with her so it seemed like a bit of a betrayal. But then, when he tried to put himself in her position, he understood that Clare's death would have made it difficult for her. A man who was conducting an affair was a clear suspect if his wife was murdered. She must have felt it her duty to inform the police. How could he really blame her?

'Dad, are you listening?'

Wilcox came back abruptly to the present. 'I'm sorry, I was miles away; it's happening all the time at the moment.'

'Never mind. I was just reminding you that we agreed to go to register Mum's death today. Are you still OK to do it?'

Wilcox frowned. 'Yes, it has to be done. We can't put it off any longer.'

'And then tomorrow morning, the funeral director is coming. It won't be an easy couple of days, but you'll feel better when it's all done.'

'You're right. Just give me a few minutes and I'll be down. I'll have some toast and some more tea, if that's OK?'

Fiona smiled; it was good to see her father a little more animated. 'Of course, Dad, I'll pop a couple of slices into the toaster for you.'

When she'd left, Wilcox sat in bed a little longer, sipping his tea. His daughters were being so supportive and helpful and he'd come to a decision about one thing. He wasn't going to say anything about his affair until at least after the funeral. How could he add that pain to his daughters' grief at losing their mother? Maybe he was being a coward, but he just couldn't do it. There was still the risk that Fiona and Jenny could find out from someone else or that it could come out in the investigation, but he would have to take that risk. The chief inspector seemed a decent man and Wilcox trusted him not to reveal anything unless it was absolutely necessary. He felt relieved that he could defer telling his daughters for the moment.

'Dad! Toast is ready!' came the call from Jenny.

'Coming!' he replied, and began to quickly get dressed.

∼

Knaresborough's public library was housed in a modern building in the Market Place. Oldroyd walked across from St Anne's, wearing some stout walking shoes and wrapped up in his overcoat. He was glad to get inside to the warmth of the library. He made for the reference section, where a helpful assistant confirmed that they had a local history section.

Oldroyd introduced himself and showed his warrant card. 'I'm in charge of the investigation into the murders connected with St Anne's.'

'Oh yes, terrible business; how can I help?' she asked in a brisk manner, as though detectives came in regularly to do research relating to murder enquiries.

'There are some curious aspects of this case connected to that church, and I'm looking for a history of St Anne's; there's a particular event that I'm interested in, which is the unusual death of someone in the church in the nineteenth century. It would probably have caused a bit of a stir at the time.'

'Oh, you mean the last murder by the ghost of the monk,' replied the assistant with a smile.

'Maybe I do,' said Oldroyd, looking pleased. 'Can you tell me about it?'

'Yes, and I'll find you a book which gives a clear account. You'll have to read it in here, I'm afraid. It's non-lending. All the books in Reference are and I don't think we have a copy in the lending section.'

'Fine. Well, if you have a moment, could you tell me the outline and then I'll read the book?'

The assistant looked around the room and saw that, so far, it was empty on this cold Monday morning. She sat with Oldroyd in a corner and spoke in a quiet voice.

'I think the year was 1851. The victim was a churchwarden, a Mr Samuel Walshaw if I remember rightly. I have a good memory for this sort of thing because I've lived in Knaresborough all my life and I'm fascinated by local history. Anyway, he was found dead in the church with terrible wounds, apparently, which no one could explain.'

'I see.'

'I think in the middle part of the nineteenth century, superstitious ideas and belief in ghosts and evil spirits was still quite strong. The prevailing view seemed to be that Walshaw was killed by the ghost. Have you heard that story?'

'Yes, the monk put to death for heresy in the Middle Ages. Austin Eliot told me about it.'

'Mr Eliot? Who runs the bookshop?'

'Yes, that's the man. He was very helpful when I paid him a visit.'

'I see. He stocks a number of local history books but he's not a native of the town, and his knowledge is not as deep and reliable as other people I could mention.'

'Do you have any particular people in mind?'

'There's a local history society; quite a few people from the church are members. Patrick Owen, the archdeacon, is a very knowledgeable man. He's made it his business to find out about the history of all the churches in his archdeaconry. He's been in here a lot over the years.'

'I see,' said Oldroyd, listening intently.

'To get back to the ghost story . . . as you will know, he was put to death by being thrown from the top of the gorge, and after that the story is that people started to die with similar injuries to his own. You can read about all this in the book I'll get for you. So the point is that Walshaw had the head and neck injuries which the monk must have sustained, so people believed that it was another case of ghostly revenge. People started to come forward and say that they'd heard noises like banging and scraping in the church at night and seen ghostly lights. The whole thing grew, and there was something approaching hysteria, with people refusing to attend church.

'Interestingly, the more enlightened clergy of the time resisted the idea of a haunting. The bishop refused requests for an exorcism of the church, and said the whole thing was nonsense. But as

186

nobody was able to find out who killed Walshaw, the idea of the vengeful ghost was impossible to lay to rest.'

And people like Violet Saunders are still asking for an exorcism in the twenty-first century, thought Oldroyd. 'Do we know where in the church the body of Walshaw was found?' he asked.

'Not exactly, but it was somewhere near to the west tower. He's buried in the churchyard.'

'Right.' Oldroyd nodded. This was all very interesting.

'There's a curious epilogue to the story. The vicar of the church at that time, I think his name was Rev Marshall, moved on to a different parish, and some years later was expelled and defrocked for stealing a valuable church plate and replacing it with a fake. It made some people wonder whether he'd been up to anything like that at St Anne's, especially as a silver communion cup had gone missing about the same time as Walshaw was murdered. Maybe the churchwarden had discovered what was going on and the vicar had silenced him.'

'Well, that's tantalising, but unfortunately we'll probably never know.'

'Perhaps not. Anyway, I'll leave you with the book.'

Oldroyd looked at the title: *A History of Knaresborough Churches*. 'There was just one more thing. Can you remember if this book covers alterations to the building at St Anne's? I'm thinking particularly about the construction of the east tower and the removal of the clock and the bells from the west tower.'

'Yes, I believe it does. That was the time when the wooden ceiling in the west tower was constructed. I'm not sure you'll find out any more than you already seem to know.'

'Maybe not, but thank you again. You've been extremely helpful.'

Back at St Anne's, Andy had spent the morning organising further statement-taking and alibi-checking, as well as sending information on the suspects to Steph for further investigation. The forensic team were at work on the west tower.

He thought ruefully about his boss spending some quiet time reading books in the library, but that was one of the perks of power. Maybe someday he would be in that position himself, but he didn't feel he would ever match the brilliance of his boss. If Oldroyd went to look at a book in a library, then it was for a good reason. He would probably return with some amazing insight into the case.

Oldroyd arrived back in a cheery mood. Maybe Andy was right after all? 'That was very useful, Andy; put the kettle on, will you? A helpful librarian directed me to the book I needed, which was a detailed history of this church.'

'Really, sir?' said Andy, with a tiny edge of sarcasm in his voice. 'Anyway, the kettle's just boiled.'

Oldroyd, in his enthusiasm for what he'd discovered, failed to pick up on that edge, however, and kept going: 'Yes. I have a theory about that tower, the wooden ceiling and the pendulum. You remember how some of the metal fittings, like the pulley, seemed as if they'd been there a long time?'

'Yes, sir.' He handed Oldroyd a mug of tea.

'Thanks.' Oldroyd took a drink and continued. 'Well, I don't think much of the construction of that devilish device was done by our murderer. It was previously constructed by a nineteenth-century vicar called Marshall. And for the same reason: he wanted to stage a murder that looked as if it was the work of the ghostly monk. A churchwarden called Walshaw was found dead in the same spot, and with the same injuries as Rev Wilcox. Rev Marshall was a thief and the churchwarden had probably found him out. It seems his scheme worked, as no one was ever arrested for the murder.'

'That would explain why that big old cupboard was stuck in front of the door to the staircase, sir. If that had only been put there recently, people would have known that there was a staircase behind it, wouldn't they? And someone would have gone up there to investigate after Rev Wilcox was killed.'

'Exactly. I suspect that cupboard has been there a long time, even before the Rev Marshall came here. When the west tower was decommissioned, that staircase had no further use and someone decided that it was OK to block it off. That was some time before Marshall came. He must have done his research, like I've done and our murderer did, and discovered the staircase. It's mentioned in early descriptions of the church, when it still led up to the bells and the clock.

'There are some contemporary accounts of people hearing noises in the church at night which they thought was ghostly activity. I think it was the sound of the vicar, Rev Marshall, constructing that removable back in the cupboard and then later installing the pulley and working on that wooden ceiling. I wouldn't be surprised if he'd been a joiner before he was ordained. Forensics will tell us more about it. Are they working in there?'

'Yes, sir.'

'Good. Marshall's big advantage over our murderer was that superstitious beliefs were much stronger in those days, and many in the congregation must have believed the ghost to be a rational explanation for the death. Anyway, our murderer discovered the clever work that Marshall did and decided to use it in the same way. With a few repairs and a bit of greasing, it was all ready for use.'

'It would all make sense, sir. We'll see what Forensics say.'

'Yes. Did you get that stuff over to Steph?'

'I did, sir.'

'Excellent. Well, let's see if her research also turns up something significant.' Oldroyd finished his tea and looked at the mug. 'Do you know? Drinking that has only made me thirst for something a bit stronger. Let's go down to the pub and have a spot of lunch there.'

Andy was only too willing to agree.

As they walked yet again through the cold churchyard, Oldroyd had a spring in his step. At last he had a sense that they were getting somewhere.

Six

'Whilst the girl stood still, half smiling, with her hands clasped over her heart, the boy, a thin shape, with black hair and ragged clothing, raised his arms in the air with an appearance of menace . . . The moon shone upon his almost transparent hands . . . the nails were fearfully long . . . As he stood with his arms thus raised, he disclosed a terrifying spectacle. On the left side of his chest there opened a black and gaping rent.'

From 'Lost Hearts', M. R. James, 1895

These were especially testing times for Donald Avison and Maisie Baxter. They shared the responsibility with Robin Eastby, the curate, for keeping the church functioning in a situation of unprecedented horror and disruption. The church had now lost its rector and a long-standing active member of the congregation to a vicious killer. The whole of the congregation and indeed the town were in shock.

The three were at the curate's house. Eastby had served coffee in a very subdued and sombre atmosphere, and now began the meeting.

'Thanks for coming. I just wanted to reassure you both that Patrick and I are engaged in planning how St Anne's is going to cope in the next few months. Clergy from other churches, and some living in the diocese who are retired, are rallying round. We shall be able to provide our normal pattern of church services when the police allow it. On the administrative side, I'm sure you and I can work together with help from Patrick or even from Bishop Michael if necessary. I thought it would be a good idea if we looked at what tasks there are – ones which Clare used to take responsibility for – and if there are any pressing issues facing us at the moment. We can try to divide these between us. I'll make a written record of what we decide. I know it's difficult, but the church is looking to us for leadership and I think you'll agree that we have to respond.' Eastby was actually enjoying his opportunity to step up.

The churchwardens nodded, and there followed a discussion of various practical matters which needed attention. At the end of this, after they had all taken a rest, Avison glanced at Baxter a little nervously and then looked across at Eastby.

'This might not be the right time to bring this subject up, Robin, but Maisie and I want to make our views clear about Clare's successor.'

Eastby raised his eyebrows. He did indeed think it was hardly appropriate to discuss this even before Clare's funeral. It seemed to be taking future planning a little too far at this stage. 'Go on,' he said.

Avison took a deep breath. 'Well, I've said this many times, as have all of us in the church who share this view: Clare was wonderful in her pastoral role and she was an astute administrator, but some of us cannot accept a woman as a full priest and celebrant. There's no point going over the arguments again, but we would hope that Clare's successor is a man. A male priest will be acceptable to everyone.'

'He may be less acceptable to progressive reformers, who might want another female rector.' Eastby frowned and narrowed his eyes.

'Yes, Robin,' said Baxter, 'but they've had their turn so to speak, so why not have a person around whom we can all unite? Anyway, we realise that this would have to be approved by the PCC and we intend to raise it at the next meeting.'

'Hmm, well, I don't think it's appropriate to discuss this any more now, but it's clear that the issue is still very controversial. You've stated your views, but I don't think they necessarily represent the majority feeling in the church.' His tone was rather curt and the two churchwardens did not respond.

The meeting ended shortly after, with the atmosphere rather soured. Eastby was shocked that the succession question had been raised, and that some people thought of it as groups having 'turns' to have the gender of priest they preferred. It made him realise how strongly wedded many people in the church were to conservative ideas about the priesthood and Christian doctrine, and how deeply divided the church was on the issue. This was something he was going to encounter in other churches during his career. It was a sobering thought.

~

It was torture to Oldroyd, limiting himself to one pint in the old pub in the Market Place; the beer was so good. But as it was against the rules to drink at all while on duty, he made the best of it, as he and Andy ate their ham and cheese sandwiches and reviewed some aspects of the case. They were sitting in a bar with low beams and there was a roaring fire in the grate. It was a cosy winter scene, and it was going to be difficult to wrench themselves away when they'd finished their lunch.

'Another thing that librarian told me,' said Oldroyd between mouthfuls, 'is that Patrick Owen, the archdeacon, is an expert on church history and has done a lot of research in the library.

Archdeacons have a responsibility for supervising the upkeep of buildings in their archdeaconry, so that may be the reason for his interest – or maybe it was something else more sinister. It's going to be worth speaking to him again.'

'What could his motive be for committing those two murders, sir?'

Oldroyd shrugged as he took a long and satisfying drink of beer. 'We don't know. Nothing's turned up against him as yet, but once Steph gets to work she may discover something.'

'I'm sure she's hard at it as we speak, sir.'

'Have you heard from the team working on the tower?'

'They're saying they will have some preliminary findings for us tomorrow.'

'Good. We're a bit stuck until we get more information. If you go back and carry on supervising things at the church, I'm going to call in on the archdeacon. He lives in Harrogate. I'll check in on Steph and see how she's doing, and I'll also pay my sister a visit.'

'She must be finding it tough, sir, that vicar who was killed worked with her, didn't she? When she was younger?'

'She did, and my sister was proud of her. Rev Wilcox was destined for high office in the Church until she was struck down.'

'So it would be like you losing me or Steph.'

Oldroyd looked at Andy, thinking for a moment that the detective sergeant was indulging in a joke that was not really appropriate – but he wasn't, he was serious.

'Yes, I suppose you're right. But don't go thinking you can go off to another force for promotion yet. I'm not ready to let you go.'

Andy laughed. 'Don't worry, sir, we're both very happy to be where we are at the moment.'

⌇

Back at Harrogate HQ, Steph was getting started on the research tasks that Oldroyd had given her. Like Andy and Oldroyd, she preferred working in the field to desk tasks, but she knew that she needed to be effective at both if she was going to make a good detective.

There were significant gaps in the information she'd been given. She had the names – Olive Bryson, Harvey Ferguson, Donald Avison, Austin Eliot, Maisie Baxter – but the photographs of some were unclear and the biographical details were sparse. Oldroyd had also included the archdeacon and the bishop. Rev Wilcox and Violet Saunders also needed to be checked for anything relevant in their pasts. There was a lot to do, and she had recruited the help of DC Sharon Warner who was a young protégée of hers. They sat at adjoining desks in the work area.

'OK, Sharon,' Steph said. 'We have to do background searches on all these people who are related to the case over in Knaresborough, some of whom are serious suspects.'

Warner was already scanning the material and looking eager to get started. Steph smiled; the young woman reminded her of herself at the same age: eager to learn and to please.

'Right, Sarge. Where do you think I should start?'

'Read the stuff we have about them and then start a search of the national database to see if any of them have a criminal record; crimes which were probably committed before they came to Knaresborough. I'm going to start with church records and then we'll look at academic records and businesses, bankruptcies, things like that. We're looking for any connections between them and anything which might have given any of them a motive for killing Rev Wilcox. DCI Oldroyd believes the second woman, Violet Saunders, was murdered because she knew things about the killer, so we need to see if she had any connections with any of these suspects as well.'

Off they went, rattling away at their keyboards and scrutinising their screens. After a couple of hours of intense work, they broke for coffee and a brief chat.

'Nothing's come up for me yet, Sarge,' said Warner. 'I haven't found any criminal records for any of them.'

'Not to worry. Keep trying. It's a slow process. The only thing I've found is that Olive Bryson has filed for bankruptcy twice in the past, both retail businesses. It appears that she had a history of money problems before she came to Knaresborough. Then it happened again, and she got herself into trouble with the church.'

'I don't suppose that's adding much to what DCI Oldroyd and Sergeant Carter already know.'

'No.' Steph yawned, stretched and looked at the young DC. 'Anyway, how are you these days? How are you finding life here?'

Warner smiled. 'Oh, fine, Sarge. Everything's been great after what happened, you know.'

Steph nodded. Warner had been involved in the case of sexual harassment at the Harrogate office which the female officers had fought. It had caused the young officer a great deal of stress.

'I'm glad you find it comfortable to work here now. I think the atmosphere's a lot better. And remember, if you're ever in difficulties again, you can come and tell me straight away.'

'I know, Sarge.'

'You've been working with Inspector Nicholson quite a lot, haven't you?'

'Yes, and he's really nice.' She smiled at Steph and her blue eyes twinkled.

'Hey!' Steph laughed. 'You behave yourself; he's married with a young family.'

Sharon laughed too. 'Don't worry, Sarge, I've got a boyfriend. He's at uni at the moment, but only in Leeds so I see him regularly.'

'Good for you; I'm glad things are going well for you. Well, we'd better get back to it.' She sighed as she turned to her computer.

As they got back to work, Steph reflected on how much improved the office here at HQ had become since she first joined the force over ten years ago. She'd had to endure so much unwanted attention from male officers and had found it quite intimidating. Working for Oldroyd had protected her; he'd always created a safe environment for women. That things had improved generally was something in which she took personal pride: she'd led a group of women officers in a fight against that kind of behaviour, and people now felt able to speak out if they were being harassed, even if it was by someone of a higher rank. She'd taken on the unofficial role of policing the police, which could be seen as impertinent. But it was necessary, and it was sad to reflect on the fact that they were now working on a case concerning the murder of a woman who seemed to have been at the forefront of moves to promote women in her own field.

After a while, Steph discovered a link between one of their suspects and Rev Wilcox. It seemed that Maisie Baxter had previously lived in Leeds, in an area where Rev Wilcox had done her first curacy at the local Anglican church. The timelines overlapped. Had they known each other then? Did something happen during that period? She noted that down.

Sharon announced she'd found something. Harvey Ferguson had been arrested some time ago in connection with a fight outside a bar in Bradford, but was let off with a caution. Steph went over to look.

'He's the organist and choirmaster. It shows he's got an aggressive side. Well done,' said Steph, and Sharon beamed. 'It might not prove significant, but at least we're finding things, and you never know what's going to turn out to be important.'

Patrick Owen was surprised to receive a visit from Oldroyd in the middle of the afternoon, but he almost welcomed it as it gave him an excuse to have a break from reading one of the many reports produced by the diocese. This one on preserving stained-glass windows was especially heavy going.

'Come in, Chief Inspector,' he said breezily. 'And take a seat.' He led Oldroyd into a sitting room decorated in a rather ornate style and full of antique furniture. Oldroyd admired a tall grandfather clock with a dark, polished oak case.

'Ah yes, nice piece, isn't it? It was made in Halifax in 1781. It's not entirely original. The clock mechanism and the face are, but the case has been modified, probably in the nineteenth century.'

'It sounds like a particular interest of yours.'

'Yes.' Owen waved his hand. 'Antiques in general, as you can see, but clocks in particular.'

'I also hear that you're a bit of an expert on church history, at least in this area.'

'Who told you that?'

'The librarian down at the public library.'

'Sheila, I imagine. She's always helpful and very knowledgeable herself.' He looked rather quizzically at Oldroyd. 'I'm sure you haven't come to talk to me about church history, Chief Inspector. What can I do for you?'

Oldroyd smiled. 'Actually, you're wrong about why I'm here. What do you know about the alterations to the west tower at St Anne's, after the east tower had been built?'

Owen looked taken aback. 'Good heavens! Well, the clock and the bells were removed to the new east tower, and a wooden ceiling was constructed to seal off the cavity in the older west tower.'

'Do you know anything about a concealed staircase?'

'No, nothing. Please enlighten me.'

Oldroyd searched the archdeacon's face for any sign of alarm, but his expression conveyed only surprise and interest. 'There are two tall wooden cupboards fixed to the wall at the bottom of the west tower. One of them, which has been locked up since before anyone can remember, has a false back. Behind that is an ancient door which leads to a steep, narrow stone staircase, up to a platform where the old clock mechanism was attached to a long pendulum.' He paused and continued to fix Owen with his penetrating grey eyes. 'So you were not aware of any of this?'

'No, Chief Inspector, but it sounds fascinating. It's part of my role to conduct surveys, with incumbent clergy, of church buildings. I remember those cupboards at St Anne's, but I never took a great deal of notice of them. Aren't they used to store hymn books?'

'One is.'

'And the other has a false back, covering a door and a staircase?'

Oldroyd nodded.

'I'm staggered,' Owen said. 'Of course, I knew there must have been a staircase at one time, to allow access to the clock and the bells. But I suppose everyone just assumed that it had been blocked up at the time of the changes. That clock, by the way, was installed in the 1780s by a local man called Oughtershaw. It had a long pendulum and, because the tower is short and squat, reached down the length of the tower wall and had a wooden casing around it. It proved to be a cumbersome mechanism which needed constant rewinding, so when they built the east tower in 1850 they replaced the clock with a more modern one, and that is still working today after many refurbishments.'

'Not only is that staircase still there, but so is the pendulum.'

'What?'

'You didn't know that either?' said Oldroyd, still looking hard at the archdeacon, trying to gauge his response.

'No, I didn't. How can it be? Wasn't it removed at the time?'

'It appears not. They left it still attached to the shaft which linked it to the clock. I suspect it was tied up against the wall in a position at the top of its swing while they thought about what to do with it. It was a big job to move it. When that ceiling was put in, the pendulum seems to have been forgotten. That's the thing about churches, isn't it? The people in charge don't stay; they move on to other parishes and dioceses.'

'Well, I'm amazed, Chief Inspector, but I'm still not sure why you're telling me all this.'

'That pendulum was the weapon which killed Rev Wilcox. The murderer discovered the staircase, the pendulum, and a hinged section of the ceiling which folds back to allow the released pendulum to swing down by the side of the wall, but sufficiently far out to miss the cupboards, to near ground level. It smashed into Rev Wilcox, causing her injuries.'

The archdeacon's mouth dropped open.

Oldroyd continued: 'I say they "discovered" things, because I believe all the modifications like the false back of the cupboard and the hinged section of the ceiling were put there by a nineteenth-century rogue vicar called Marshall, in order to stage the murder of a churchwarden called Walshaw. I assume you know about that?'

'Well, I know about the murder. The killer was never found. A lot of the parishioners thought it was due to the ghost of the monk, because the injuries were the same as those the dead man had endured. And the legend did have him promising revenge.'

'Which is exactly what the killer wants us to think now, only regarding the death of Rev Wilcox. We've got a forensic team at work in that tower at the moment and I think they will confirm my theory. As you say, Sheila is very helpful. She directed me to a source for the Walshaw case.'

Owen was gripping the arms of his chair and looking stunned. Oldroyd leaned back in his chair with his head to one side, still coolly observing the archdeacon.

'But this is terrible,' said Owen. 'You're saying that someone who had a knowledge of the building used this method to commit another murder?' His eyes widened as he belatedly realised what Oldroyd was implying. 'You surely can't think it was me, Chief Inspector? That's a ridiculous idea; why would I kill Clare? I had tremendous admiration for her.'

'You tell me – if it was you,' replied Oldroyd, with brutal directness.

'Of course it wasn't me.'

'Where were you on the evening that Rev Wilcox was killed?'

For the first time, Owen seemed flustered. 'I . . . It was Wednesday, wasn't it? I was working at home that day.'

'Can anyone verify that?'

'No. Well, I don't think so. My wife's a teacher and she doesn't normally get back until after five. There's a staff meeting after school on Wednesdays, so it would have been after six when she got home. Does this mean I'm a suspect?'

'You and a number of others. How was your relationship with Rev Wilcox?'

'As I said, it was very good. The church very largely allows priests to run their churches as they wish; the senior people running the diocese don't interfere. We don't have a lot of regular contact with the clergy on a day-to-day basis, but when it came to things like the building survey, which I do with the clergy in each church, or getting involved in diocesan-wide initiatives, she was excellent to work with.'

'I take it you're in favour of women priests and bishops?'

'Very much so. I see no theological objection. Women's minis-try is badly needed, and is to be celebrated.'

'Were you aware that there is opposition within the congregation at St Anne's?'

'There is some opposition in every church, Chief Inspector, though I think it's true to say that in this diocese they are in a very small minority. No congregation around here as a whole rejects the notion of a female priest or bishop, though individuals may refuse to take communion from a female priest.'

'You were not aware of any particular problems at St Anne's?'

'No. I think Rev Wilcox enjoyed a good relationship with the people there.'

'And how do you feel about gay people in the Church?'

Oldroyd saw Owen flinch at this question, but he quickly regained his composure.

'I have no problem with that either.'

Oldroyd nodded and then stood up. 'Right, well, thank you for your cooperation. We'll contact you if we need to interview you again.' He was shown out by a rather shaken Patrick Owen, who then returned to the sitting room and picked up his phone. There was someone he needed to call.

~

While his colleague in the upper echelons of power in the diocese was undergoing an uncomfortable interview with Oldroyd, Bishop Michael Palmer was at home in the rather palatial bishop's residence in Ripon, dealing with the fallout from a double murder connected to a church in his diocese. The fact was that this was uncharted territory, and none of his friends and colleagues could offer him much advice. The general feeling seemed to be that it was best to ride it out and let the whole thing blow over as far as publicity was concerned. As regards the suffering individual church, it was vital to provide as much support as possible.

He'd spoken to the Archbishop of York, who was very supportive and raised the question of what the implications were for church membership if the killer proved to be a member of the congregation. Could it have been possible to prevent what had happened? Were churches alert to strange behaviours and mental-health issues amongst their congregations? And were they trying to provide support? These were all valid but tricky questions. It was his and the archbishop's responsibility to plan ahead and try to anticipate what the next problem might be. He had been pleased to hear the archbishop say that he still hoped that the new Bishop of Kendal would be a woman.

Palmer sat at his large oak desk, surrounded by solid wooden bookshelves that reached up to the high ceiling. He looked out on to the extensive lawn and reflected on the many possible repercussions of what had occurred. He was not the kind of church leader whose first thought was to protect the church's reputation. He was concerned about the pastoral consequences of the situation, and he foresaw that these might be deep.

On his desk was a simple Celtic cross. He found himself praying that God would guide him in leading the diocese on a way through.

～

Harvey Ferguson arrived home from York in the late afternoon to find a curious blank envelope behind his door. Inside was a sheet of A4 paper with a word-processed message:

> *I know things about you. You are a repulsive pervert I can destroy you if I want. Meet me at 7 tonight at Sir Robert's Cave if you know what's good for you. Maybe we can come to some arrangement, otherwise you've had it.*

Ferguson's lip curled in disgust. He'd received abuse before, but usually it was called out in the street. This was a person who knew where he lived. But then a lot of people did; he'd never kept his address a secret. Who could this be? Someone from the school? From church? Or just from the town?

He sat down, angry and shaking. He knew he should report this to the police, but he was so sick of this kind of thing that he felt like sorting it out himself. The police were always slow to respond. It would be very dark and quiet at the cave, which was by Grimbald Bridge over the river on the edge of town. It could be dangerous. So what? He would be there and he would arm himself. He'd defended himself before against homophobic thugs. He was tougher than his appearance suggested. If there was any aggression, he would give as good as he got.

❧

'The January afternoons are starting to feel longer,' remarked Oldroyd. He and Alison were walking across the snowy fields on a hill near Kirkby Underside. It was cold, and sheep were clustered around bales of hay dumped in the fields by the farmers. Yellow strands of the feed were lying on the snow, which was dirty and trampled by the feet of the hardy animals who could survive in these wintry conditions even through the night in the freezing out-doors. 'It's still cold though.' He clapped his hands together and watched the vapour of his breath rise into the still air.

'Well, there's an old saying: "As the light lengthens, the cold strengthens." We're in the coldest part of winter now, but it's nice that it's nearly four o'clock and there's still plenty of light,' observed Alison.

'It's also nice to get out into the countryside, see all this and breathe in the fresh air.' Oldroyd gestured at the characteristically sweeping Yorkshire landscape before them. They were looking west across the broad valley of Lower Wharfedale, towards the distant hills of Otley Chevin and Burley Moor. In the distance, the setting winter sun was creating vivid effects in the sky, in blues, greys and orange. 'What a gorgeous sunset it's going to be!' he exclaimed.

'Yes, the beauty of nature is always there to console us,' said Alison.

So far, neither of them had mentioned the case. They had just been relaxing in the outdoors and in one another's company.

Alison finally broke the silence. 'How are you getting on with it?'

Oldroyd didn't need to ask her what she meant. 'I think we're making good progress. We've worked out how Clare was killed.' He explained about the pendulum and its history and about the monk.

Alison shook her head. 'It's like a cross between an M. R. James story and Edgar Allan Poe; you know, "The Pit and the Pendulum". And everyone thought St Anne's was a sedate church in a quiet market town.'

'I know. I think we're closing in on the killer; we're waiting for some conclusive piece of evidence to turn up. It's going to be very edgy and tense until then.'

'Do you think they will strike again?'

'I still think the only planned victim was Clare, but we don't yet know why. The suspects all have different possible motives. I believe the other woman was killed because she knew things about the killer. I'm not expecting another attack, but I can't be sure. At least nothing bad has emerged about Clare, which I had warned you might happen.' Oldroyd decided this was not the time to tell his sister about Jeremy's affair.

'Good, I'm pleased about that. It's bad enough losing her, without unpleasant things being revealed.'

They reached the edge of a field and climbed over a stile in the wall, taking care on the slippery surfaces. Nearby was a stone water trough iced over and surrounded by the frozen muddy imprints of animals' hooves. The line of the path ahead was only visible as footprints left by previous walkers. Their boots scrunched on the icy surface as they made careful progress across the next field.

'How are you feeling?' asked Oldroyd.

Alison sighed. 'I'm still in shock, Jim; that this could happen in a church, and someone like Clare could be so abruptly taken away from us is . . . well . . . it's hard to take in, and then another church member killed. It feels like my whole world is turning upside down.'

'You were very close to Clare, weren't you?'

Alison nodded. She was struggling to talk about it. 'Yes. You could say she was my protégée. But I felt something deeper than that. She was like a family member; maybe the younger sister I never had. Those years when she was the curate at St Bartholomew's were some of the happiest I've had since David died.'

'She also represented something important to you, didn't she?'

Alison stopped and looked over the landscape again with a faraway look in her eye. 'Yes. I suppose I wanted her to achieve what I could never do because I was born in a different age. I was already middle-aged by the time I was ordained, and there was no possibility that I could ever become a bishop.'

'Did you want to be?'

'I'm not sure. Aspects of the Church drive me mad, as you know, but as a force for progress and an advocate of women's ministry, I think I could have achieved a lot. I wanted Clare to be able to do that instead.'

She paused, and Oldroyd saw that tears were welling up in her eyes. He put his arm around her shoulders. 'It's hard, I know. You've lost a close personal friend and someone who was shaping up to be a great champion of a cause that is very important to you. But someone else will take on that role; the tide of history is moving in your favour.'

Alison nodded. 'I know, but the opposition is well organised and can be very nasty.'

Oldroyd looked at her. 'Do you still think hatred of women in positions of authority in the Church played a part in Clare's death?'

'My instinct says yes, but you say you haven't found any evidence of it?'

'Not really, the people we've interviewed who are opposed to women priests have been very upfront about it and they don't appear aggressive. It's a small minority.'

'It always is, but they can be very fanatical.'

'No one has actually been physically attacked over this issue, have they?'

'No, but the abuse has been vicious, especially online. And there have been death threats.'

'We didn't find anything on Clare's computer to suggest that she was being harassed.'

They were returning to the village, and the path came out into a lane. They passed a pub and the warm glow from the windows looked very inviting. The streets of cottages and occasional larger houses with their snow-covered gardens looked very pretty in their winter quietness.

'That doesn't necessarily mean that she wasn't. She could have deleted it all.'

Alison stopped by one of the big houses. The formal rose gardens were covered in white, and the bare branches of wisteria curled around the front of the house.

'The problem I have, Jim, is that I still can't imagine what kind of motive someone could have to murder Clare. Surely it couldn't be money, jealousy or blackmail? You haven't found anything else really compelling, and now someone else has been killed I still think that there is something really depraved and diabolical going on.'

Oldroyd looked at her. 'Alison, you may well be right, and I'm not discounting it. It's just that, as yet, we haven't seen any compelling evidence to back it up as a theory.'

They walked on in silence, lost in their own thoughts, until they reached the rectory.

~

Olive Bryson was sitting in her dimly lit living room looking out of the west-facing window. She had a good view of the gorge, and would often sit and watch the sun set. Today the sun had left it very late in the day to appear, but had sunk in a splendour of colour behind the trees lining the gorge. That was two hours ago, but she was still sitting at the table and had not drawn the curtains. She liked to see the moonlight and any activity that took place in the street.

I'm going to become an old curtain-twitching gossiper if I'm not careful, she thought.

She was going through her accounts book by the light of a small lamp, trying to bring some order to her financial affairs, when a movement caught her eye. Someone was walking past in the street outside. This was quite rare on a winter evening in a quiet street like this. She stood up and went closer to the window in time to see Harvey Ferguson, dressed in an overcoat and wearing heavy boots, walking in a very determined manner. He was looking straight ahead with a grim expression on his face. Where was he going on a dark night like this? Harvey was not known as a keen walker. Was he in trouble? She'd been worried about him ever since these terrible events began; he'd seemed very disturbed and ill at ease.

She made a quick decision to follow him. It couldn't do any harm if she just watched from a distance without him knowing she was there. She put on an old fur coat, slipped on her boots and left the house with a torch and her phone. Walking quickly for a few minutes down the road, she soon saw him again in the distance and slowed her pace.

∽

Ferguson had left his house with a sharp kitchen knife in his pocket. He was prepared to use it if he was threatened. If they saw he was prepared to defend himself, they might lay off.

It was a long walk from his house down to the river and along the narrow Abbey Road, past fields and cottages to the cave that had been the dwelling place of the medieval hermit. It was very quiet, and he encountered no one on the empty road. A full moon shone above the winter trees, illuminating the snowy landscape with a ghostly light. He was unaware of the shadowy figure following him.

At last, he could see Grimbald Bridge. A narrow path went down from the road to the cave, which was near to the river. He'd also brought a torch, and he turned it on. The beam shone on the remains of the small stone chapel, next to the cave. On the ground was the outline of the grave in which St Robert had originally been buried, now covered with snow. The only sounds were from the river and from an occasional vehicle crossing the bridge.

Ferguson looked at the time: just seven o'clock. He turned his torch towards the river, wondering who was going to appear and from which direction. Belatedly he realised that there might be more than one person involved, but he was beyond caring. Years of anger and bitterness about how he'd been treated were welling up inside him. The more who turned up, the more he could harm. He clutched the knife in his hand.

As he faced away from the cave towards the river, a figure moved quickly towards him from where it had been hiding behind a large rock near the cave entrance. He heard the movement and was turning when he was struck on the head. Fortunately, he'd had time to instinctively raise an arm so the blow was partly parried. It was still sufficiently forceful to send him heavily to the ground. The assailant was raising an arm to deliver a second blow when there was the sound of shouting.

'What yer doin'? Leave 'im alone!' A man appeared out of the cave. It was David Tanner. He'd seen the attack from the cave entrance. The figure whipped round and immediately ran off, up the path, skidding a little on the ice, and on to the road. At the same time a person appeared from the other direction, holding a torch. It was Olive Bryson.

'Is he OK?' She knelt down by Ferguson. There were some splashes of blood on the snow.

'Ah didn't hit 'im,' said Tanner.

'I know you didn't, I saw what happened. Did you get a look at them?'

'It was that bloody monk again. They were dressed t'same as before wi' a great big hood on. Ah told t'police about it. Ah couldn't see a face.'

'What do you mean?'

Tanner told her about seeing the figure coming out of the church the day Rev Wilcox was killed, while she examined Ferguson, who was conscious but moaning. There was lots of blood on his head. She stood up.

'OK. I'm going to call an ambulance and the police. What were you doing here?'

'Ah kip down in t'cave sometimes if ah don't fancy goin' to th'ostel. Ah've got an old sleeping bag. Ah 'eard people movin' about outside and when ah came to t'doorway as ah call it, ah saw t'monk hit this bloke. Ah think he had a 'ammer.'

'Well, you saved his life. I was too far away to stop them hitting Harvey again.'

'Yer know him, then?'

'Yes, he's a friend of mine, and I was afraid he was going to be attacked so I was following.' She looked at the unkempt man and repeated: 'You saved him. Thanks.'

'Ah didn't do owt really. Yer can't just let someone bash a bloke's head in and not say owt.'

'Right. Could you bring out your sleeping bag and lay it over him until the ambulance arrives?'

'Aye.' Tanner went back into the cave and brought out a grubby sleeping bag, which he placed over Harvey. It wasn't long before the appearance of flashing blue lights indicated the arrival of the ambulance. Bryson's fears had been realised, but at least Ferguson was still alive.

~

'We need to thank you again for what you did. You undoubtedly saved his life. Another blow like the one he received would have been the end of him.'

Oldroyd was addressing David Tanner, who was sitting in a chair outside the ward in Knaresborough General Hospital, where Harvey Ferguson was receiving treatment. He and Olive Bryson had been allowed to travel in the ambulance with Ferguson for the short distance to the hospital. Bryson had insisted that Tanner should be allowed in as he had saved the patient's life.

'Aye, that's what that woman said. What's 'er name?'

211

'Olive.'

'Aye, that's reight, Olive.' He looked about curiously; eyes still screwed up in the bright light. He appeared out of place in this clean, highly organised environment, in which people were wearing uniforms or smart clothes.

'Can you tell me what you saw?'

Tanner fidgeted uncomfortably in his chair and drank from a plastic cup of tea that Bryson had brought him. 'Not much. Ah wa' in t'cave and ah heard people walking abaht. Ah went to t'door and saw that monk again. He wa' just smashin' that bloke over th'ead with a 'ammer, so ah called out to 'im. He shot off; yer should 'ave seen 'im run; as if he 'ad t'Devil followin' 'im.'

'Do you think it was the same person you saw coming out of the church when Rev Wilcox was murdered?'

'Ah couldn't say for sure, but it were abaht same 'eight, same clothes, same 'ood, couldn't see t'face. It must be t'same, don't tell me there's lots o' folk goin' round dressed up as monks.'

Oldroyd laughed. 'No, I think you're right; it's highly likely it was the same person. Do you think he got a good view of you?'

'Ah shouldn't think so, it bein' dark and that.'

'I just wanted to warn you to take care until we find who this person is and catch them. They've killed two people and attacked another with the clear intention of killing them. If they think you saw them and could identify them, you may be in danger. Understand?'

'Aye, but ah'm scared o' nobody.'

'I'm sure you're not, but be on your guard; stay where there are other people around, especially at night.'

Tanner nodded. 'Aye, ah will.'

'Do you want a lift back to the hostel?'

'Aye. Ah think ah need to get inside now after all that. It'll be warm in there.'

212

'And you'll have a story to tell.'

'Aye.' Tanner laughed.

Oldroyd arranged for DC Robinson to drive Tanner back to the hostel, and went back inside the ward. Andy was outside a small side room off the main ward. The call had come at about eight o'clock, disrupting the restful evening being enjoyed by the detectives. They both looked tired and sombre: this was the development in the case that they'd feared the most, but at least the victim was still alive.

'Is he conscious?' asked Oldroyd.

'I think so. The nurse said there was trauma to the head and a lot of blood. They're checking for signs of concussion. She said not to talk to him for very long and we should all leave soon to let him rest.'

Oldroyd sighed. 'He was damn lucky. Fancy two people coming to your rescue.'

'I know.'

'I'll just take a look.' Oldroyd slipped quietly inside the door and shut it behind him. Olive Bryson was sitting in a chair by the bed. Ferguson was lying with his head bandaged and his eyes closed.

'Is he awake?' whispered Oldroyd. She nodded. Oldroyd sat on a chair at the other side of the bed and leaned towards the prostrate figure. 'Mr Ferguson, can you hear me?' There was no response.

'Don't disturb him; I think he's gone back to sleep,' said Bryson. 'I was speaking to him a little while ago before you arrived. He told me that he got an anonymous threatening letter with homophobic insults. The writer said to meet him by St Robert's Cave. Harvey realises that he shouldn't have gone, but he was very angry, and wanted to confront whoever it was.'

'I see. Did he consider that it could be the killer we're looking for who sent the letter?'

'I don't think so. He just thought it was more homophobic abuse like he's suffered in the past.'

'Did he get a look at the attacker?'

'No, none of us did. It was very dark, and they were wearing a hood. They ran off up to the road and disappeared. The weapon was metal, probably a hammer.'

'Yes. David Tanner said the same.'

'He was very brave. He came out of that cave unarmed and foiled the attack. I was too far away to do anything.'

'Why were you there?' said Oldroyd.

'I've been worried about Harvey for a while. He hasn't been himself. Then, at about half past six, I saw him walk past my house which is on his route to the site of the cave. I just wondered where he was going on a dark winter evening like this. I was suspicious and uneasy, so I followed him at a distance. It's a good job I did because Mr Tanner didn't have a phone to call the ambulance.'

'Why were you worried about him?'

'Harvey's very conscious about his sexuality and the things people say about him. I'm one of the few people, maybe the only person, at church who knows he's gay. I'm a bit of a maverick character and he trusted me. As I said, lately he's been very edgy.'

'He told us about this when we interviewed him. There was something going on at church, but of course I can't tell you any specifics.'

'I see. Well, I'm so relieved he's survived. I'm very fond of Harvey. He's a talented musician and I'll bet he's a good teacher too. Why can't the church and society just celebrate those talents? It's beyond me.'

'I'm sure a lot of people in the church would agree with you.'

'Yes, but it doesn't feel like that a lot of the time.'

Oldroyd stood up. 'I don't think we can do any more here tonight. I'll send someone round to speak to him tomorrow. Would you like a lift back?'

'Thank you. That would be nice. I feel exhausted.'

'I want you to take extra care. I told David Tanner the same. If the killer thinks you might have recognised them, you could be in danger.'

'Don't worry, I'll be on my guard. Who knows when they'll strike again?'

Oldroyd asked her to wait in the entrance while he had a word with Andy, who looked very grave. Oldroyd told him what Bryson had said to him.

'This is bad news, isn't it, sir? Apart from the victim surviving that is.'

'It is. It takes us back to looking for motives and we don't know who else could be at risk. The whole thing's starting to look more random.'

'But every victim has been connected to that church, sir.'

'True, but if we're right about Saunders being a blackmailer, what do the other two have in common? Apart from being the rector and the choirmaster of the same church?'

'Was Ferguson blackmailing someone too? We've only got his word about receiving an anonymous letter. Maybe the person he was blackmailing tried to get rid of him,' replied Andy.

'But as the assailant was most likely the same person who killed Saunders and Wilcox, that would mean that two people have been blackmailing the killer. Maybe Rev Wilcox was blackmailing them too, so that makes a record three.'

Andy knew this was not a serious suggestion and that his boss was in a grim mood.

'We'll have to hope that Steph can uncover something soon.' Oldroyd sighed and ran his hand through his hair. 'The media are going to kick off big-time tomorrow, and Matthew Watkins will be on to Superintendent Walker.' He shook his head in frustration. 'What the hell am I missing?'

'It's a funny case, sir. Perverse, if you know what I mean. A killer dressed up as a monk and killing people from a church. It's weird.'

Oldroyd said little else as they went to their cars, with Olive Bryson getting into Oldroyd's. He was silent too on the drive back into the town. Something Andy had said made him wonder if his sister had been right all along about the motive behind the murders.

~

The weather continued to be cold. Snowploughs had cleared all the major roads and were starting work on the side roads, which had been impassable for days. As Oldroyd drove to Knaresborough the next day, under a grey sky, the snow seemed to have lost its magic, lying in dirty heaps at the side of the road and covering the fields in monotonous dull blankets.

Maybe it's my mood, he thought, as he looked out across the rather desolate landscape. He hated it when the criminal they were pursuing was always a step ahead. It became a personal battle, which was potentially dangerous, as the stress and the urgency to make progress could lead to mistakes being made. It had happened many times in the history of policing, and Oldroyd was always on his guard against it.

When he arrived at the church, he was pleased to see Andy already there and at work, reading something on his laptop.

'Morning, sir. I've got the report from the forensic team who examined the tower. It looks as if you were right, as usual.' He smiled at his boss. 'The ceiling is hinged, but that's not visible from below. The hinges and the pulley are old, nineteenth-century they

216

say, but still in working order and everything's been oiled and generally restored recently. The wooden ladder down to the ceiling has been repaired, and that great pendulum has been tied up securely with nylon rope replacing whatever was holding it before. It all confirms your theory that the whole thing was set up by someone in the past, and then used again recently.'

'Good. Well, at least that's something,' replied Oldroyd.

'The less-good news is that there were no fingerprints on anything, and nothing else which could be used to trace somebody, so I'm afraid it doesn't take us much further towards identifying the killer.'

'No, I didn't think it would. The person we're dealing with is far too clever and careful to leave us any information like that. I think that they half expected the staircase and the pendulum to be discovered once we started ferreting around. They would have hoped that it wouldn't be, and that the case would remain unsolved and ascribed to the ghost by some people, but they would be realistic. They thought that, even if the trick was revealed, it couldn't lead to them. I suspect the thing only really started to go wrong with Saunders, and now I feel that the whole enterprise, as it were, has changed. Has Steph found anything?'

'Some news on that front, sir, but I don't know how significant it will be.' He told Oldroyd about Ferguson's caution and Baxter and Rev Wilcox probably being part of the same church in Leeds.

'That's interesting, Baxter never mentioned that she already knew Rev Wilcox before they both came to Knaresborough. We'll have to follow that up. So, Ferguson's been involved in a fight before. No wonder he was prepared to take on the writer of that note. You're right though, I don't know whether any of it takes us any further.'

'They're still working at it, sir.'

'Good.'

There was a knock, and their old helper Donald Avison peeped round the vestry door. He looked very grave. 'Good morning gentlemen. Are you all right for everything? I . . .' He shook his head and for the first time seemed to be at a loss for words.

'Come right in, Mr Avison,' said Oldroyd. 'I'm sure you're shocked by what happened last night.'

'Me and lots of others, Chief Inspector.' He sat down on a chair near the door. 'Everyone's wondering what's next? Or, more precisely, who's next?'

'Yes, I can understand that, but tell the people you're in contact with that we're working as hard as we can, and we will bring this person to justice.'

'Yes.'

'Do you know if Mr Ferguson had any enemies?'

Avison stared at Oldroyd for a moment, and his face was set in a grim expression. 'That's partly why I've come to see you this morning, Chief Inspector. I know you've been questioning everyone and finding out about us all. You'll know that Harvey Ferguson is a . . .' He paused and enunciated the word with difficulty, as if he found it extremely distasteful: '. . . a homosexual.'

Oldroyd and Andy flinched.

'Yes,' replied Oldroyd warily. 'How do you know about this? He told me he is very careful about keeping it a private matter, especially from people in the church.'

Avison licked his lips nervously and avoided answering directly. 'I know society is tolerant of such . . . things nowadays, and I don't wish to go back to the times when people were persecuted and arrested, but for some of us in the Church, this . . . this behaviour is a problem. You see, it is against the teachings of the Bible and we are particularly concerned when . . . such a person is working with children.'

In case they 'catch' homosexuality? thought Oldroyd. Or because homosexuals are inherently dangerous? He was starting to understand Harvey Ferguson's feelings a little better.

'You haven't answered my question,' Oldroyd said, with increasing firmness in his tone. He was beginning to realise that the helpful churchwarden had a rather bigoted side to him.

Avison swallowed and looked away. The tough ex-soldier was rattled. 'We knew that he visited a gay bar – I . . . I think that's what they're called – in Leeds.'

'How did you know this?' asked Oldroyd. Andy wanted to ask Avison if it was because he went there himself, but decided to remain quiet.

'There is a network of people in this area who share the same beliefs, Chief Inspector. When we suspect that a person in a responsible position in a church is homosexual, we . . . have them followed. Harvey Ferguson was seen at this bar.'

'I see,' said Oldroyd, unable to keep the contempt out of his voice. He wasn't in the mood for this. 'So, you were the one who reported him to Rev Wilcox?'

'That's right.' He looked away from Oldroyd, whose eyes were now fixing him in a glare. The only thing in Avison's defence was that there was no defiance. He actually seemed sorry and ashamed.

'And what did you expect her to do?'

'We weren't asking her to do anything specific, just informing her of the situation and that a number of people in the congregation would not be happy if they found out that the choirmaster and organist was a homosexual.'

'Who's "we"?'

'Myself and Mrs Baxter, who you've met, and one or two others.'

'I will need all their names.'

'Yes.'

'And what was Rev Wilcox's response? Did she refuse to do anything? Is that why one of you killed her? Or maybe you planned it together. You know all about the history of the church, don't you, Mr Avison? I think you knew all about that secret staircase and the pendulum.'

There was the first sign of real anxiety in the normally unflappable Avison. He put his hands to his face.

'No! We didn't! I had no idea until you found that staircase, I—'

'And maybe you took matters into your own hands with Harvey Ferguson, and tried to kill him too?'

'No, that's not . . .' Avison couldn't continue. Andy watched with admiration as Oldroyd tore the man to pieces. When his boss was in this mood, he was a sight to behold.

'So, where were you last night between six o'clock and seven?'

'At home, my wife was with me. I . . .'

Oldroyd eased off a little. 'OK. So why are you telling us this now?'

Avison made a big effort to pull himself together. 'I'm really sorry about what happened to Harvey. It was terrible that someone tried to kill him. I wanted to make it clear that although we reported him to Clare, I don't believe any of us wished him any harm.'

'And maybe you're beginning to realise that people like Mr Ferguson do face hostility and that your attitudes and behaviour don't help.'

Avison looked at Oldroyd as if he'd been startled by the detective's perceptiveness.

'Yes, I suppose you're right, but I definitely didn't attack him.'

'Very well, Sergeant Carter will take the details of your little "group", shall I call it? And in answer to your first question: yes, we are fine for everything, thank you.'

'What a rat, sir,' said Andy after Avison had left. 'Is that what the average churchgoer is like if you scratch beneath the surface?'

'No, it wouldn't be fair to say that; they are mostly very decent people, like my sister, but as in many other areas of life, the church attracts some people who have very rigid beliefs which they seem to prize above common humanity. Anyway, what did you think of what he said?'

'I don't trust him, sir. I think you were right to suggest he knew all about the tower. He crumbled when you pushed him about it. He could be the killer, maybe with some help from these other people who feel the same way as him.'

'That would mean his wife is lying to provide an alibi for him.'

'Maybe she's part of it. He discovered the body of Rev Wilcox, which means he had the opportunity to kill her.'

Oldroyd leaned back in his chair with his hands behind his head. 'But why report that straight away? Why not just leave the body to be discovered the next day instead of drawing suspicion to yourself by calling in the police?'

'Maybe it was a kind of bluff, sir; you know, the whole business of him being helpful and reliable conceals the fact that he's the killer. You said yourself that hanging around here enables him to watch what we're doing.'

'I did, and you could be right. We need to search his house and examine his computer and phone, and see if anything turns up.'

'Like a monk's outfit?' Andy laughed.

'Maybe.' Oldroyd sprang up from his chair. 'Right, let's get moving. Avison did give us some useful material. I think we need to start looking beyond our original group of suspects and consider more of the people on Avison's list. Perhaps we should have done this before. Blast it!' He banged his fist on the table in frustration.

'It's not even a week since the first murder. How can we be expected to move any faster than we have? Especially with the weather hampering us.'

'We couldn't, sir.'

'But it doesn't make any difference; two people have been murdered and one seriously injured, and everyone wants answers. The press will be around harassing us again, but I'm dodging them today. I'm not sure I could keep my cool if they start asking ridiculous questions.'

'I'll speak to them, sir, and say you're unavailable. It'll give you a bit of a break.'

Oldroyd raised his eyebrows. Andy had not taken responsibility for handling a news conference before, but maybe it was time.

'OK, why not? That would be helpful. Knock any conspiracy theories on the head and don't let them lead you into saying more than you intend. You've seen me at work. I'll have to go back to the hospital and speak to Ferguson, and then . . .' Oldroyd's phone rang. 'Oh bugger, it's Tom Walker. I knew he'd be calling me.' He hurriedly accepted the call and put the phone to his ear. 'Morning, Tom.'

'Jim, how are you?' Walker's tone was apologetic, which meant that he was being harassed by Watkins and didn't like the idea of passing his boss's instructions on to his detectives in the field. 'You can guess what I'm ringing about. I can see you're having a tough time over there but you-know-who is eager for progress. Some high-ranking cleric has been on to him – I don't know, the Bishop of Pontefract or something – asking what's happening with the case and saying it's giving the Church a bad name. I said to him that what's giving the Church a bad name is what people are getting up to there, not the way our officers are conducting themselves. But he won't have it. He'll be in some kind of club with this bloke. Watkins is a social-climbing little so-and-so.'

'But Pontefract or wherever has nothing to do with Knaresborough; why didn't Watkins tell him to mind his own business? We've spoken to the Bishop of Ripon and he's a decent chap; he hasn't caused us any problems.'

'Jim, you're making the big mistake of assuming that Watkins would want to defend his own people and show some loyalty. Quite the opposite: he'll side with any Tom, Dick or Harry who wants to have a go at his own force, if he thinks it will benefit his career. Personally, I think he's after some kind of gong, OBE or something, and what a bloody travesty that would be. Anyway ... bring me up to date, will you? There was a third attack last night, wasn't there?'

Despite his weariness, Oldroyd patiently explained to Walker what the investigation had uncovered. 'I think it's only a matter of time, Tom. I think the killer is getting more reckless and we're narrowing the field down. I've got Stephanie Johnson doing background searches at HQ.'

'Yes, I saw her yesterday. She's got that new lass helping her. Warner, is it?'

'That's right – DC Sharon Warner. She's got good potential and Steph's bringing her on. I've got DS Carter and DC Robinson here, and some officers from the Knaresborough station.'

'Well, what can I say? If you and those people can't solve it, nobody can. And I'll tell Watkins if he gets on to me again. You know, one of these days I'm going to completely lose it with him. I'll say what I really think about him in very colourful terms, and that will be the end of me.'

'Don't do that, Tom; we'd all miss you. We might get someone like Watkins in your position and then where would we be?'

This punctured Walker's anger, getting a laugh out of him.

He defused the tension by using a bit of dialect, a standing joke between him and Oldroyd. 'Aye, well, don't worry, lad,' said

Walker, chuckling. 'Ah'll keep a lid on it for thi. Let me know when thi get a breakthrough.'

'I will.'

The call ended. Oldroyd sighed. Sometimes the literal life-and-death responsibility of the job was hard to bear.

~

At the rectory, the Wilcoxes had just finished the painful task of organising Clare's funeral service. The undertaker, a genial and portly man very skilled at putting people at their ease, had just left, and the family were sitting in the lounge.

Jenny slumped on the sofa and sighed. 'Well, I'm glad that's over. I never realised how many decisions there would be to make about the coffin, the flowers, the hymns, the music. I thought it would never end.'

'He was a very nice, helpful bloke, wasn't he?' added Fiona. 'I couldn't do that job, dealing with death and people's grief all the time, but I suppose someone has to do it.'

'You were brilliant, Dad,' said Jenny. 'That was really hard and you stuck with it. You deserve a rest now before the funeral.'

'I'm resting all the time,' replied Wilcox with a weak smile. 'I'd rather do something. I think I'll go back to work in a few days' time. I can't just go on sitting here and feeling sorry for myself.'

'Do you think that's a good idea, Dad? You don't want any extra stress from work at the moment,' said Jenny.

'It's more stressful being here in the house all the time with nothing to distract me. I'm expecting your mum to walk in at any moment, and everything here has an association with her.'

Jenny gave her father a sad smile. 'I can understand that. It's up to you; I'm sure they'll be very understanding at the surgery.'

There was a knock at the door. Fiona answered it and brought Robin Eastby into the sitting room.

'I've just come over to see if you've heard the latest news,' he said, looking rather shocked.

'No,' replied Fiona, 'we've been with the undertaker most of the morning. What's happened?'

Eastby sat down and then told them about the attack on Harvey Ferguson.

'What?' said Wilcox. 'Do the police think it's the same person who killed Clare and Violet Saunders?'

'I'm not sure, but I think so. Olive Bryson and a homeless man saved Harvey's life.'

'Really?'

'Yes, I've spoken to her. She saw Harvey going past her house in the dark and was concerned about him. She followed and witnessed him being attacked. It was by the river, down at St Robert's Cave. The homeless man was sheltering inside the cave, saw the attack and rushed out. The attacker ran off, and Olive called the police and the ambulance.'

'Wow! Good for her,' said Fiona. 'Was Harvey hurt badly?'

'Olive said he was hit on the head with a hammer; he was taken to the hospital, but she thinks he will be OK.'

'Good on that man for risking himself like that.'

'That's what I thought; people like that get so much criticism, I hope that good deed is properly reported in the media.'

Jenny put her hands up to her face. 'This is the third time you've brought bad news, Robin. We've got enough to deal with without all this. It just seems to get worse.'

'I know,' said Robin. 'I'm sorry; I just wanted you to hear it from me. We'll just have to take even greater care, all of us. Don't go out alone, especially at night.'

'Are the police making progress, do you think?'

'I don't know; it must be difficult for them. Things have happened so quickly. It's only a week tomorrow since . . . well, you know, and then we've had this snowy weather. They seem a sharp team of people. I'm sure they'll find the person responsible.'

'I hope you're right,' said Wilcox. 'And the sooner the better. Once thing is certain: it's going to be a long time before this town recovers from the traumas it's been through, and that's assuming that there's no more.'

Seven

'His back was now to the door. In that moment the door opened, and an arm came out and clawed at his shoulder. It was clad in ragged, yellowish linen, and the bare skin, where it could be seen, had long grey hair upon it.

Anderson was just in time to pull Jensen out of its reach with a cry of disgust and fright, when the door shut again, and a low laugh was heard.'

From 'Number 13', M. R. James, 1904

When Oldroyd returned to the hospital, he found Ferguson sitting up in bed looking rather groggy, with a fresh bandage on his head.

'I'm glad to find you conscious,' Oldroyd said.

'Thank you,' replied Ferguson in a weak voice, and then he winced; even moving his face to speak caused pain.

'Did you manage to sleep well?'

'Not particularly.'

'Well, I won't keep you long, but can you just explain what happened? We've had an account from Olive Bryson, so we know the outline. Why were you there, by the river, at that time of night?'

Ferguson explained about the note. His speech was halting. 'I know I shouldn't have gone alone but I was so angry, I just wanted to sort it out myself. I took a knife with me in case I was threatened but I never got the chance to use it; they sprang on me from behind.'

'You shouldn't have been carrying a weapon like that, but I'll see if we can overlook it in the circumstances. Did you get a look at the person who attacked you?'

'No, they came from behind and they were wearing a hood. I just caught a glimpse and raised my arm before I felt this bang on my head. I heard a voice shouting and after that nothing, until I came round in here.'

'I know you've encountered homophobic abuse many times, but was there anyone in particular who had threatened you recently?'

Ferguson shifted in the bed and grimaced again. He was not only uncomfortable in the bed, but also with what he was about to say. 'No one has threatened me lately, but . . .' He stopped and sighed. 'I have something to confess to you, Chief Inspector.'

Oldroyd sat up. Was this going to be the breakthrough? 'Go on.'

'I've been blackmailing someone; not for money but for protection.'

'Who?'

'Patrick Owen, the archdeacon.' He looked relieved that he'd finally said it.

'Over what?'

'Patrick's bisexual; we knew each other several years ago before he became archdeacon, and we had a brief relationship. He was over in Leeds then. I don't know whether his wife knows or not, but generally he's kept his sexuality a secret, like many of us have to. We met up again when he came to Knaresborough but kept quiet about the past.

'When things started to get difficult here, especially when someone reported me to Clare, I went to see him and made it clear that he had to do everything he could to protect me and keep my sexuality a secret. As I've said to you before, there's no coming out in churches like St Anne's, even though there are lots of good people like Olive, and I also had my job to think about.'

'So, you threatened to expose him if he didn't help?'

Ferguson looked away. He was clearly ashamed. 'Yes. I wanted him to use his authority to prevent anything damaging being said.' He sighed again. 'I shouldn't have done it, but I was desperate. Here I am doing all this work free of charge for the church, and then nasty interfering bigots want to denounce me as a pervert. I thought: why shouldn't I try to use some of the power in the church to my own advantage?'

'Did he cooperate?'

'Yes. I even think he sympathised with me. It wasn't nasty, but of course I made it clear that ultimately I had this power over him.'

'And what happened?'

Ferguson gave a grim laugh. 'That's the irony: nothing. You know about the meeting where I got angry and left. Then Clare was murdered and here we are.'

'If the issue comes up again with the new rector and they aren't sympathetic, you could always call on Owen's protection?'

'That was the idea.'

Oldroyd paused and thought about what he'd been told. 'So why are you telling me this now?'

Ferguson looked even more agitated. 'The reason I didn't sleep last night was that a terrible idea was going round in my head. Could it have been Patrick who lured me out there and then attacked me? Maybe he wanted to get rid of his blackmailer. Then, when Olive told me the person had been wearing a monk's habit with the hood, I had a shocking thought: could Patrick have killed Clare and Violet? I don't know why, but maybe he's gone insane. I just don't like it.' He was getting agitated; he slammed his arms down on to the bed and winced again with pain.

'OK, calm down, Mr Ferguson. You'll only damage yourself. You did the right thing to talk to me and I realise it was hard. We'll investigate what you've told me. You just need to concentrate on getting well again.'

Ferguson nodded and laid gently back against the pillow.

～

When Oldroyd got outside the hospital, he immediately called Andy.

'We've got a number-one suspect, Andy: Patrick Owen, the archdeacon. Ferguson has confessed that he was blackmailing him. He could have been the assailant last night. I know he has a detailed knowledge of the St Anne's building, so he could be our killer. I can't say I'm clear what his motive might be for killing Rev Wilcox, but hopefully we'll find out, or maybe Steph will.'

'Good God, sir, so that makes two blackmailers in one church?'

'Maybe.'

'But, sir . . . if Violet Saunders was killed because she was blackmailing the killer and that was Owen, then that means that he was being blackmailed twice.'

'Yes, I know; it seems unlikely but not impossible. We're going to have to go with it, because it's the only firm lead we've had so far. We at least need to thoroughly eliminate him. I've got his address from Ferguson. I want you to drive over and meet me there.'

'The press are coming at three o'clock, sir.'

'Blast it! I forgot about them. Put them on an hour; tell them there's been an important development. That will pique their interest. You should easily be back in time. I'll get a sandwich for you on my way over.'

'OK, sir, can you get me a chicken one, please?'

'No problem. No cakes or biscuits, though.'

'Fine.'

The call ended with Andy thinking how hectic things could be when working with his boss. But then he had intensified the pressure on himself by volunteering to do the press conference. Not to worry, he needed to challenge himself out of his comfort zone, and it was good to know that Oldroyd had faith in him.

～

Down at Knaresborough Men's Hostel, David Tanner was about to receive a hero's treatment. DC Robinson had brought him back the previous night, cold and hungry. Robinson had explained to Trevor Wood what had happened while someone sorted out a bed for Tanner.

A number of the men, including Tanner, were in the communal area, eating toast for breakfast. Most of them were regulars. A smiling Trevor Wood asked for their attention.

'Right, lads, I've got something great to tell you about. Our very own David here saved a man's life last night.' He pointed at Tanner, who was sitting at a table drinking tea. He looked away, shyly.

Heads turned in his direction. There were calls of 'Eh?' and 'Bloody hell!'

'He stopped a man being assaulted by someone with a hammer, and stayed with him until the police and ambulance were called. I'm pleased to say that the victim is now recovering in hospital. So, now I think we should all show David our appreciation.'

There was enthusiastic clapping and calls of 'Good on you, Dave!' and 'Brilliant!'

Tanner smiled and nodded his head to acknowledge the applause.

Afterwards, Wood took Tanner into the little room he used as a makeshift office, where he could talk to people in private. Tanner stood shyly by the door.

'Come right in, David.'

Tanner edged a little further inside.

'I just wanted to say I'm proud of you. It shows what a good-hearted, brave bloke you are.'

Tanner looked embarrassed, and beneath his thick black beard his face was red. 'Ta,' was all he said.

Wood continued. 'You're going to beat this drink thing. We'll try to get you somewhere permanent to live and some job training. Look at what everyone thought of you.'

'Aye, that wa' good. Ah've niver been clapped for owt in me life.'

'Well, you take it from me, David; you're on the way up from now on.'

Tanner looked at his mentor and smiled. He felt some self-esteem at last, and for the first time in many years he really believed that he could rebuild his life.

~

Oldroyd and Andy arrived at Patrick Owen's house, which was located in a secluded and leafy part of Harrogate. It was a little less cold, and a slow thaw was underway. Rivulets of water from melting piles of dirty snow ran down the sides of the road.

Oldroyd looked at the house. It was in a rather gloomy position, surrounded by dense evergreen shrubbery. 'I'll do the talking;

keep an eye on him all the time, because if he is the killer, he's a dangerous man.'

Everything seemed very quiet as Oldroyd rang the doorbell wondering if anyone was in, but soon a figure loomed up in the hall, indistinct through the frosted glass of the front door.

'Chief Inspector?' Owen looked very surprised.

'Yes. Can we come in, please? We need to ask you some questions.'

Without a word, Owen beckoned them in and showed them into the sitting room where they all sat down.

'I'll get straight to the point,' said Oldroyd, fixing Owen with a stern expression. 'I don't know whether you've had any news about last night's attack on Harvey Ferguson?'

Owen's eyes widened. 'No, I haven't. What happened? Is he all right?'

'He was hit over the head with a hammer by an unidentified assailant. He's in hospital at the moment, but he'll be OK.'

'Thank you for informing me; I will go round to see him. But what's this got to do with me?'

'We know that Ferguson was blackmailing you. He's confessed to us.'

Oldroyd saw that Owen was shocked at this news, but he held himself together.

'I see,' was all he said.

'How did you feel about it?' asked Oldroyd.

'Not badly enough to want to do him any harm, Chief Inspector; and before you ask, I was at home here last night and my wife can corroborate that.'

'Very well, but you must have felt a lot of animosity towards him.'

Owen frowned. 'Strangely enough, I didn't. Obviously I resented it, but I understood why Harvey was doing it, because I have the same problems myself. He didn't blackmail me in a nasty way for money or anything like that. It was the desperate act of a desperate man.'

'You would describe yourself as gay?'

Owen shrugged. 'Bisexual in my case. What do these labels really mean? Sexuality is a spectrum, isn't it? I'm happily married, but my wife knows I'm also attracted to men.'

'Does she accept it?'

'These are very personal questions, Chief Inspector, but yes. I don't have any sexual contact with men any more. The last man I was with was Harvey, which was several years ago. I told my wife about that and we've moved on.'

'So you shared with Ferguson the need to conceal your sexuality from the world?'

'Yes, in a nutshell. I'm sure that Harvey has told you that it's not really possible to come out in the Church and maintain your position.'

'But there are a number of openly gay clergy, aren't there?'

Owen smiled. 'Yes, some have taken the brave step of being honest about their sexuality. For this they have been accepted and praised by some people in the Church, but rejected and treated ever after with suspicion by many others. Harvey and I, though we never talked about it directly, felt that we had something to contribute to the Church and we didn't want that to be compromised. We would rather our sexuality remained a secret so we could get on with our work in peace.'

'Isn't that perhaps a bit morally dishonest?'

Owen took a deep breath in and shook his head. These were issues that had clearly tormented him for many years. 'You could say that. It's a balance between total honesty about yourself and damaging the good you can do in the Church. It's not that we're criminals pretending to be virtuous. That would be grossly hypocritical.'

Oldroyd was fascinated by the debate and would have liked to continue it, but he knew this was not the time. 'How, exactly, did Ferguson expect you to protect him?'

'He wanted me to interfere with the church's procedures, and this is the bit I felt bad about. It seemed wrong and deceitful, but he was trapping me. He was in a panic after Clare told him that he'd been reported by some bigoted busybody. Imagine? You've nothing better to do with your Christian life than ferret out gay people at church. If that's your Christianity, then God help you!' It was the first time Owen had shown his feelings, which were normally well under control.

'He wanted me to speak to Clare, and somehow stop any enquiry. I don't think he appreciated how difficult that was. I may be the archdeacon, but I can't go round preventing the proper processes in a church. Clare would not have accepted it, and rightly so.'

'Do you think he ever would have outed you, if it actually came to it?'

'I don't know. He feared he would lose everything: his job as well as his position in the church. But anyway, Clare was murdered, so the problem was deferred.'

'That was convenient for you, wasn't it?'

Owen looked sharply at Oldroyd. 'So you still think I killed Clare and assaulted Harvey? What kind of person do you think I am, Chief Inspector?'

'Maybe a desperate one, like Harvey Ferguson.'

'And did I also kill the other woman? I forget her name.'

'Violet Saunders. Maybe you did, if she saw you in the church and had some control over you.'

Owen laughed sarcastically. 'So I was being blackmailed twice over? Really, Chief Inspector, it's all getting a bit far-fetched, don't you think?'

'I've known much more unlikely things to occur. Just because the odds are against something doesn't mean that it couldn't happen. So, where were you on Saturday evening?'

'I was here preparing my sermon. I was preaching on Sunday over in Wetherby. My wife was here with me again.'

'It seems like the only person providing your alibis is your wife.'

'I work a lot from home. Most senior clerics do. I go into the diocesan office occasionally and visit parishes, but it's mostly from home.'

'And you're sure you knew nothing about the staircase and the pendulum before I told you?'

'Absolutely. By the way, on that, after you came last time I did a bit of research at the diocesan office; we have a small archive there with bits and pieces about the diocese and the area. I found an old book about tradespeople in the nineteenth century. Some local antiquarian must have researched the accounts of local businesses. I photocopied a page for you. The book's called *Knaresborough Trades 1840–1880*; not bedtime reading but it has some useful information about the alterations that vicar must have had done in the tower, and the unfortunate joiner who did it. It's a kind of trade directory with extras.' He went out of the room and came back with a sheet of paper which he handed to Oldroyd, who glanced at it quickly.

'Who has access to this archive?'

'Any of the staff there, and any clergy in the diocese who ask to see it from Bishop Michael down. Any historian or researcher would have to make a special appointment. Some of those books are valuable and they are kept locked up.'

'Is a record kept of those appointments?'

'I'm not sure, but they'll be able to tell you at the office.'

'OK, thank you for this. We'll be sending someone round to take a statement and to interview your wife. You need to stay in the area for the time being.'

'That's fine.'

~

Outside in the car, Oldroyd read the page carefully and then turned to Andy.

'Listen to this,' he said. '"Riley's Joiners. Family firm established in Brooks Yard 1845. Often employed to work in ecclesiastical settings. Herbert Riley senior was paid a significant amount to install cupboards and work on the wooden ceiling in the west tower; also various ironworks." That's it, all right. That's the man who did the work for Rev Marshall. I thought the work was too good for Marshall to have done it himself. And listen to this: "Herbert Riley junior took over the business after the tragic death of his father in 1851, his body being found in the River Nidd below the castle."'

'Wow, sir! Do you think the old rector got rid of him? He knew too much, didn't he?'

'It looks like it. He would have told him not to say anything about what he was doing and probably paid him for his silence, but he would be even quieter when he was dead.'

'God, some vicar he was!'

'Yep, a real wolf in sheep's clothing. It looks like that book was the key to working out that there was something concealed behind those cupboards. We need to find out who else might have read it.'

'Are you moving away from the idea that Owen is the killer?'

'Not necessarily. He tells a convincing story, but we can't eliminate him as he had a motive. We need to look wider as well, to consider other people who have not come under suspicion so far and who have accessed that book.'

'Do you think there's someone else out there, sir, that we don't know about? Who had a motive to kill Rev Wilcox and the others?'

'I doubt it, but what can we do at the moment except follow up all leads, however weak they seem?' Oldroyd gripped the steering wheel and sighed. 'Anyway, we'll have to get you back to that press conference.'

The detectives headed back to Knaresborough, still feeling a sense of frustration at the lack of a breakthrough. And beneath that feeling was the fear that the killer could strike again.

~

Back at Harrogate HQ, Steph and Sharon were still doggedly pursuing their research, anxious to help the investigation to make progress. This task was more urgent now that the person responsible had seemingly attacked a third victim. They had trawled through records of convictions, and they had consulted church records. The lives of the suspects before they came to Knaresborough had been examined as far as was possible. It had all yielded nothing of significance.

'OK,' said Steph, as she and Sharon were sitting together in the office again in front of their screens. 'I think we should change tack. I'm wondering if we're looking in the right places. Andy mentioned to me that DCI Oldroyd's sister thinks that anti-women attitudes in the Church might be behind at least the murder of Rev Wilcox. Let's explore websites which oppose women priests and see if anything emerges.'

'Do you think someone would murder a woman simply because she was a priest, Sarge?'

'Not a normal person. But we may be dealing with some deranged fanatic. Anyway, we'll try. We need to access any sites which have been identified by the police as extreme.'

Almost as soon as Steph began the search, which took her on to the dark web, what she saw shocked her. There were terrible levels of misogyny: people arguing that women could not be trusted because Eve was responsible for the fall of mankind in the Garden of Eden; that a woman in any kind of position of authority in the Church could not be tolerated; that it was blasphemous for a woman to administer communion; that women were unclean due to menstruation and were created as inferior and secondary beings to men; that a woman's role was as a homemaker. There were dire warnings of how these upstart women would bring the wrath of God down upon the Church. Biblical passages were quoted in support of all these ideas.

This was sickening, but then she followed references to a more obscure site, which featured shocking images and foul language, with women priests denounced as dangerous witches and controlled by the Antichrist. There were images of women in dog collars with their eyes torn out and nooses round their necks. Appalling threats, often sexually perverted, were scrawled all over their bodies. She had to get up and take a break after viewing this.

As she returned, Sharon gasped and said, 'Sarge, look at this!' Steph looked at Sharon's screen. She was on a site similar to the one Steph had seen. It was called 'Alliance for the Protection of the Church and Priesthood', which seemed reasonably mild until you saw the rampant hatred expressed on its pages and the calls for the deaths of women priests. Sharon was pointing to a photograph showing someone giving a speech at a meeting. Their face was contorted, and their eyes blazed with fury, but it was still possible to recognise who it was.

'Oh my God!' exclaimed Steph, and put her hand to her mouth. 'I must inform DCI Oldroyd straight away. Well done, Sharon.'

Oldroyd had returned to the vestry office, leaving Andy to deal with the press. He could hardly sit there with him when the message to the reporters was that DCI Oldroyd was unavailable. Anyway, he was sure Andy would do better if his boss weren't looking over his shoulder.

He called the diocesan office, asking if there were records of people who had consulted the archive. The speaker said they would enquire and then ring back.

He made a cup of tea and sat down to think. Did they really have to go back to square one and start looking for new suspects who had found out about the west tower and the pendulum from the church archive? That could mean many people in the congregation, and what about motives? He sat there for some time, and eventually shook his head and was thinking what a mess it was when Steph rang.

'Please tell me you've got something for me,' said Oldroyd in a tone of desperation. 'We're struggling here.'

'I think I have, sir. I'm sending a photograph to Andy's laptop, along with a link to a website. Is he there?'

'No, but his laptop is. Go ahead.'

It took a few seconds for the items to come through, but when he saw them, Oldroyd's eyes lit up. 'I see! Well done, that's extremely useful.'

'Sharon found it, sir, not me.'

'Did she? Well, pass on my thanks and tell her I'm impressed.'

'I will, sir; she'll be delighted. By the way, it looks as if your sister was right.'

'Yes, I should have listened. I didn't really think that men were capable of such . . .' For once, words failed him.

'Unfortunately, they are, sir. It's the kind of thing we're up against all the time.'

Oldroyd knew she meant as women. 'Yes, I think I've grasped that a little more,' he said as the call ended.

When Andy returned shortly afterwards, he found his boss looking serious but more upbeat.

'Your partner's done it, Andy! Or should I say her assistant, young Sharon Warner.'

'What have they found, sir?'

Oldroyd showed him the photograph.

'Well, of course, I should have realised.'

'*We* should have realised; we were taken in by—' Oldroyd's phone went. 'Yes?'

It was the diocesan office returning his call. They did have a list of people who had consulted the archive.

'Good,' replied Oldroyd, and he smiled at Andy. 'Now, can you tell me if the name Austin Eliot appears on the list? It does, and when was that? . . . A year ago. Thank you, that's very helpful.' He ended the call. 'Austin Eliot saw that book when he was researching, and that's him speaking to that extremist group in the photograph. It almost certainly means that he's our murderer. Yes, and David Tanner said something which now makes sense. Let's get down to that bookshop straight away.'

~

It was late in the afternoon and the sun was going down when Oldroyd and Andy arrived at the bookshop by the river. The trees across the water were casting a shadow over the old building. Dirty meltwater was trickling down the sides of the road.

The old Saab drew up outside the shop, which was in darkness. Oldroyd got out and looked around the empty side road. A car went past and over the bridge. He knocked on the door with no response, and then tried the handle. It was locked.

'Get your shoulder on that, Andy, we can't stand on ceremony.' A few powerful shoves from the burly detective broke the lock from the wooden casing and they went inside.

'Mr Eliot! Chief Inspector Oldroyd and Sergeant Carter. We need to talk with you.' The shop was eerily quiet. The rickety shelves of books could just be made out in the gathering darkness. 'Can you find a light switch, Andy?'

'Here, sir.' The light suddenly illuminated the shop, including where Oldroyd had sat with Eliot debating theology. A search of the ground floor with its warren of little rooms revealed nothing. There was a staircase marked 'Private'.

'Let's go up here,' said Oldroyd. 'Mr Eliot!' he called again with no reply, as they walked up the creaking steps. Andy, behind his boss, found another light switch.

'Oh my God!' cried Oldroyd, who had reached the top. Andy went swiftly up the remaining steps. They were in a small room, which was obviously an office. On one side were more shelves containing box files. On the other was a desk with a computer. The wall behind the desk was covered with photographs and slogans of the type Steph had seen on the anti-women-priests website. Slogans demanding that medieval brutality be inflicted on women priests because they were destroying God's church. Women depicted as witches having sex with the Devil; women priests shown with the heads of wolves.

'Bloody hell, sir!' Andy was deeply shocked.

'Yes,' replied Oldroyd as he took a deep breath. 'I don't think we need to look any further than this to know who our killer is.'

Andy shook his head. For a time, he was utterly stunned, as he scanned the wall with a horrified fascination. 'How the hell can men think like this, sir? It's disgusting!'

'I don't know,' replied Oldroyd, 'but they do. And look here, there's a section on gay people.' He pointed to pictures of gay men with phrases scrawled on: as 'disgusting perverts', 'sinners worthy of eternal damnation', 'evil sodomites' and so on. 'So we know he was deeply homophobic as well as misogynistic, which would explain the attack on Harvey Ferguson.'

'And we're still assuming the murder of Violet Saunders was to keep her quiet?'

'I would think so. We'll find out when we catch him. It was you who put me on to this when you said there was something perverse about the case. My sister was right all along; it was nothing to do with money or extramarital affairs or anything like that. It's the work of a deranged and violent misogynist and homophobe who thinks he's crusading for God and to save Christianity. He—'

'Sir, oh bloody hell! Look at this!'

Oldroyd rushed to where Andy was looking at material on another wall. There was a heading in red letters, depicted as dripping in blood: 'Women Bishops: A Divine War Against Satan's Whores'. Underneath was a photograph of Rev Wilcox with a red cross scrawled across it. But it was what was underneath that caused Oldroyd to gasp: a picture of his sister, Alison, with the phrase 'Our Arch Enemy: Die Bitch!!! Now!' printed above it. Oldroyd staggered and Andy had to grab hold of him.

'We've got to get out there quickly, sir, she's in great danger. "Now" could be today.'

'Yes,' said Oldroyd, struggling to remain composed. 'Call Harrogate HQ to explain the situation, and get them to send armed support up to the vicarage at Kirkby Underside. Let's go now, and you'd better drive.'

They rushed down the steps and into the car, which took off at great speed as Oldroyd, in his anguished state, wondered why he hadn't taken Alison's ideas more seriously from the beginning? If she paid for his mistake with her life, he didn't know how he would ever forgive himself.

At Kirkby Underside, Alison was again sitting in prayer and meditation before her window, looking out on the bedraggled winter garden. The shrunk and deadened state of the plants reflected her mood, especially after recent events. Clare's death had had a profound impact on her, also provoking some remnants of the grief about the loss of her husband. Maybe this was good, as it was telling her that there were things she still needed to work on in relation to her first bereavement. Her faith told her that at some point renewal would come, just as spring would bring new growth to the shrubs and flowers out there.

It was very quiet in the vicarage until she heard a noise. It seemed to be coming from the kitchen, and it sounded like someone or something tapping on glass. She ignored it for a while and then reluctantly got up to investigate. The light was rapidly fading outside as she switched on the light in the kitchen. She looked at the window but there was nothing there. Was the wind causing a branch from one of the trees near the house to scratch against a window? She stood still for a moment and listened. Suddenly there was a crashing noise outside the back door, which led into a yard. It sounded as if a bin had fallen over, and sometimes foxes did this when looking for food. She opened the door and peered out into the dim twilight. Yes, the bin had been overturned, and so she stepped out of the door intent on lifting it back up. The figure that had been lurking in the darkness at the side of the door immediately came up behind her and flung an arm around her neck. The hand on the other arm held a knife to her throat.

'Don't scream,' said the voice of Austin Eliot. 'Let's just go quietly inside and have another nice discussion, shall we? Before I rid God's world of your blasphemy and evil.'

~

Oldroyd held his phone with a shaky hand, as he called Alison's number again and again without success. After a while he gave up and called DC Robinson, telling him to secure the bookshop and search Eliot's nearby house. When he ended the call, he put a hand to his head. 'I just hope to God we're not too late,' he groaned. 'Why is she not answering her phone?'

'It happens, sir. Maybe it's out of battery, or it's switched off and she doesn't realise it.'

Oldroyd shook his head.

'And anyway, sir, we don't know for sure that Eliot's headed for there, he may have just gone out somewhere else.'

'Maybe, but he knew it was only a matter of time before we were on to him. He wants to do as much damage as he can before we arrest him.'

Andy couldn't think of anything else to say, and they both remained silent as the car sped along the winter roads and the sky darkened.

~

Alison stared defiantly at her captor from the chair in the kitchen to which she'd been bound with nylon cord. She was facing the locked door to the yard and the window above the sink. Austin Eliot sat nonchalantly in a chair across the table, on which lay another piece of cord and the knife. His long hair was blown wild about his head and his eyes gleamed. He was about to speak when Alison heard her phone, which she'd left in the living room.

'Just ignore that,' said Eliot. 'We don't want any interruptions of our little meeting, do we?'

Alison didn't move and tried not to betray her feelings. Internally, she was praying hard and fighting to stay calm. She knew, from what Jim had told her, that many deranged killers like this actually wanted their victims to break down and plead for their lives.

'You won't get away with this, you know.'

Eliot smiled. 'I know. I haven't much time left before they catch me, if I let them. But I'm happy with what I've achieved.'

'And what is that?' Alison knew that the only way to delay him attacking her was to keep him talking and engaged in what they were saying to each other.

Eliot looked at her and his eyes narrowed. 'I'll have eliminated two female servants of the Devil, and nearly got rid of one disgusting pervert. I think God will be pleased.'

'How have you convinced yourself that murdering people is the will of God?'

Eliot's expressive eyes lit up. He was eager to talk about this. She was succeeding in getting him involved. He smiled at her. 'I'm glad I didn't kill you straight away. I enjoyed our debate the other day, and I want a little more of it now that I can tell you what I really think. It will be very satisfying to explain it all to you, one of the arch-demons.'

'Why am I so bad?' Ask him questions, she thought; give him opportunities to talk but don't provoke him.

'I've followed your career for many years. We know about everyone who's been sent by the Devil to undermine the Church.'

'Who's "we"?'

'The Alliance; we're all sworn to fight for God's truth and His Church against the upstart spawn of Eve.'

Alison flinched: it was a truly chilling way to describe women. 'Does it all go back to the sin of Eve, then?'

Eliot picked up the knife and pointed it at her. Alison returned his malevolent stare with a composed and dignified look.

'Eve gave in to Satan and persuaded Adam to disobey God. Women's weakness brought evil into the world and so God placed men in charge of the weaker sex. Jesus chose only male disciples. Then people like you came along and upset the divinely ordained order. We know you've been around since the beginning, campaigning for women to be priests – mock priests, the Devil's priests!'

He got up from the chair as his anger increased, and Alison held her breath. 'And that's why you are an arch-demon, one of the first to preach this infernal message of equality in the Church.'

Alison saw Eliot's demonic energy and hatred increasing in intensity, and fought hard against desperation. She had no idea how she might escape from this nightmare.

~

By good fortune, Oldroyd and Andy arrived in the village of Kirkby Underside at the same time as the police van containing the back-up team. When he saw the van, Oldroyd got out and flagged it down. He knew all the officers from Harrogate HQ. He told them to stay here in the main street of the village and remain quiet until he and Andy had investigated. Then the two detectives left the Saab and walked to the vicarage. There was a car parked by the entrance to the driveway.

'That's very suspicious,' whispered Oldroyd. 'Take care; if it's Eliot, he must still be in there; I hope to God we're not too late.'

They crept along the edge of the drive, keeping to the shadows provided by the rhododendrons and laurel trees. Oldroyd noticed the kitchen light was on.

'He would have gone to the back of the house, where it's secluded. Let's move slowly around the wall to the door.'

When they eventually got near to the kitchen door, Oldroyd was relieved to hear voices, including a female one which must be his sister's. But what was actually going on in there?

He signalled to Andy to stay in the shadows while he crouched down and scuttled across the yard to the kitchen window. He could hear the voices clearly now and they were definitely those of Eliot and his sister. He moved to the very corner of the window and brought his head up very gradually until he was able to glimpse into the room. To his horror, he saw Alison tied to the chair and Eliot wielding a knife. From what he could make out, it seemed as if they were talking about the Church and women priests, and he understood what Alison was probably trying to do: to keep him talking in the desperate hope that someone might come and rescue her.

Oldroyd ducked down and went back across the yard to Andy.

'So, this is what we're going to do. Over there at the side of the house is a manhole, which leads down into the cellar. If we can get the lid off quietly, I want you to drop down into the cellar and find the steps up into the house.'

'I'll use the light on my phone, sir,' whispered Andy.

'Good. So, the door from the cellar comes out in the hall, and then you turn right back towards the kitchen. The door has a Yale lock, but there is a key hidden at the top of the steps in a crevice behind a brick. I went through all the security with her once. I advised her to change the lock for something more secure or to get this manhole sealed, but luckily I don't think she ever got round to it. I'm going to try to get Eliot's attention and I want you to try to creep up on him from behind. Got it?'

'Yes, sir, I'm on it.' Andy fiddled with the metal cover, which opened without a great deal of effort. The only noise was a slight grating of metal on stone, too faint to be heard in the house. Andy gave Oldroyd the thumbs-up sign, dropped through the hole and disappeared into the darkness.

Oldroyd phoned the back-up team and ordered them to surround the vicarage, as discreetly as possible because of the risk to life. There were to be two armed officers in the backyard. Then he paused and thought about what to do next.

∼

In the kitchen, Alison was continuing to listen to Eliot's ranting. She tried to ask questions that would keep him talking.

'Why was Clare Wilcox a target? There were plenty of other women priests around.'

Eliot slammed the knife on the table. 'Don't use the words "women" and "priests" together – it's a horrendous blasphemy!' he yelled, and Alison flinched again. 'You know as well as I what was about to happen. She was about to become a bishop: an even greater blasphemy. Imagine! A member of the sex who led us into evil acting as the shepherd of the flock; a wolf in charge of the sheep!'

'Was it the idea of a woman in that role,' said Alison carefully, 'that finally spurred you into action?'

As she said this, she caught a brief glimpse through the window of a figure outside. Luckily, Eliot was facing away from the window so he could see nothing. She made a supreme effort not to look in that direction. At least now she had some hope.

'Of course! Women with such authority in the Church? There is clearly a plan to take over the Church completely. It'll be a feminist Church, not a Christian one.'

Alison struggled with the wild confusion of this idea, but continued to ask questions. 'I hope you don't mind me asking, but why do you not join the Roman Catholic Church, where women can't take on these roles?'

Eliot looked very sly, as if he'd been expecting Alison to make this point. 'We're not going to join the Church run by the Antichrist from a European city! We want our own Church; the Church of England to be returned to purity and to observation of the Bible and the will of God. Anyway . . .' A spasm of fear went through Alison as Eliot picked up the cord from the table. 'I think I've had enough of this. You now know why you have to die.'

Alison dived in quickly with another question. 'Wait! That was the first thing I asked you: why do we have to die? Can't you just leave us alone and go to churches that don't have women in that role?' Again she chose her words with care.

Eliot laughed. 'As if it were that simple! The integrity of the whole Church is at stake. We've been reasonable and opposed these changes, but no one has listened. God is calling us, as he did people in the Old Testament, to cleanse the land of evil and make a fresh start. This is a disobedient generation.'

Suddenly there was a loud knocking on the door, and Alison was intensely relieved to hear her brother's voice shouting outside in the yard.

'Austin Eliot, we know you're in there! Do not harm your captive, but open the door and walk out with your hands raised. The house is surrounded by armed officers. There is no way for you to escape.'

Eliot looked furious. 'That's that damned brother of yours, isn't it? I didn't think he would be on to me so quickly.' He looked at Alison with an evil grin. 'It's a good job I came when I did.' He came over to her with the knife and Alison braced herself, determined to make no noise. But Eliot only cut the cords that bound her to the chair and pulled her up. 'I was going to use the cord to avoid the mess, but it's too slow. I think cutting your throat in front of your brother will be a fitting end. Yes, I like it!' He almost giggled. 'Two fingers up to feminism and to the police.'

He put the knife to her throat again and moved her to the door, which he flung open with his other hand. Alison saw Oldroyd standing across the yard with two armed officers, who took aim with their guns.

'Jim, be careful! He's got a knife to my throat!'

Oldroyd took in the situation immediately. He couldn't risk angering Eliot, so he tried to keep his voice calm and talk him down. 'Eliot, stop! Listen to me. You might get killed here. Are you sure God will judge you mercifully if you kill another person? You've already got Clare Wilcox and Violet Saunders on your conscience. I know exactly what you think about women in the Church, but killing is against God's law. If you drop that knife now and surrender, you will have a chance to make peace with God and ask forgiveness. Don't you fear for your immortal soul?'

To Oldroyd's great relief, as he was talking, he could see Andy walking stealthily through the kitchen towards Eliot from behind.

'Why should I?' declared Eliot, clearly revelling in this moment of possible martyrdom. 'God has made his will clear in the Bible and he will reward me for my courage. Sometimes blood has to be shed to defend righteousness.'

'How much blood?! How many people?!' shouted Oldroyd frantically, but Eliot had turned to Alison and seemed to be preparing to use the knife.

'Go, Andy!!' screamed Oldroyd, and Andy pounced on Eliot from behind, knocking him to the ground and grabbing for the hand that held the knife. The back-up officers piled in and Eliot was soon overcome. But Oldroyd had seen blood.

'Alison!' he cried as he ran over to where she'd been knocked on to the ground. There was blood on her neck.

'It's all right, Jim, I think it's just a bit of a cut, not deep. I think I'm all right.'

Oldroyd knelt down beside her. 'Thank God!' he said. He rang for the ambulance and then put his arms around her. They were both crying as Eliot was handcuffed and bundled off to the police van.

∼

Next morning, Oldroyd faced Austin Eliot across a table in an interview room at Harrogate Police HQ. Andy sat next to his boss, and a duty solicitor was next to Eliot. A PC sat in the corner. Alison was in hospital recovering from her neck wound and the shock of the attack. A search of Eliot's house and the bookshop had revealed a great deal of incriminating evidence of his involvement in extremist groups. There was some forensic evidence linking him to the crimes too. However, it seemed that he was not going to contest his guilt, and showed no remorse. It was an attitude that Oldroyd had seen before in deranged killers: they felt that what they'd done was right.

Oldroyd didn't know exactly what to make of the man opposite him. Eliot had killed two people and attacked two more with intent to kill. He was clearly insane. Or was he? The man wasn't going to plead diminished responsibility, although it was very doubtful that any jury would find him 'not guilty' on such grounds. The attacks were all well planned and he hadn't displayed any particularly strange behaviour in between.

'Your strategy worked for quite a long time,' began Oldroyd. 'It was an excellent double bluff. You were so open about your hostility to women's ministry that we almost discounted you, but there you were in plain sight actually telling us the truth: you hate women priests and bishops. You also told me how much research you'd done on the history of the church and all about the story of Rawcliff the monk and the haunting. You seemed to be incriminating yourself. Why tell us about the monk if you were using the haunting to divert people away from who was really carrying out these murders?'

'Correct,' said Eliot, as matter-of-fact as if he were confirming his name. 'You see, I knew you'd find out about it all anyway, but you wouldn't expect the guilty person to be telling you things like that.' He smiled unpleasantly. 'But then, why wouldn't I? I'm a historian, Chief Inspector, and it's historical continuity and faithfulness to its founding principles that the Church needs.'

Oldroyd ignored this. 'You had an alibi, but I suspect Mrs Henderson was quite easy to deceive.'

Eliot laughed. 'Oh yes. When she was in the kitchen brewing tea, I moved the hands forward an hour on her little carriage clock on the mantelpiece. When I left, she thought it was five o'clock but it was really only four. I drew attention to the clock so she would remember what time I had apparently gone from the house. She would either not notice or forget that other clocks gave a different time.'

'You also made a reasonable job of covering your tracks. We wondered where you'd been before you arrived in Knaresborough, but it took my staff a long time to unearth some evidence of your activities.'

'I lived down in Hertfordshire for a long time, and that's where I joined the Alliance. The local police kept harassing us when we picketed churches and things like that, so I decided to move a distance away to where I wouldn't be known. I was never convicted of anything, so there was no criminal record for you to track down on your system. I was well integrated at St Anne's and carrying on in secret with the Alliance. There was not much going on locally until Clare Wilcox was appointed to St Anne's. I wasn't the only one to object, but the others are weak; they're not prepared to take action to defend God's word.'

'Did you ask them?'

'Certainly not. We in the Alliance trust no one except those who have shown loyalty and commitment over the years, and have never revealed anything to our enemies.'

'So no one was involved in these murders except you?'

'Correct again.'

'But you were working under instructions from this organisation you're part of?' asked Oldroyd.

'No. We use our own initiative, and we act alone. This was all my effort.' He seemed very proud of what he'd done.

'Rev Wilcox was in her position for quite a few years before you took action.'

'Yes. I explained this to your sister. It's not easy to mount the operations we would like to see round the country.'

Oldroyd frowned at the thought of what those operations might be.

'But when it was announced that she was to be made a bishop, I knew that I had to do something.'

'So, explain to me about the tower and the pendulum.'

Eliot's face became animated. 'Ever since I heard about the story of the ghost of the monk, I thought, as you said, that it would act as a wonderful cover for a terrible death which people would blame on the haunting, especially if the attack seemed impossible.'

'And then you discovered the staircase?'

'I did.' Eliot was almost giggling with excitement over his plan, which made Oldroyd doubt the man's sanity again. 'I'd done a stint as churchwarden and became interested in the building. The stock I inherited at the bookshop contained some volumes on church history, and the one I showed you about hauntings in the area. I thought it was a clever idea to tell you all about it as you would be less suspicious of me. I knew you would discover the legend sooner or later anyway.'

'And you read about the alterations to the tower in the nineteenth century?'

Eliot leaned forward with his elbows on the table, as if this were a casual conversation in someone's kitchen. 'Yes, and it was very intriguing. When I considered the tower, I wondered how people in the older days had accessed it to get to the clock and the bells when they were there. It was assumed that everything was just blocked up when the alterations were made.

'Then I read about the last supposed death due to the haunting; that of Samuel Walshaw, and the obviously crooked nature of Rev Marshall who was vicar at the time. And I thought: did someone have the same idea as me? I did some more research at the diocesan office.'

'Where you found a very intriguing entry about Herbert Riley the joiner, and the work he did for Rev Marshall.'

'Yes. And I had a good idea that something was being concealed behind those tall cupboards at the base of the tower. I started to make nocturnal visits to the church, and I discovered everything: the false panel, the staircase, the pendulum, the ladder and the part of the ceiling which hinged back. It was so ingenious, and just what I wanted. It was clear that God was telling me to go ahead. You see, Marshall had used this device to cover up his wrongdoings and murder an innocent man, but this time I would be using the same device to carry out the will of God, so that would absolve the device from evil and make it a thing of goodness. Do you see?'

Oldroyd said nothing in response to this twisted and devilish logic, but continued with his questioning. 'You had to do some repairs and restoration?'

'I did, also at night; fitting some locks and tying up the pendulum more securely, things like that. I was able to get in at night through the door into that boiler room. I changed the lock without anyone knowing and made it look as if it was boarded up.'

255

'Yes, we saw that, and if people heard anything they might attribute it to the ghost. No one would feel like going in to check. In fact, you told me you had heard things going on in the church yourself, and that maybe there was something in the idea of a ghost. That was another part of your double bluff.'

Eliot giggled. 'I know. That was very audacious of me, don't you think?'

Oldroyd ignored this too. 'How did you get Rev Wilcox to go into the church that afternoon?'

'I arranged to see her there. I told her I had discovered something important and unusual which I wanted her to see, which of course I had. I asked her not to tell anyone and I would explain why. She was a bit puzzled, but I persuaded her. I left Mrs Henderson's at about four o'clock and came in through the boiler room door, though the church was open. I checked there was no one around and then put on my monk's outfit. Then I switched the light on in the room behind the tower so she would walk towards it. I went up into the tower, opened the hinged section of the wooden ceiling and waited.

'I heard her come in and she stood right below me. I released the pendulum and it worked beautifully, smashing her to pieces with one swing.' Eliot, wide-eyed and looking demented, almost chuckled with glee, while everyone else winced. 'I hauled it back up and fastened it, closed the ceiling and went down to check. She was dead all right. I left her there in a pool of blood and walked out of the church.'

Oldroyd felt sick hearing the details of Clare Wilcox's death and the relish with which Eliot recounted them.

'Why didn't you go back out through the boiler room?'

Eliot raised a finger as if he were particularly proud of this part of his scheme. 'Ah! You see, I was in my monk's outfit with the hood up so no one could see my face, and I was hoping someone might catch sight of me from a distance and report it. That would add to the idea that the killing was the work of the ghost. Unluckily, there was no one in the churchyard, so I went quickly back home. I don't think anyone saw me.'

Well, someone did, thought Oldroyd, and smiled. Eliot would not be pleased when he learned that it was the same person who had prevented him from killing Harvey Ferguson.

'I imagine that you were pleased with how things had gone. I assume it all started to unravel with Violet Saunders.'

Eliot's expression changed abruptly. The smugness disappeared and was replaced by a ferocious scowl.

'That prying little witch ruined everything. I had actually used her: let her see me from a distance in the church before I disappeared into the boiler room. I thought she would do a good job of telling people she'd seen the ghost, keeping the whole story alive. It turns out we were wrong about her. I don't think she believed in the ghost at all; that dottiness was a cover to enable her to find things out about people and information to be used against them.

'I wasn't planning on killing anyone else. I'd eliminated a potential member of the Devil's Episcopacy, as we call it. But then that woman hid in the shrubbery around the church and watched me that night I paid you a nocturnal visit and she got a sight of my face.' Eliot stopped and smiled. 'Did you enjoy my visit, by the way?' he asked. 'I was hoping to scare and confuse you a little. I got out of the boiler room before you had time to follow me.'

'I never believed in the ghost, either. You were wasting your time,' replied a stony-faced Oldroyd. He wasn't going to pay this man any compliments about his plans.

Eliot shrugged and continued. 'Then she had the audacity to try to blackmail me. It wasn't difficult to lure her to her death. Her and her blasted cats. She had a good death compared to what she'd have had in the Middle Ages; she would have been burnt at the stake for witchcraft.'

And you would have been there lighting the fire, you sadistic religious maniac, thought Oldroyd in a spasm of anger. He paused to calm himself down.

'You said you didn't initially plan to kill anyone other than Rev Wilcox, but you were forced to get rid of Violet Saunders. So why did you try to kill Harvey Ferguson?'

Eliot's lip curled. 'That disgusting pervert. I'm not a fool, Chief Inspector, I knew you were a clever man and would track me down eventually, especially after the second murder which suggested the killer was someone Saunders knew, so I wanted to make the best use of the time I had before you got to me.'

'By killing a man because of his sexuality?'

'A bestial sodomite!' Eliot abruptly raised his voice, and the PC stirred in his chair. 'Cursed by God. Read the Old Testament, it's clearly spelled out in Leviticus.'

'I'm sure it is, but your attack on Ferguson was thwarted, wasn't it?'

'Yes. I thought there was no one around, but some bearded man ran out of St Robert's Cave, so I thought I'd better disappear.'

'Well, let me tell you, that man David Tanner not only saved Ferguson's life, he also saw you walking across the churchyard after you'd murdered Rev Wilcox. He couldn't see your face, but he said the monk figure with the hood had long hair. That made us think that we might be looking for a woman, but of course your hair is long so there's another little piece of evidence.'

'Huh,' snorted Eliot. 'Damned riff-raff wandering around; they all want locking up.'

'So your final attempt was on the life of my sister?'

'Yes, it was a race against time and I just lost. I worked out at the beginning that she was your sister. I'm sorry from your point of view, but it would have been good to have got rid of one of the high priestesses of women's ordination and equality. She's been our bitter enemy for years.'

Without knowing it, thought Oldroyd, who was shocked at the nonchalant way Eliot described the attempt to murder Alison. He stopped and looked at the man, who seemed completely devoid of guilt, regret or basic human feeling.

'You know,' he said at last. 'You were born in the wrong century. You would have enjoyed being a witchfinder, or a member of an ecclesiastical court sentencing people to be burnt to death. I can see you standing and watching them suffer as the fire illuminated your violent and fanatical face. You might even have thrown that monk off the cliff into the gorge.'

'Oh no, I would never have done that, Chief Inspector. I admire that man. As a Lollard he would have fought for what he saw as the true Church, a Church much closer to the Protestantism of today. The Lollards were the first to really question the—'

'Yes, yes,' said Oldroyd impatiently. He'd had enough of lectures in theology and morals from a vicious and heartless bigot who had nearly killed his sister. Andy's comment that there was something perverse in the case had finally made him think that Alison was right: sheer, diabolical nastiness and perversity were at the heart of what had happened. 'Take him out,' he said, and watched with revulsion as Eliot was removed.

～

After the interview, Oldroyd and Andy walked back up to the general office.

'By the way,' said Oldroyd, 'I never asked you how the press conference went.'

'Oh, fine, sir. I kept to the line, as you suggested. I wasn't derailed by any fanciful questions. Anyway, it hardly matters now, does it? It's all been superseded as we've caught the killer.'

'Never mind, it was a good experience for you. Well done, and thanks again for last night. You saved my sister's life and I'll never forget it.'

'That's OK, sir, you're welcome.' Andy shook his head, thinking about the interview he'd just witnessed. 'What did you make of him then, sir?' he asked, nodding back at the interview room. 'He seemed a complete nutter to me, justifying murdering women and gay people by quoting the Bible and stuff.'

'Yes, he's a dangerous character who doesn't show any remorse. One of those types who think they're on a mission. We'll need to check that no one else in his organisation was involved but I think not. He took pride in this being all his own endeavour. Ah, look who's here. More people I have to thank.'

They reached the office and found Steph and Sharon.

'Well done, you two,' said Oldroyd. 'You found the vital bit of information which enabled us to identify the killer, and only just in time.'

'Thanks, sir,' said Steph. 'It was Sharon here who found the website and identified Eliot from the photograph you gave us.'

'Well done again, I can see you're coming on well,' said Oldroyd to the young DC, who went rather red in the face, mumbling her thanks and hardly able to look at her boss directly. Oldroyd winked at Steph and left Andy with the two women as he went into his own office. He had to call Tom Walker, which was always a bit tricky. Calling was usually better than going up to see him, because it was hard to get away if he began one of his rants against his *bêtes noires* – principally Watkins and the press. He sat down at his desk and called the number.

'Ah, Jim, I've been expecting you to call. You've sorted it, I see.'

'We have, Tom. I'm just sorry we couldn't have got on to him a bit earlier and saved him from assaulting another church member and my sister. He was a wily character; played the double bluff on us. Anyway, those two will be OK.'

'I'm sorry about your sister. How did she get involved? She's a vicar, isn't she?'

Oldroyd explained about the murderer's misogynistic hatred of women priests.

'So he's some kind of religious lunatic? Well, I must say, you see life, warts and all, in this job. I'm sure it won't have gone down well with the Church establishment; people in a church in Knaresborough bumping each other off. What's the world coming to, eh?'

'I know, Tom. Anyway, I just wanted to put in commendations for Andy Carter, whose action at great personal risk saved my sister's life, and for Sharon Warner, who uncovered some vital information in her research.'

'Good for them. I'm proud of the people we have in this force. That young lass has been a good addition.' Walker seemed to be in a reasonably good mood, and Oldroyd was hoping to escape but then his heart sank. 'Do you know what the latest is, Jim? At great expense that idiot Watkins has commissioned some firm of consultants to do a full inspection of our HQ here to . . . What is it? I've got the bloody quote here; oh yes, "to optimise working practices and eliminate waste in terms of time and resources". I can't believe the cheek of that bugger. What does he think we bloody do all day? Sit on our arses like him and stare into space? This is where the real work gets done. I mean there's young Carter, risking injury and even his life to save your sister; how dare that man send round some ridiculous form-filling . . .' By this time he'd worked himself up into such a rage that the diatribe went on for several minutes, and Oldroyd had no opportunity to intervene.

It was difficult, but Oldroyd always remembered that, fundamentally, Walker was a good boss to work for and his heart was in the right place.

Eight

*'Suddenly he came to a cross-road. At the corner two fig-
ures were standing motionless; both were in dark cloaks;
the taller one wore a hat, the shorter a hood. He had no
time to see their faces . . . Yet the horse shied violently
and broke into a gallop, and Mr Wraxall sank back into
his seat in something like desperation. He had seen them
before.'*

From 'Count Magnus', M. R. James, 1904

It was a bright and mild morning for the funeral of Rev Clare
Wilcox at St Anne's. It was now the end of January and the strength-
ening sun and the birds singing amongst the still-leafless branches
of the trees gave a hint of the spring that was still some time away.
The snow had melted, returning green to the fields beyond the
Nidd Gorge. The river was reflecting the blue sky again. In the tall
trees behind the church, rooks were cawing and beginning to build
their nests.

There was a huge number of people waiting outside St Anne's.
Oldroyd in his dark overcoat and wearing a black suit and tie stood
with Deborah, whose preference for colourful clothes meant that
she was wearing a borrowed black woollen coat. She had insisted
on coming to support him and Alison, who was conducting the

service. He looked up at the west tower and reflected as they waited for the family and close relations of Clare to file into the church ahead of them. How strange that the negligence of people long ago in not removing that pendulum had resulted in two bizarre and seemingly inexplicable murders!

The cortège arrived, the hearse and two black funeral cars sliding slowly up the drive and curving round to stop outside the entrance. The coffin was brought out of the hearse and taken into the church by the pallbearers, followed by Jeremy Wilcox who walked unsteadily into the church supported on either side by his two daughters. Close relatives got out of the second car and followed them in. As the slow organ music was played by Harvey Ferguson, those waiting at a distance filed in to fill up the seats at the rear of the church.

Oldroyd and Deborah took their places, picking up the order of service booklet which had a picture of a smiling Clare Wilcox on the front. Funerals were never easy, reflected Oldroyd. Even if you had little emotional connection with the deceased person, the heavy presence of sadness and grief was overwhelming. He remembered the funerals of his parents and of David, Alison's husband. Was this the first funeral he'd been to of a victim of a crime he'd investigated?

The organ stopped and Alison stepped forward. She still had a bandage on her neck. The wound inflicted by Eliot had turned out to be quite deep and she'd lost a lot of blood. However, nothing could persuade her to allow someone else to conduct the funeral instead of her, even though she knew it was going to be very difficult.

It turned out to be a heroic and moving performance. Not only did she lead the prayers and say the words of the commendation and blessing, but she delivered the eulogy in which she spoke about Clare's talents and her personality; what a warm and generous person she was; what she had contributed to St Anne's; how she was a pioneer for the cause of women serving at the highest level of the Church. It was impossible not to feel a sense of loss about that, thought Oldroyd, as well as the trauma for her family and friends. People would never know just what kind of impact she would have had on the Church and the community.

At the front of the church, Jeremy Wilcox was struggling as he heard further short eulogies from his daughters and Clare's friends, who spoke about their memories of Clare and their personal loss. He glanced around the church and caught the eye of Sylvia Addison, his practice manager. She immediately looked away without smiling. Jenny and Fiona were being so wonderfully supportive and he was very proud of them. The presence of Sylvia was a painful reminder at a time he could have done without it – that he had unfinished business with his two daughters.

Harvey Ferguson left his position at the organ to conduct the choir singing one of Clare's favourite hymns, watched with ambiguous feelings by Patrick Owen. He was not pursuing the blackmail business with the police. He was too much in sympathy with Harvey's situation to want any action taken against him; action that would most likely result in his own sexuality being revealed. He glanced at the coffin, and was reminded that insane misogyny had taken the life of an outstanding woman who had so much to offer. He looked at Harvey and thought how the same kind of bigotry had nearly claimed his life too. Owen took a deep breath and looked up into the inspiring medieval splendour of the church ceiling. Then he prayed that the Church and society and the whole world would become more tolerant, more inclusive and more diverse as time went by. But for now, he and others like Harvey would keep certain things secret.

Olive Bryson found the service unbearably moving, and tears fell down her face as conflicted feelings moved within her. She was so relieved that she had been able to save Harvey's life, and at the same time she was so devastated about Clare. She was now revolted by the idea that she'd been attracted to Austin Eliot. Recent events had shaken her faith in the Church to the point where she was really questioning whether or not she wanted to continue attending St Anne's or any traditional church. What was the future of an institution that was so socially conservative? Maybe it was different in London and the big cities, but in little towns and villages across the country, the churches seemed to her to be stuck in the 1950s. There was a Quaker meeting house in Knaresborough. The Quakers were famous for their tolerance and commitment to social issues. It could be time for her to try that.

Another person for whom this funeral heightened a sense of personal crisis was Donald Avison. Throughout his adult life, rules and standards of behaviour had been central to him, whether determined by the army or by the Bible and the Church. Anyone questioning these rules of respectability was undermining moral standards and threatening society. Now, when he thought about the shocking things that had happened and his part in them, he was no longer so sure. Rev Wilcox, a lovely woman and a good priest, had been murdered by a fanatic who, like himself, opposed women priests. There was clearly something wrong when a thing like that could happen. Was the idea of a woman priest actually so bad? Was the Bible really so clear about this as some people argued?

He watched Harvey conducting the choir. The man had contributed so much to the church. Avison was now utterly ashamed that he'd got involved with a group of self-righteous individuals who rooted out gay people. It was cruel and unnecessary. What damage did Harvey's sexuality do to anyone? Those passages in the Old Testament about Sodom and Gomorrah were used as an excuse for bigoted people to be outraged and to appoint themselves the moral guardians of the Church and of society. It was very uncomfortable for Avison to be forced to question a lot of his assumptions and beliefs. He'd prayed about all this, and felt that he was being led in a different direction, away from inflexible rules and standards and towards greater love. It was never too late to change.

The service reached its climactic moment of the committal, and the family gathered at the door of the church as final prayers were said and the body was taken off to be cremated. They had decided not to prolong the process by conducting further ceremonies at the crematorium. The attendees then filed past the family to pay their respects before making their way across to the rectory for the reception.

At this point, things began to relax a little. It was mild enough under the pale blue sky for the French windows to be opened out on to the patio, where people gathered in little groups with cups of tea and coffee and engaged in quiet conversation.

Inside, Jenny and Fiona circulated, welcoming everyone and encouraging them to partake of the buffet lunch, which was spread out on two tables placed together. Jeremy Wilcox was sitting in his usual armchair, looking tired but talking to a group of relatives. In the crush of people, Oldroyd found himself next to Robin Eastby.

'I want to thank you, Chief Inspector,' he said. 'I can't tell you what a relief it is to have some answers and not to feel that there is still a threat out there.'

'You're welcome. I imagine you're going to have to go through a long healing process before the church gets anywhere near back to normal again,' replied Oldroyd.

'Absolutely. The shock of finding that the killer was one of us, the deaths of two of our church family and the attack on a third is profound.' He shook his head. 'I'll be honest with you, I had dreams that I could succeed Clare and I'm a bit ashamed of those thoughts now, but I realise that the situation needs someone with a lot more experience and someone new to the town. I was too much a part of what happened. I've spoken again to Bishop Michael and to Patrick, and we agreed that I will stay at St Anne's as curate for a while even though it would be normal for me to move on soon. That will give the congregation some continuity, you know, the fact that I went through all this with them.'

'It sounds very sensible to me.'

'Yes. Can you excuse me? My wife's waving to me.'

Eastby moved off. Oldroyd noticed that Deborah and Alison were in conversation with a group of women, whom Oldroyd recognised as women priests. He had asked Deborah to keep an eye on Alison. He knew that she had been under enormous stress recently, despite appearing to be as calm and composed as usual.

He heard a voice at his side. It was Olive Bryson.

'I always knew you'd do it, Chief Inspector. You have a very perceptive mind.' She was drinking from a glass of wine and leering at him, smiling broadly. 'You and that lovely sergeant of yours, you're unbeatable.' She raised her glass to him.

'Thank you,' replied Oldroyd, thinking again that Olive was certainly not your average churchgoer. 'You played your part in saving Mr Ferguson. You showed perception too, in realising that something was wrong.'

'That's very kind of you. It was that homeless man who saved him. I was too far behind to have stopped Eliot.' She leaned forward and whispered to him. 'Why isn't that man here today? He's a hero, but he wouldn't fit in, would he? Not middle-class enough.' She pronounced 'class' with the long southern vowel. Oldroyd didn't think this was really fair, but understood the sentiment. 'I never liked that Austin Eliot; cold and arrogant man. You never knew what he was really thinking.'

'In some ways it was probably better that you didn't; how appalling to be inside a mind like that.'

'Yes.' She grimaced. 'Anyway, if you'll excuse me, Chief Inspector, I must have a word with Fiona and Jenny, they've done such a wonderful job.'

Oldroyd ate a plate of food and then wandered outside to get some air. It was beautifully calm on this sad day. Fleecy clouds were crossing the clear sky. He could see part of the viaduct over the Nidd and a train was gliding across it to the station. The river moved smoothly underneath. In the distance there was a glimpse of the hilly country further north, in the Dales. The beauty of nature was always there, regardless of what was going on for good or bad in the human world. And it was possible on a day like this to imagine that the terrible things through which they'd all just lived had never happened.

Inside, Bishop Michael and Patrick Owen were in conversation.

'Alison did a wonderful job, didn't she, Patrick?' said the bishop.

'She did indeed,' replied the archdeacon. 'We're very fortunate to have her in the diocese.'

'You know, with people like her around, we're going to get through this and move forward. It's what Clare would have wanted. We're going to create a better atmosphere. We've got to be much more upfront about challenging bigoted attitudes and not be afraid of bad publicity. Do you know Ian at Pontefract complained to the chief superintendent at Harrogate about how the police were handing the case? The archbishop told him off and rightly so; the police were doing their best, and now they've solved the case and one officer took a great personal risk. We've got to stop being so concerned about our image and speak out about what's right.'

'I couldn't agree more, Michael. It's amazing, isn't it? Even something as dark as this can have a positive side if it brings us all closer together and makes us more loving and tolerant.'

'Absolutely! Oh, there's the chief inspector. I'm just going over to thank him again.'

The bishop caught Oldroyd as he was coming back into the house. 'I'm glad I've seen you before you left, Chief Inspector,' he said with an affable smile. 'I know many people will have already thanked you, but I wanted to express my gratitude too, on behalf of the whole diocese. It's been a very difficult time for us, and it's been a great help that you've managed to bring the whole dreadful business to an end in a very short time. So, thank you.'

'You're welcome. I had a personal interest as you know, with my sister being involved.'

'Yes, and thank God she's safe.'

'Indeed, so I can understand how people were feeling. I was saying to Robin Eastby that it's obviously going to take a long time for everyone to recover from this, but the healing process can begin now.'

'Yes.'

'I think these events have also healed something that's been around for a long time.'

'Oh?'

'I'm thinking of the old story of the monk and the hauntings. The second victim, Violet Saunders, told me that she'd tried to have the ghost exorcised from the church. She said she'd sent you letters requesting it.'

'Really? I don't remember that.'

'Well, I'm not sure how serious or honest she was being, but I think that, after all that's happened and been revealed, we can say that the ghost of Thomas Rawcliff has finally been laid to rest.'

~

It was dark outside as, in the early evening, Oldroyd, Deborah and Alison relaxed in the Harrogate flat, each with a glass of wine. Alison was staying the night after a hugely demanding day. Deborah had made a spicy Mexican bean stew the night before, which was now being heated up for tea.

'I have to say again, I thought you were magnificent,' said Oldroyd to his sister, and Deborah agreed.

'Thank you again,' replied Alison. 'I can't say it was easy, despite having conducted lots of funerals in the past. It's completely different when you're personally involved, but I really wanted to do it. It was important for Clare's memory and for the movement of which she was such an important part. It had to be a woman and it had to be me in the circumstances.'

'It might be an awful thing to say, but I think what's happened will create sympathy for the women's cause in the Church, and more generally for that matter,' observed Deborah. 'The fact that such terrible misogyny and homophobia existed in a church member is shocking, and it shows that those attitudes are not confined to weird dysfunctional people hidden away from mainstream society. It will make people think and hopefully do more to tackle the problems.'

'Actually, I agree,' said Alison. 'We always have to look for any good which can come out of a situation, however bleak it is – and this one has been truly diabolical.' She shuddered slightly, put down her drink and leaned back into the sofa. For a moment her emotional exhaustion was showing, despite her stoical efforts to continue. Her neck was sore, and she put her hand up to it.

'Are you OK, sis?' Oldroyd asked, looking concerned.

'Yes. It's taken it out of me today. And my neck is still painful, but I'll be fine.'

'Don't underestimate the trauma of what you've been through,' said Deborah. 'Being brutally surprised like that and then held in your own kitchen tied to a chair and expecting to be murdered at any moment will have made a deep impact. Expect some PTSD symptoms, maybe anxiety and flashbacks; hopefully they'll be mild.'

'Yes, I know you're right.'

'You can always come and stay here with us if you're feeling bad.'

Alison smiled. 'I know.'

'Talking about trauma, I think that church will take some time to recover from the trauma of Austin Eliot,' remarked Oldroyd.

'They will,' said Deborah. 'In addition to the horror and the shock, there will be a deep sense of betrayal; that all this was done by an active member of their own congregation who had even served as churchwarden. It may take a long time for them to trust people again.'

'Yes,' said Oldroyd. 'I'm interested in what you think of the extreme misogyny and homophobia, of the kind that was in Eliot.'

'There are many psychological theories about it, and like most severe psychological problems they locate it in childhood trauma. Sometimes men who were abused and made to feel powerless exert their strength over less powerful groups in society, to regain a sense of power and control. Some extreme religious groups still teach that women and gay people are inferior or evil, so if someone is deeply conformist through wanting to please, they may internalise those attitudes at a very deep level and at a young age. Then, of course, we've got the problem of continuing negative attitudes to these groups in society generally, which will tend to reinforce the more extreme attitudes. How much more do you want?' Deborah laughed.

'That's fine; it's all very interesting.'

'Of course, a case like this is very complex and there will be more than one pathological condition at work. It sounds to me as if Eliot had a kind of egotistical, crusading belief that God had called him to rid the Church of the "evil" of these women priests and gay people. He may have suffered from psychosis and heard voices telling him to do things.'

'I see. What do you think, sis? Sis?' Alison had fallen asleep in the chair.

'Oh, look at her!' said Deborah. 'She must be exhausted, poor thing! Why don't I bring the food out here on trays and we'll sit with her? If she wakes up, she can have some.'

Oldroyd got up to help. 'Come here,' he said to Deborah, and he gave her a kiss. 'You're wonderful; so kind and considerate. Maybe it's because I've been lucky with the females I've known, but I've always liked women. In fact, to be honest, I prefer their company to men.'

'Who wouldn't? The best thing about you as a man is that you know your place and do as you're told!' She laughed again as Oldroyd chased her into the kitchen.

~

'There is really nothing more to tell, but, as you may imagine, the professor's views on certain points are less clear-cut than they used to be. His nerves, too, have suffered: he cannot now even see a surplice hanging on a door quite unmoved, and the spectacle of a scarecrow in a field late on a winter afternoon has cost him more than one sleepless night.'

From 'Oh, Whistle, and I'll Come to You, My Lad',
M. R. James, 1904

Acknowledgments

I would like to thank my family, friends and members of the Otley Writers' Group for their help and support over the years.

My friends Rev Brian Harris and Rev Alison Harris gave me important guidance on procedures, structures and terminology in the Church of England.

The fictional St Anne's Church is based on a number of Yorkshire churches, although I did have in mind the general position of St Mary's Church above the gorge in Knaresborough. There is a church in Yorkshire that has a giant pendulum concealed within a wall, but I prefer to keep its location a secret! The bishopric of Kendal is fictional, as is the West Riding Police, which is based on the old riding boundary. Harrogate and Knaresborough were part of the old West Riding, although they are in today's North Yorkshire.

The House in the Rock, the Chapel of Our Lady of the Crag, Mother Shipton's Cave, the Petrifying Well and Sir Robert's Cave all exist in the remarkable Nidd Gorge beneath the town of Knaresborough.

About the Author

John R. Ellis has lived in Yorkshire for most of his life and has spent many years exploring Yorkshire's diverse landscapes, history, language and communities. He recently retired after a career in teaching, mostly in further education in the Leeds area. In addition to the Yorkshire Murder Mystery series, he writes poetry, ghost stories and biography. He has completed a screenplay about the last years of the poet Edward Thomas and a work of faction about the extraordinary life of his Irish mother-in-law. He is currently working on his memoirs of growing up in a working-class area of Huddersfield in the 1950s and 1960s.